MW01206264

The Spiral Bridge

Alvin H. Franzmeier

PublishAmerica
Baltimore

First printing

ISBN: 1-4137-0953-2
PUBLISHED BY PUBLISHAMERICA, LLLP
www.publishamerica.com
Baltimore

Printed in the United States of America

In memory of my parents
Alvin W. and Thelma Franzmeier

Acknowledgments

During the better than two years it took to prepare this work I was cajoled, flattered, prodded, pushed, encouraged and supported by the members of my writers' group, affectionately known as *Writers in the Hat* of The Woodlands, Texas. I thank them for their patience and persistence. Members included Bonnie Blink, Carol and Rick Dennis, Jim Elledge, Mike Huckaby, Pepper Hume, Lee Stoiser, Martha Swearinger and Pete Wessner. I owe a special debt to my mentor and friend, Kristl Franklin. Thanks also go to Carol Dennis for her patient editing as I prepared to submit the text to the publisher and to my wife Sylvia for her patience, encouragment and comments during the entire process.

Chapter 1

Sweet Rosie O'Grady

He muttered to himself as he walked down the basement stairs. "Michael Arthur Murphy needs you, little bottle. This Irishman needs you tonight. He needs you really bad, sweet flask of mine. Now don't be a naughty bottle and play hard to find."

So lonely. He needed her, but she was gone; one way or another she was always gone. Soon the pain and the hurt would disappear. Too many times she had refused him, shut herself off. Too many excuses, always sick, tired, whatever. What's a wife for anyway? Now she was gone, taking care of her sick mother.

He reached under his work-table, pulled out a five gallon paint pail stuffed with old rags, pushed his hand deep within and there it was, his forbidden fifth of whiskey. "Ah, there you are, me darlin'. I been lookin' for you."

He took a long swig, smacked his lips and took another. He began to dance a little jig and sing. "Sweet Rosie O'Grady. My dear little rose." He paused, took another long nip and continued to sway and hum. He hummed and drank, drank and hummed, hummed and drank until the pain was gone and that familiar warm feeling filled him.

Images and thoughts washed over his mind, dark, alluring and hungry. The pain disappeared, but the desire grew, the desire long denied and long rejected. He laughed and swayed, kissed his bottle and rolled his head back and forth. "Shweeet Rosie Oooo'Graaadeee. Me deeear li'l rooose." He laughed again. "Oh, Rooosie, where aaaare you? Come to me, Rosie."

He lurched to the stairs. Where did all those steps come from? How was he going to make it up so many? Did somebody build ten extra while he wasn't looking? So what. He would make it up. Rosie was up there. She was waiting for him. I'm coming, Rosie, sweet little Rosie. I'm coming to you.

He stumbled again and again as he moved up the stairway, pushed open the door to the kitchen and laughed. "Oh Rooosie. Are you there, li'l darlin'?"

He stood in the doorway to the living room, swaying, looking at his niece on the couch. "Hello, Helen. Have you seen Rosie? I bet you haven't seen Rosie, eh?" He laughed at his joke.

Helen stared at her uncle. "Uncle Michael, what's going on?"

"Oh, nothing much. I just had a few sips from me little bottle." He held up his fifth and patted it with his hand.

"Uncle Michael, you're drunk!"

"Oh, maybe a little, but not so drunk that me and you can't have a good time. Would you like to have a good time with me, sweet li'l Helen?" He laughed again. "I been thinkin' a lot about you, me little darlin'. We're goin' to have a good time."

"Uncle Michael, go away. Don't do this!" He heard the panic in her voice, but ignored it.

He staggered across the room to where his twenty-one year old niece was now huddled. She wrapped her hands around her knees and began to whimper. He stood before her, struggling to keep his balance, his head cocked to the right, his red hair disheveled, a lazy smile on his mouth and his eyes bloodshot. "You're a good teacher, li'l Helen. Let me teach you how to have a good time. Me and you need to have a good time. You'd like that wouldn't you, li'l Helen?"

Helen's voice cracked. "Uncle Mike, stop this. Go away! Leave me alone!" she screamed. Fear was written on her face. Sweat covered her quivering body. He continued to ignore it. "Uncle Mike, please. Go to your room and sleep it off! Leave me alone!"

"Oh, no, me dear. I don't want to sleep it off. I want to sleep with you!" He laughed at his wonderful sense of humor.

"You don't know what you're saying!" Helen's entire body was shaking. Tears flooded from her dark green eyes. She started to stand.

She was trying to get away. She mustn't get away. He seized her by her shoulders, shoved her back down on the couch. Then he held her there as he sat beside her. With his arms around her and his face next to hers, he said, "Don't go away, li'l Helen. Have a li'l nip. You know how much I love you, li'l lady. I need you tonight, me sweet li'l Helen. I need you to love me." He reached out and pulled her face toward his.

She struggled to push him away, but he was too strong. "Uncle Michael, don't! Please, please, go away!"

She tried again to get up, but this time he slammed her, face up, all the way down on the couch and crawled on top of her. She was much smaller than he was. His weight pressed her down. He could taste his own foul, stale breath, but hers was sweet, alluring. She tried again to crawl away, but he held her firmly. "Me and you are going to have some fun," he began to chant, "Some funny fun, some funny fun. Me and you are going to have some funny fun."

Suddenly his hands were all over her, tearing open her blouse, pulling up her skirt, ripping off her panties. His knees pressed against her thighs. She fought and kicked and screamed, but he was too strong, too big. She couldn't stop him. Not now. His face was against hers, his lips on hers, kissing her. He kept laughing and chanting and then he was inside her, deeper and deeper and deeper until he collapsed, his full weight smashing her down, down into the couch, suffocating her, his breath coming in gasps. He laughed, hysterically, in a wild and uncontrolled manner. In a couple minutes he began to calm. Slowly he raised himself up from her battered and bleeding body. She was sobbing irrepressibly.

"Now, wasn't that fun, wasn't that fun?" he gasped again and again as he rolled off her and fell to the floor. Then he struggled up, swaying as before. He glanced down at his niece, coiled in a ball. Everything was a blur. He couldn't think. The passion was gone and he was tired, so very tired. He turned away from her and shuffled to his bedroom, humming to himself. "Sshweet Roseee O'Gradeeee, my deeear li'l rooosie!" He slammed the door, collapsed on his bed and in a few seconds was sound asleep, snoring loudly.

The next thing he knew it was morning. The sun was shining in through his bedroom window. Michael Murphy's eyes hurt as he tried to open them. He couldn't stand the light and his head was throbbing and pounding. "Oh me head," he mumbled. "Oh mercy, me achin' head. I need some aspirin."

Slowly, carefully he placed his feet upon the floor, holding his head with both hands. With his eyes barely open, he walked one step at a time to the bathroom. Screwing off the top of the aspirin bottle with shaking hands he poured several into his mouth and swallowed them with a glass of water. Then he stumbled back to his bed and fell on it, burying his head in his pillow.

Little by little his mind began to clear. At last he felt able to sit up. As he sat on the edge of his bed an avalanche of memories came crashing down into his mind, memories of the previous night.

"I was drunk, wasn't I?" he mumbled. "Helen was screaming."

Then it hit him. Terrible, dreadful reality buried him under its weight. He held his hundred pound head in his hands. What had he done to his niece? The pain intensified. A powerful waterfall of guilt and self-loathing followed the avalanche, filling every crevice of his being. What had he done? What would he do now? What could he do?

With agony in his heart and pain in his head, he rose and staggered to the bathroom. Upon relieving himself, he washed his face and walked carefully to the kitchen where he made a large pot of coffee. After his second cup a muddled plan came into his mind. He began to realize that his whole life stood in the balance. If Helen told what he had done, his career and his marriage would be over. He must stop her. He must shut her up. He must. How could he do that? Then he knew. The plan was simple. He would warn her, put the fear of God in her. He would even threaten to kill her if he had to. He had no other choice.

By the third cup his plan was clear. He would not only threaten her, he would arrange for her to move out. He could not have her around, yet he would be close and she would know that he could find her at any time. This was the only way.

The throbbing in his head subsided to a mere pounding headache. It was Sunday. He must continue with his day. He must attend Mass. After all, as the Superintendent of Independent School District 132, he must keep up appearances.

He stripped off his disheveled clothes, shaved and washed his face, arms and upper body. He pulled on clean underwear, a fresh shirt, his Sunday suit and shoes and combed his hair. He was ready. Let the week begin. He still had time to make the 11:00 a.m. Mass.

Before leaving, he must speak with Helen. He climbed the stairs and stood before her bedroom door. Was she awake? He knocked on the door.

"Helen! Are you awake? It's time for Mass. Are you coming?"

Not a sound.

"Helen, I said it's time for Mass."

"Go away!"

He pushed open the door. She was curled in a ball on her side with the covers pulled to her chin. Her light brown hair lay in knots and tangles around her bruised face. She stared at him with red, swollen eyes. "You monster!" she screamed. "I hate you! Get out of my room!"

"No, I won't get out!" he screamed back. "Shut up and listen! Last night never happened! Do you hear me? IT NEVER HAPPENED! You will never tell anyone about it!"

"Go to hell!"

"No, you listen and listen good!" His voice was trembling, even as he raised the pitch. "You will say nothing about this to anybody, especially your Aunt Mary. If you do, if you ever tell her or anybody else about last night, I'll kill you! Do you hear me? As sure as I'm alive, I'll kill you!"

Helen stared at him with wide, unblinking eyes and said no more. He turned from her and stumbled down the stairs. He pulled on his hat, marched out the front door, slammed it behind him, got into his car and drove to St. Cecelia's for the eleven a.m. Mass.

Michael Murphy was waiting for his wife as the Greyhound Bus lumbered up to the front of Grady's Café on Main Street on Monday afternoon at fifteen minutes past four. He could hear the wild beating of his heart in his ears. His panic simply would not leave. He paced back and forth as he waited for the door of the bus to open. Would Helen say anything? Did Helen believe his threats? Could he carry them out if she didn't? She had said nothing to him since he threatened her the day before. They had eaten separate meals and carefully avoided one another. Now his wife was home.

He smiled when Mary Murphy stepped from the gray coach. If he smiled broadly she would not notice the sweat on his forehead. She couldn't hear the pounding of his heart. She wouldn't notice his nervousness. Walking up to her, he took her face in his hands and kissed her gently. She tensed when he touched her, but said nothing.

As he reached down to pick up her small suitcase he asked, "How's Mother doing?"

"She seems to be better, but the doctor says she's going to have to take it easy for quite a while. She's really weak."

"But she's able to get by on her own?"

"Yes, as long as she doesn't push it."

"Good. We'll keep in touch with her. It's good to have you home, Mary."

"I'm sure you missed me, Michael, missed me cleaning your house and making your meals. Three weeks is too long to be gone. You didn't have your little slave around. I'm just glad you had Helen to keep you from wrecking the place."

"For God's sake, Mary, let's not get into that right off the bat. And, yes, it was good to have Helen around. I want to talk with you about Helen, but that can wait until you get settled in again."

They said no more as Murphy drove his wife to their modest home on a small side street in the little town of Rosemount, Minnesota. Their niece, Helen Shattuck, was waiting in the living room when they arrived. She ran to her aunt with a tense smile on her lips. "Aunt Mary, it is so good to see you. I really missed you." Helen gave her aunt a big, tight hug.

"My goodness, Helen, you didn't miss me that much, did you?"

"Aunt Mary, you'll never know how much I missed you." Helen's eyes caught her uncle's for a second before she looked back at her aunt. Michael Murphy's face was passive, unreadable, his eyes cold.

"I made supper. Get your coat off and come sit down."

After the evening meal the two women chatted in the kitchen as they cleaned up the dishes. Murphy sat in his favorite living room chair, within earshot of their conversation.

"How is school coming along?" asked Aunt Mary.

"Fine, just fine."

"Just a week to go, right?"

"Yes."

"You seem troubled, Helen. Anything wrong?"

"No, nothing's wrong."

"I'll bet you'll be glad when this year is over."

"Very glad. Very glad."

"You sure nothing's wrong?"

"Yes, Aunt Mary. I'm sure. I'm tired. I think I'll go to bed. Big day tomorrow."

"Of course, dear. Good night."

After Helen had made her way up to her room Murphy invited his wife to sit on the couch. He spoke in a low voice.

"Mary, I need to say something. It's about Helen."

"What about Helen? She seems so quiet. She's not herself tonight."

"Please. Keep your voice down. What I have to say is not for Helen to hear."

"Is something wrong?"

"No, nothing is wrong. It's just that I've been thinking. It's time for Helen to get out on her own. She's been living with us nearly two years. She's not our daughter, after all. She needs to grow up, learn to take care of herself."

"Michael, what are you saying? She's my sister's daughter. We promised to look after her. You know she doesn't have any money."

"Oh, Mary. She does too. You know we've helped her to set up a little savings account. Why, I think she has nearly $200 in that account. It's time for her to learn how to manage her own affairs. We've helped her through the rough times, her dad's running off, the whole business of your sister getting a divorce and the dirty shame of it all. Now we got this depression and all that. I think it's time for her to be having her own room, grow up."

"But where would she go?"

"I've checked into that. Now that Clarence Wilson is dead Norma has sold the store and is turning her house into a boarding home for girls. She has four rooms. I've talked with her already and told her that I thought Helen would probably want one of them. She has it reserved."

Mary frowned as she looked at her husband. "Sounds to me like you settled it all without even discussing it with me, just like always. Did you talk with Helen about this?"

"No, but I'm quite sure she'll agree."

"How do you know?"

"For goodness sake, Mary, it's a feeling I have. I think she wants to get away from this house, get out on her own, start being an independent adult."

"Perhaps, but I'm thinking she should have a say in this. I don't want to throw her out."

Murphy's heart was pounding again. Did he dare let Helen speak before her aunt? Would she confront him? He had to risk it. "We're not throwing her out, Mary. Tell you what. Let me call her down this very minute. See what she thinks about it. If she agrees it's a good thing, I'll pay the first three months rent and help her move her things over to the Wilson place right after school ends."

"Seems terribly abrupt to me," sighed Mary Murphy. "I don't see how this will help her. It's lonely around here without the children. Helen and I have gotten to be quite close."

"Mary. For God's sake, it'll not be her moving to Minneapolis. She'll be a couple blocks away, that's all."

"I don't know, Michael. It seems so quick. We have the room ... Call her.

If this is what she wants, I'll do it, but I want to hear it from her."

Murphy called his niece down to the living room. When she had settled next to her aunt he began. "Helen, your Aunt Mary and I have been talking. We're thinking that you might want to move out on your own, have your own place, not be under our thumb. We want to hear what you think."

Helen said nothing. She stared at him with hard, unblinking eyes. Murphy continued, "I've spoken with Norma Wilson. She's starting a new boarding home for girls. She says she has a room if you like. I've asked her to reserve one for you. I'm even willing to pay the first three months rent. What do you think?"

Before Helen could speak Mary broke in, "Now Helen, dear, I want you to know that you don't have to do this. I'm happy for you to stay here. You are family. We love you, you know."

Helen said nothing for a long moment. She continued looking at her uncle with an icy stare as she spoke. Her voice was even, firm. "Yes, Aunt Mary, I know that you *both* love me—very much! Each of you *loves* me in your own way." She paused for effect before continuing. "It's strange that you should bring this up, because I've been thinking about the same thing myself. I was wondering how I could do it without hurting you." She looked at her Aunt and smiled. "Now that you bring it up, I agree. It's time for me to move. Moving to Mrs. Wilson's place sounds good."

Uncle Michael Murphy stood and smiled as he looked down at his niece. She was sitting on the same couch she had occupied two nights earlier. A fuzzy memory of that time seeped like damp fog into his mind. He clasped and unclasped his hands in front of him. He took a couple of deep breaths. "Very good. It's settled then. You'll only be teaching another week. As soon as you put everything away, we can get you moved. I'll give Mrs. Wilson a call right now to let her know we're taking the room."

Mary Murphy's eyes were sad as she spoke. "Still seems awfully quick to me, but maybe, if that's what you want, Helen."

"Yes, Aunt Mary, that's what I want. I really do need to get out on my own. And this is a good start."

Chapter 2

Foolish Step

One Year Later, 1934

The long week was over for Tillie Tilden. The long ride from Hamline University to the west side of St. Paul, Minnesota was nearly over as well. She transferred to the Smith Street bus, settled her petite frame next to the window in the fifth seat from the front, pushed her dark brown hair away from her face and watched the houses and businesses slip by.

What was next? Perhaps it was best to turn down the offer from the College of Education and finish her senior year. Mother kept telling her it was foolish not to finish college. Perhaps she was right after all.

As Tillie entered the front door of her parents' home on George Street, her mother was lounging in her accustomed chair. As usual, Iva Tilden did not look up when her daughter entered, but continued to stare out the large picture window at the neatly manicured lawn.

"I'm home," Tillie said. "Any calls?"

As if on cue, the black cradled phone, resting on a metal shelf covering the hot water radiator next to Mother, started to ring. At the third ring Mother picked it up, spoke briefly and then motioned to Tillie. "It's Dr. Johnson from the University."

"Tillie Tilden, here."

"Miss Tilden. Good news. Rosemount Schools' Superintendent Michael Murphy has agreed to supervise you if you are willing to take the job."

"Oh, great!"

"The department also agrees to your request. You can complete your student teaching requirements during the year and the university will give you credit."

"Wonderful!"

"You'll be full time and this will mean extra work, reports and, of course, weekly meetings with your supervisor."

"I understand."

"Very good. You'll only have one semester left to complete when you return. As you requested, the University has agreed not to charge you for those hours."

"This is perfect."

"So, you will accept the assignment then?"

Tillie was quiet for a moment, lost in her thoughts. The warm afternoon sun shone through the living room window on her dark hair, fine featured cheeks and hazel eyes, causing her to squint. A few minutes ago she had ridden a city bus west across the High Bridge over the Mississippi River to her part of town. A hundred different memories played out on the streets of West St. Paul flitted across her mind as she stood there. In that moment it seemed as if she was about to cross another river on another bridge, a bridge leading to a new time of life. To cross that river meant leaving childhood behind forever. All her friends, favorite teachers, choir tours, piano lessons, football games, dances in the gym, speech contests, dates with nervous, pimpled boys, years of singing and celebrating, of reading and writing, of listening and learning, would be left behind. Another bridge. What was on the other side? Should she cross over?

"Dr. Johnson, thank you for working out the details. I appreciate the University's cooperation and help. Right now I can't give you a final answer. It's the weekend and I need to talk some more about this with my parents. I'll have my answer first thing Monday morning. Is that agreeable?"

"Absolutely, Miss Tilden. We understand. I'll see you in my office first thing Monday."

Tillie hung up and turned to her mother. "He has it all arranged, supervision, credit, everything, just as I asked."

"I see," said Iva Tilden in a stiff, sullen voice. "Whatever you want they give you—as long as you agree to put off college and go out to the country to teach a bunch of farm kids." She rose slowly from her chair, more slowly than one might expect for a woman in her late forties, but who can say when or why a woman might have arthritis in her spine? She rubbed her heavily corseted back and straightened her flowered cotton dress. "You know how I feel about this Tillie."

"Mother, please. We've been over and over this. I didn't ask for it. Dr. Johnson called me into his office. They desperately need a teacher out at Rosemount. Last year they lost a teacher in one of their schools and had to make do with an assortment of substitutes. In these depressed times they're just not graduating enough teachers."

"My point exactly," replied her mother as she adjusted her glasses and pressed down her reddish-brown hair with both hands. "Graduate and you will have the pick of any decent school in the city. What sense does it make to go out to the country? Finish college first. Then you'll have all kinds of other opportunities."

"I know how you feel, Mother. That's why I told Dr. Johnson that I needed to talk about this with you and Poppa."

"What's to talk about, Tillie? You are too smart, too talented, to waste your life in some one room school house with a group of farm kids. Don't throw it away on a bunch of hicks."

"Mother, for goodness sake, you grew up on a farm."

"I'm not living there now, am I? And I'm never going back."

"Poppa still thinks of himself as a farmer."

Iva Tilden reached down and picked a wilted leaf off the flowers arranged in the middle of her dining room table. "I've heard all his speeches about farmers. Nonsense. People are farmers because they aren't smart enough to do anything else besides slopping pigs and picking corn."

"You're always so negative."

"Am I? How about some thrilling quilting sessions with the ladies' aid society to gossip about how Mrs. Schwarz's husband beats his children or why the preacher had such a boring sermon?"

"Okay, you made your point, but what's one year going to hurt?"

"One year? That is my point. It's the waste. The years go so fast."

"Mother, please. I'm only twenty years old. I won't be twenty-one for another month. I've got time."

"Think so? Every decision affects everything else later."

"I know."

"Do you? Did you ever stop to think about why we're living here in West

St. Paul?"

"Because Poppa got a job at the stockyards and he wanted us to have a nice place to live."

"Hardly. It's because I insisted we move here."

"You never told me that."

"No, but maybe it's time you got some family history straightened out."

"What're you talking about?"

"Your father wanted to be a vet from the time he was a little boy. All he wanted was to help cows deliver calves. That was his dream."

"I know all about that."

"You don't know the whole story. When we fell in love, I didn't have the courage to tell him how I felt about farming. So when he graduated from Iowa State, we got married and moved to a little fifty-acre place of our own not far from Ames, with a small house and barn. We had a garden and a couple milk cows."

"You showed us pictures of that farm. That's where I was born."

"Sure. He was a partner with another vet. His dream was coming to pass."

"You've never said much about that."

"That's because I don't like to think about those times. I got really depressed out there. Nothing your father said or did helped. I sat around day after day staring out the window. I couldn't do my housework. I wouldn't even change your diapers until you were screaming. He kept asking me what was wrong, but I couldn't tell him."

The memories of those dark days pressed Iva Tilden down again. She settled back in her lounge chair with a sigh. Tillie sat in her Poppa's chair opposite and listened attentively.

"One evening, after you were sleeping, I finally found the courage to tell him. I said, 'I'm leaving. I'm taking the baby and moving to Ames. I'll find a job somewhere. I can't take this any more.'

'What can't you take?' he asked.

'I can't take this country life,' I told him. 'I feel trapped, alone. I have no friends. I'm not going to spend the rest of my life pulling weeds in some stupid garden. I'm not going to can tomatoes and raise chickens any more. And I'm not raising my daughter this way.'"

Iva gazed up at the ceiling, her hands folded in her lap, remembering that night. "Your father got all panicky. I can still hear his voice. 'But this is what I do,' he said. 'I'm a country animal doctor. I treat horses and cows and pigs and sheep. I work with farmers. This is what all the years of study and sacrifice were all about.'"

'Fine,' I said, 'Be a horse doctor, but do it without me! I can't and I won't take it any longer!'"

"Did you really leave?"

"I did. I took you and moved to Ames with my sister, gave her a little money to take care of you while I worked in a grocery store and tried to save enough money to move to Minneapolis. It was a bad time for our marriage, but I was never going back to live on that farm again."

"So how did you and Poppa get back together?"

"He came to me in Ames and told me he had applied for a government meat inspector's job in the South St. Paul stockyards. He said he'd do it my way because he loved me and didn't want to lose me and not see his daughter grow up."

"And that's how we came here to West St. Paul?"

"Right. Now you know why I keep telling you to be careful about the decisions you make."

Tillie said nothing. She sat with a frown on her forehead, looking at her shoes.

Mother pulled herself forward to the edge of her chair and carefully stood again. Looking down at her daughter she continued, "I've never told this to you or your sister before. I only tell it to you now, because you are making some extremely important decisions. Please, think this through very carefully." She turned toward the kitchen. "Right now I have to get supper started. We'll talk more when your father comes home."

Dr. Stephen Tilden arrived home about an hour later. He parked his gray 1929 Desoto in the detached one car garage at the back of the family lot and walked slowly across the small yard. His work day at the South St. Paul stockyards was over and his evening with his family was about to begin.

A big man with a square face and a muscular build, he carried his six foot frame easily, even as he struggled inwardly with his usual mixture of confused feelings, some happy and satisfied, others tense and angry. He knew his two daughters would hug and kiss him and talk excitedly about their day's activities. He would joke with them and share a story or two of his own. He also knew he would try to give his wife a kiss and she would permit it, but only on her cheek. She would not return his kiss. Instead, she would ignore him while silently going about preparing their supper.

He knew that all through the evening Iva would continue to take no notice of him. After the meal was over, the girls would retreat to their rooms to study and he and Iva would sit in their individual chairs, she with her knitting, and he with his newspaper and journals. At nine-thirty they would listen to the evening news on the radio. By ten they would both climb the stairs and retreat to their respective rooms for the night.

Dr. Tilden loved his daughters. They were his life. They helped him make sense out of the humdrum and often boring work of inspecting slaughter animals at the stockyards. He often chuckled at their remembered jokes as he tested cow and pig carcasses for diseases. He made up stories in his head to tell them as he certified that the railroad meat cars were properly refrigerated.

He pondered his sixteen years at the stockyards. Three years after they had moved to West St. Paul, Mattie, their second daughter was born. They had given her the name of Iva's mother, Madeline. She was dark haired like her sister, but a much bigger girl. She favored her father's side of the family.

Now Tillie was a junior in college and Mattie a junior in high school. He dreamed about their futures. He prayed his daughters would one day be freed from the bleakness of the city. He prayed they would meet young men who would bring them back into touch with the wonders of God's creation and the marvels of living plants, animals and birds. He prayed for them, but doubted that his prayers would ever be answered.

He opened the door to the back porch with these prayers in his heart. As he stepped into the tiny kitchen, his older daughter wrapped her arms around him. "Poppa. You're home." She kissed him and stepped back, still holding his hands. "I've got some good news. Dr. Johnson called. Everything's worked out. All I have to do is say yes."

"Great. So you're moving to the country."

"No she's not!" insisted Iva Tilden as she turned over a pork chop in the frying pan. "Nothing has been decided. We all need to talk about this. It's a family matter."

The Tilden family members took their usual places at the dining room table and the evening meal began. The conversation soon turned to Tillie's proposed move to Dakota County to teach in a one-room grade school between her junior and senior years of college. She reviewed the phone call from the Dean of the College of Education and said, "Now that they have agreed to my demands, I'm really thinking I should do it."

"I agree," replied her father. "It will be a welcome break from the city and from college, a chance to learn about a whole different way of life, a time to meet some new people."

"And waste a year of her life!" said Mother. "This whole thing is crazy. Why stop college now? Tillie, you're so close to graduating. You have so many better things to do than to teach in a dumpy little one-room country school."

"Hey, Till, maybe you can meet some new fellas out there," said Mattie. "There's got to be some men more interesting than those stuffed shirts you been dating from Hamline."

"Mattie, don't be silly," replied her mother. "The only thing a young farmer finds interesting is tomorrow's weather forecast. Most of them can't even spell the word university, let alone engage in any conversations more meaningful than the price of eggs."

"What would you do for eggs if those same farmers didn't know how to raise chickens?" asked Stephen Tilden.

When the meal was over, they carried their dishes to the kitchen. Setting his into the kitchen sink, Poppa turned to Tillie. "As far as I'm concerned, this is a great opportunity. If you decide to accept it, you have my blessing ... And now I've got to mow the yard."

When he had left the kitchen, Mother turned to her and snapped, "Tillie, do whatever you want. Just remember your father and I have always guided you in ways we thought best. This business of going to the country is a foolish step."

That decided it.

"So I'm a fool if I go this way?" Tillie fought to control her emotions, but knew she was losing. Her voice grew louder and rose in pitch. "You don't trust me at all, do you, Mother? You still treat me like a ten-year-old."

She gave in to the torrent boiling up within. "This isn't about me at all, is it? It's that old quarrel between you and Poppa. Now you want to control me just as you've controlled him all these years. He thinks it's a good thing. He believes in me. Foolish step? I love you Mother, but there are times when we all get to make fools of ourselves. My time has come!"

She slammed the back porch door, bounded down the sidewalk and ran toward the High Bridge. No one said any more about her future throughout the rest of the weekend. On Sunday evening Tillie announced that she was going to take her 'foolish step' and accept the position. Poppa gave her a big hug. Her mother scowled, continued with her knitting and said nothing.

On Monday morning Tillie met Dean Johnson in his office.

"I'll do it, but mind you, only for the one year. After that, I want to finish my final semester and complete my degree. I appreciate the effort of the University and I look forward to meeting Superintendent Murphy."

Chapter 3

_____

Moving to Rosemount

Tillie arrived in Rosemount to begin her duties as the temporary teacher of Dakota County Independent School District 132's one-room school at the end of August, 1934. Poppa drove her out in his Desoto. Mother said she couldn't come because she was having another of her terrible migraines.

As they approached the little town south of St. Paul, Tillie said, "You know, Poppa, I've never been all the way out here from South Robert Street before."

"No. We always take Highway 52 … So, what do you think, Tillie, about moving to the country, I mean?"

"I'm excited. Meeting new people, teaching in my own school and everything … Scared though."

"You're my Tillie. You can do this."

"It's good to know you believe in me. I don't think Mother does."

"Mother has her own ideas. I can't change them."

Stephen Tilden's heart ached with regret that his daughter had missed growing up in the country. Life in the city was sterile. So much asphalt and concrete, so many machines and loud noises, so many glaring lights and ugly signs. His daughter should have smelled fresh clover on a hillside in spring. She should have heard the songs of meadow larks and killdeers. She should have tasted warm milk, fresh from a cow's udder, and bit into a ripe red apple, right from the tree. She should have seen a tiny chick pick its way out of an egg shell and watched a little piglet slurping hungrily from the teat of its mother sow. She should have felt the sweet joy of leaping into a pile of new mown hay. She should have caught a bullhead from a lake down the road.

She had none of these wonderful memories. She had known nothing but the barrenness of urban existence. He wanted her to have so much more.

Tillie stared out the window as they approached Rosemount. The rolling, green farm land, with its fields, some plowed, others still covered with corn and grain stubble, faded into the outskirts of the town. A few small houses with neatly kept yards greeted them. A John Deere Implement store appeared on the left. A little further on the right a Standard Oil Filling Station looked out at them with dirty front windows and a broken down car seat leaning against the wall beneath. An overflowing trash can stood next to the door.

"Rosemount reminds me of other little towns," she said. "One main street, a bunch of small shops and businesses. The people live in little frame houses. Their high school is a lot smaller than ours–Home of the Fighting Irish."

"Lots of Irish Catholics settled around here when Minnesota was just becoming a state around the end of the last century," replied Poppa. "They own many of the farms in this part of the country. They pretty much run this little town."

"Look at the size of that Catholic church."

St. Cecelias was a large, dark brown brick structure, built in imitation of European Gothic Cathedrals, with stained glass windows and a high bell tower. Behind it stood a large parish hall and an attached rectory. The sign in front proclaimed, 'Sunday Masses 8,9:30 & 11:00 a.m. Holy Days 7:00 a.m. Confessions Saturdays 2:00 - 7:00 p.m.'

"Ever been to a Catholic Mass, Tillie?"

"Just once. Remember Edna Sternitzki?"

"Who?"

"That little kid that used to live across from us. I think her dad was a truck driver."

"Oh, them. So?"

"When she was confirmed she invited me to Mass. Remember how you and Mother made a big deal about my going? That's the only time I was ever at a Mass. Really strange, with all that Latin, incense, bells and chanting … Who was St. Cecilia, Poppa?"

Poppa laughed. "Now how in the world am I supposed to know that Tillie? I think she was some kind of Roman virgin way back in ancient times."

"Okay. I'm going to live here so I ought to know something about the people. By the way, are there any Methodists out here?"

"Don't think so.

"Well, if there are no Methodists, where will I go to church?"

"I think there's a Methodist church seven or eight miles down the road in Farmington. How about going to that Baptist church over there? Ever been to a Baptist church?"

"Goodness no, Poppa," she laughed. "Mother'd have a kitten, maybe another of her migraine headaches."

"Guess she would, all that hand clapping and loud preaching. I used to go to a Baptist church when I was younger, down in Iowa, before your mother and I got married. Rather enjoyed it. Don't mention it to Mother if you do drop by some Sundays."

"Too wild for Mother."

"Probably. A couple times a month I'll come on Saturdays and pick you up for the weekend, bring you to our proper Methodist Church. Okay?"

"Sure."

By this time they were approaching O'Dell Street. "This is the street," said Tillie. "Are all the streets named after Irishmen?"

"Guess so."

At the end of O'Dell, near the eastern edge of the town, they found Mrs. Wilson's boarding home for young ladies. Tillie knew it at once, both by the size of the building and by the neatly painted sign planted among flowers in the front yard.

Tillie felt she already knew Mrs. Wilson when she met Tillie and Poppa at the front door. She was of medium height, with gray hair pulled back in a tight bun on the back of her head. She wore round, rimless glasses. Her matronly figure more than filled her cotton print dress. Her black laced shoes were worn, but polished with care.

She led them up the front stairs to the last of the four rented bedrooms in her large, frame house.

Tillie followed, struggling with her heavy canvas suitcase full of clothing and shoes. Dr. Tilden tagged after, arms weighed down with two large cardboard boxes of books. They piled the boxes and suitcase on the single bed.

"You don't need me getting in your hair, so I'll leave you two to get settled in," said Norma Wilson. She disappeared down the stairs.

"Not very big, is it?" asked Poppa.

"A little smaller than mine at home. At least I have a dresser, four drawers, too. And a bookcase. Try the chair, Poppa."

Poppa sat down on a well-worn wooden chair with a faded paisley cushion and took a deep breath of the flowers on the dresser. "Mmm. Smell those. Mrs. Wilson must be a gardener. I'll bet she cut them this morning. Very nice. Smells like the country."

Tillie pulled open a door on the other side of the bed. "Not a very big closet either. Guess it'll do. The window looks out on the back yard. I see a whole garden full of flowers and a couple apple trees. Lots of green grass. Very pretty. I'm going to like this place."

One more trip to the car for both Tillie and Poppa and all of her belongings were moved in.

How weird and yet how wonderful, she thought. *A new town full of strangers, a new home. In about a week I'll be standing in front of a classroom of children I know nothing about. Will they accept a girl from the city? Will I be able to teach them anything? What will these Catholics say about a Methodist? Of course, they're not all Catholics. They have their own school in town. Baptists, Methodists and Lutherans live around here too, I believe. And farmers. What are farmers like? Mother says they're dull, boring, uneducated. Poppa says they're loving, dedicated, fascinating people. Strange. I'm both excited and anxious all wrapped in one.*

Poppa's bottom lip quivered as he stood before his car, preparing to leave. He reached out to his daughter. "Time to go, baby. You're going to be fine, just fine. Give me a hug."

Tillie gave her Poppa a final hug and wiped away a tear rolling down his cheek with her index finger. "Don't cry, Poppa," she said as she choked back her own tears. "It's not like I moved across the ocean."

"I know, Tillie. I knew my little girl would grow up one day and leave home. I'll miss you not being there each night to give me a big smacker. Love you, baby."

With that he dropped down into his Desoto, started the engine and drove off. Tillie wiped her own tears and made her way up to her room.

Ten minutes later Mrs. Wilson appeared once again at the door to Tillie's room, glowing with her most charming, benevolent smile. She waited until she was certain Tillie was looking at her.

"Welcome again, Miss Tilden. We're glad to have you here."

"I'm glad to be here too."

"This is a home for young women. We're in our second year. The other girls are wonderful. I'm sure you'll fit in."

"I'll do my best," Tillie smiled.

"I'll do my best too. Clarence and I raised six children, two boys and four girls. I have a pretty good idea what young people need."

"I haven't met Mr. Wilson. Is he at work?"

"No, dear. The poor man passed away a little over two years ago."

"I'm sorry."

"I miss him. We ran Rosemount's hardware store for nearly thirty years."

"Do you still own the store?"

"Goodness, no. Couldn't afford to keep it. Too many bills. Sold it and decided to turn this big place into a boarding house."

"Good thing for us girls."

"I like to think so. Now I don't want to throw the book at you, but I must give you a word or two about our house rules."

"I'm used to house rules."

"Good. Here's ours. We encourage our girls to attend the church of their choice. Each girl is expected to care for her own linens. The washing machine down in the basement is for you to use. Sign up for your turn on the sheet posted next to it."

"Sounds fine with me."

"Breakfast is always served at seven o'clock. You may, of course, prepare yourself a daily lunch. The evening meal is served promptly at six o'clock. On Sundays the main meal is always served at noon."

"I like home cooking."

"Fine. Do you have any questions?"

"One or two. The church of my choice is Methodist. Is there a Methodist church in town?"

"Sorry. None here. Our family attends a nice little Baptist church. Perhaps you'd like to visit with us one Sunday."

"Perhaps."

"There are several Lutheran churches out in the country. There's a Methodist church in Farmington, but it's too far for anyone without a car."

"I certainly don't have a car. One question about social affairs. Men friends may call on us, right?"

"Of course, as long as you meet in the parlor. Men are never allowed in the bedrooms."

"No problem. I'm accustomed to rules. There's one that you didn't mention." Tillie's eyes twinkled as she asked, "What about alcohol, Mrs.

Wilson?"

"Oh dear, Miss Tilden, I'm surprised you should ask such a question, you being a Methodist and all. Absolutely no alcohol allowed in this house. If I ever hear of one of our young ladies acting inappropriately in public, well, I may have to ask her to leave."

"You and my mother agree on that one. She doesn't just keep alcohol out of the house, she's an active prohibitionist. She's really angry that prohibition has been abolished. I've heard speeches and stories about the dangers of demon rum as long as I can remember."

"Looks like we're both on the same page, Miss Tilden. I'm happy to see your mother raised you to be a proper young lady."

"She did that. Yes, she did that." Tillie laughed. Then casting a glance back at her room she said, "By the way, thank you for the beautiful flowers. They smell so good. Poppa said they reminded him of all the wonderful things about the country. I agree. It's wonderful here."

"Very good. Get yourself settled in. Supper will be served in about two hours. I'm sure you will want to meet the other girls."

One of the three other girls didn't wait for supper time to introduce herself. As soon as Mrs. Wilson went back down the stairs Tillie heard a little tap on her door. She opened it to find a slim, smiling blonde-haired young woman about her own age and a couple inches taller than her own five feet, four inches.

"Hi, I'm Eila, Eila Stricklund. I'm in the next room. Couldn't help but hear Mrs. W. lay out the house rules. Makes you feel just like home, huh?"

"Yup, now that you mention it. I'm Tillie, Tillie Tilden. I'm from West St. Paul. Where're you from?"

"From Minneapolis, a nurse. Been working here at a little clinic with a couple of these hick doctors now for a year. Sorry about calling them hicks. They don't keep up."

"I'm familiar with the term. My mother calls all country people hicks."

"Sounds snobbish, doesn't it? I should stop using it. Lots of good people around here."

"Right. So far I've met one. You're the second. Neither one of you seems to be a 'hick'."

"Got your point. Now what brings you to our little town?"

"I'm the new teacher for District 132's country school."

"Oh yeah? The new country school teacher. Right..." She paused, searching for words. "Okay. Your first teaching job?"

"First one. Actually I'm not certified yet. Just finished my Junior year at Hamline. They couldn't find a teacher for out here, so to make a long story short, I'm it. Just for one year."

"One year and then back to college?"

"That's the ticket. This year will serve as my student teaching experience."

"Sounds good. Looks like we'll have lots to talk about. By the way, you like to dance?"

"We studied ballroom dancing at the University, if that's what you mean."

"Naw, I mean real dancing, like polkas and schottisches and stuff like that."

"My mother, ah ... No, I never learned about that kind of dancing. I'd like to."

"Good. Count on learning something new."

"Where?"

"Got a good dance hall right here in town. I'll invite you."

"I'd like that. One more thing. Where do you go to church?"

"Don't much. I'm a Swede. Grew up in a Swedish Lutheran Church in Minneapolis, Augustana Synod. Ever hear of it?"

"Not sure. I'm a Methodist. No Swedes out here?"

"One or two. Mostly Germans, German Lutherans and a little handful of German Catholics."

"So why don't go to the German Lutheran church?"

"They talk German. I no *spreche Deutsch*. I get back to the Cities about once a month though. Go with my family up there ... So, see you at supper." Eila disappeared back into her own room.

Here's a girl I can relate to, thought Tillie. *We're going to be friends, good friends, even if she is a Swede. Now if I only knew what a schottische was.*

27

Chapter 4

First Day at School

Tillie's opening school day was scheduled for the first Tuesday after Labor Day. Promptly at eight a.m. on Monday the week before, Emil Wunderlich picked her up at the Wilson house. He was taller than Tillie by an inch or two, mostly bald, with white hair around the edges and a rotund figure that reminded her of an illustration of one of Snow White's dwarves in her copy of *The Young Folks' Treasury of Fairy Tales*.

He greeted her with a happy laugh, "So, Miss Tilden, we meet."

"Good morning, Mr. Wunderlich." Tillie climbed into his Chevy pickup, plunked an armload of books on the seat beside her, closed the door, and continued. "You live close by?"

"Yah, about two blocks away. Lived there most of my life."

"Really. What do you do besides drive teachers to school?"

"I'm retired. I was a shop keeper for thirty years on Main Street. We sold groceries, dry goods and all sorts of odds and ends."

"You must know everybody around here then."

"Pretty much. Momma and I was born here, yah. So we know most of the people."

"How'd you end up with the taxi business?"

"Superintendent Murphy says he needs somebody to drive his teachers to school. I'm not real busy. So I get the job."

"How far is it?"

"Just about six miles one way."

"You pick me up again in the afternoon?"

"That's my job."

Tillie noticed that Wunderlich spoke with a decided German accent to his words. She thought he sounded like Gerhard Spiegel, the butcher who ran a shop up on Smith Street in West St. Paul. He was, however, a lot shorter and smiled often.

Wunderlich continued. "Your first year teaching, I understand, Miss Tilden."

"Yes. Lots to learn. Please, call me Tillie."

"Okay, Tillie it is. Yah, and everyone calls me Emil. It's 'Mr. Wunderlich' when I'm in trouble, yah."

"So, Emil, tell me about 132's previous teacher. Did you know her?"

"Ach, maybe we talk about that another time. Not good to gossip."

"What do you mean? Something I should know?"

"*Nein*. Don't worry about it. It won't … You don't want to get into all that … You've got some good students and some good parents to work with.

"Excuse, me, but are we changing the subject?"

"Yah, it's best. The school board wants to look after you. That's why they hired me."

"Why? Why don't you want to talk about it?"

"*Ach*, it was a sad time. Let it be over … Anything else you need, just let me know."

It was obvious that Emil was not going to say any more about last year's teacher. Tillie shrugged her shoulders and frowned deeply. First Eila and now Emil. What was so sad, so strange?

In a few minutes a little white school house appeared, perched on an acre of land at the intersection of two country roads. Emil turned into a graveled driveway to park in a tiny front lot.

Tillie gazed with wonder on the little building before her. It wasn't much to look at, just a small building with three windows on either wall and a roof covered with graying wooden shingles. Nevertheless, this was her school, her very own school. *Before long those walls will be filled with children, my students*, she thought. *I'll be their teacher. We'll be on this journey together, right here.*

She looked at the flagpole next to the front steps and imagined her little troop standing before it, pledging allegiance to the flag and to the country for

29

which it stood, one nation, indivisible, with liberty and justice for all. On the either side was a lawn of mostly dandelions and weeds. She wondered who kept them cut back. The playground stretched out beyond the building to meet a plowed field. She saw her students playing tag out there and sliding down the rusty metal slide during recess.

"This is your school," said Emil.

She piled her arms full of books from the seat beside her, stepped from Emil's faded red truck and followed him to the front door. He opened it with his key and ushered her in through a coat room to the single classroom. The air was hot, stuffy and stale. As she walked toward the front of the room between the rows of desks, she ran her finger across the dust that had accumulated over the summer.

A little cloud of dust rose also from the sill as Emil raised one of the windows. He said, "Here you will change the hearts and lives of young boys and girls. You will open their minds to reading, writing and mathematics. You will be their honored teacher."

"Emil, you're quite a philosopher."

Emil raised a second window and turned toward Tillie with an impish smile. "Yah, maybe I wanted to be a teacher once."

"So why weren't you?"

"*Ach*, what a long story. Too much work to do on the farm. My Poppa needed me. No time for higher education."

"But you wanted to teach."

"Yah, I always loved children and I love to read. I still read many books."

"Emil, I bet we'll have lots to talk about. I'll need your wisdom."

"Yah, if I can help, let me know."

Every day throughout that first week Emil picked her up at the Wilson home and drove her to the Rich Valley school. As they made their way she plied him with questions. "Emil, what crops do the farmers raise? When do they plant them?"

"One question at a time, Tillie. Yah, they raise hay and sweet corn and field corn and oats and barley. They milk cows and raise pigs and chickens."

"Lots of work, right?"

"Yah, and it's hard work. Everybody works hard."

"Do they all hate the work, Emil?"

"What you mean? I do not know."

"Do they wish they lived someplace else, like St. Paul?"

"Why you should ask that question?"

"My Mother hates farms. She grew up on one and couldn't wait to get away."

"*Ach*, these people don't want to get away. This is their life. For generations they live this way."

"The farms pass on from father to son, I suppose."

"Yah. Many sons live with their poppas and mommas and work the farms."

Through each day of that first week, after Emil dropped her off, Tillie poured over the lesson plans left by the former teacher, Helen Shattuck. Helen had signed those plans, but who was she? Tillie was puzzled about why no one wanted to talk about her. Emil and Eila continued to avoid her questions. Mrs. Wilson shrugged her shoulders. What had happened that no one dared to talk about? Even Superintendent Murphy put her off when he dropped in for his initial visit on the Thursday of her preparatory week.

"Good to meet you, Miss Tilden. Sure I've heard a lot about you from the University."

They didn't tell me much about you, Mr. Murphy, she thought. *They didn't talk about your carrot red hair and all those freckles. Depression or not, it looks like you never miss a meal, either. Now that I see you, I guess I'll have to figure you out myself.*

"Good to meet you too, Mr. Murphy. I hope what they said was not all bad."

An impish smile crossed Murphy's freckled face. "Well now, there were a few things they warned me to be watching out for."

"Really. Like what?"

"Too many questions. Watch out for her, they said. She's full of questions. It's in a corner with her questions, she'll put you, if you don't be on your guard."

My, but you sound like some kind of leprechaun. Does that mean you're into tricks as well? "Too many questions? Now who in the world said that?"

"Ah, see. There you go. Just like they said."

Tillie began to laugh. "Got me. Sorry. It's just that I have so many things I want to learn about."

"Indeed, Miss Tilden. Now there's the other thing they warned me about."

"The other thing?"

"Yes. She's a smart one, they said. With a mind as sharp as a tack. She'll be giving you a run for your money, Michael Murphy."

At least he has a kind of charm about him. Perhaps we'll get along just fine, she thought. "I'm sorry, sir." Tillie smiled broadly. "I'll try to behave."

"I'm sure you will, Miss Tilden. I'm sure you will. I want you to know from the start how happy I am to be having you here."

"Thank you, Mr. Murphy. I'm really looking forward to this year."

"Fine. Fine indeed. Now if there's anything you need, just be letting me know."

"I will. You can be sure of that."

"I'll be by every week. Would Thursday afternoons be a good time?"

"Yes. That will work out well. I'll save up my questions."

"Sure and I'm certain you will. It's just for a moment that I'm here today. Is there anything you will be needing from me at this time."

"Not really. Emil has been very helpful and I believe I've got my plans pretty well worked out for the first week."

"Good. I've brought a list of your students with me, I have. You'll be wanting to memorize their names."

He handed the list to her. She scanned them and then commented, "Mostly Germans."

"That they are. Most of the people in this neighborhood are of Germanic backgrounds. We Irish live mostly over near Rosemount."

Tillie continued to study the list for another moment. Then she looked up at Murphy again. "There's one other thing I wanted to ask about."

"Sure, if I can answer it, I'll try."

"It's about Helen Shattuck. I see her name on all the lesson plans and papers around here. Can you tell me about her? Everybody around seems to avoid my questions about her."

"Helen's dead. An unfortunate accident."

"I know she's dead, sir. What I don't understand is how it happened."

"That'll take some explaining, it will. I'd rather not be getting into it today." Murphy's voice was quiet, intense. "We'll discuss it later, Miss Tilden," he said. "Right now, 'tis best you be focusing on the tasks at hand. Be getting your classroom ready for the new year. Everything you'll be needing to get started should be here. As I said, I'll be by weekly. If you have any other questions, feel free to call me office."

Tillie noted that Murphy's smile had turned into a frown. His teasing manner had melted when she asked about Helen. His voice was now stern, business-like. He tried another smile, but it would not come. "I must be on my way now. Again, good to meet you."

Murphy took Tillie's hand for a moment and then turning on his heel, disappeared swiftly out the front door. As she heard his car drive away, she pondered her first encounter with her new supervisor. *What a strange man. Not only sounds like a leprechaun, even looks a bit like what I would imagine one to be. Needs a green suit though. Taller too, but he has the red hair and freckles. I wonder why he is so nervous.*

During the week Tillie made notes and prepared her lesson plans. Emil helped her find paper, pencils, chalk and crayons at his former store. She decorated the walls, hung pictures and posted a bulletin board for the approaching start of school.

The first day of the new school year began as planned, on the Tuesday after Labor Day. She greeted it with fear and excitement. *Will I be able to teach them anything? Will they accept me? What if I am a total failure? Maybe they won't obey me. Oh, silly girl. I'll do fine. In a few weeks they'll be running to get to school. They'll love it. This is going to be tremendous.*

She stepped from Emil's truck and stared at the building as if she were seeing it for the first time.

"So, Tillie, now it starts," said Emil. "A good job you will do, I know. Have a good day. I'll see you this afternoon." He drove off.

Good bye for now, old Philosopher, she thought. I do hope you can help me to understand these children, these Germans, these farmers and, yes, this strange Irishman who runs the show.

She unlocked the front door, went to her desk at the far end of the room to ponder her list of students. She pulled the list from its brown envelope, put it on her desk and tried to picture each one of her students in her mind, but realized at once that she had no idea who these German children were: Baumgartner, Gerber, Kramer, Metzger, Neunaber, Switzer, Wagner and Zimmermann. There were a couple Scandinavians: Lundgren and Swenson. And an Irish child, Brent Sullivan.

Who were these children? What were their families like? In less than an hour all twenty-three would march in the front door, deposit their lunch pails in the coat room. They would find seats in the rows of desks. Those scratchy old desks kept looking at her. What secrets did they hold?

She put her list down, rose from her chair and wandered again to the far corner where a large, wood-burning stove with its surrounding wrought iron screen, stood. The screen obviously kept the children from touching the hot stove. A pipe crawled from its top and disappeared in the chimney behind it. The dark black stove, with its big iron door, seemed too large. At least nobody will be cold with a big fire stoked in there, she thought.

A rear door led from the classroom to the attached back storage room. The wood-room mocked her. She hated that room with its huge piles of wood scraps, split logs, dried corn cobs ... and spider webs! She was terrified of spiders, especially the big black-widow kind that had woven their webs in every corner. They seemed to claim that dark and dirty room as their private territory.

Emil told her that he would help her start a fire in the stove at the beginning of the approaching cold days, but she would have to keep it going during the day. Tillie knew that in October the temperature would drop below freezing at night and the following days would get progressively colder as she and her students trudged through the icy Minnesota winter and on toward spring. Already, those days were marching toward her, like a menacing army. To drive back their arctic attack she would have to go out to the spiders' domain and bring in wood. The spiders would die in the cold, but their wretched webs would still be there, filled with eggs of new spiders for the coming year. Yuk!

What did she know about tending to fires anyway? At home Poppa always did that. Never in her life had she built a fire in a stove. Yes, Emil said he'd help, but nobody at the college ever said anything about her having to stoke fires. Maybe she would get one of the two eighth grade boys on her list to help. Did the eighth grade boys like to keep fires going? She doubted it.

And at the end of the day, who was going to clean up the floor, wash the chalk boards, dust the shelves and knock the chalk out of the erasers? One guess. Nobody at college said anything about those things either.

Her self pity was interrupted by the sounds of children's voices. The list on her desk suddenly came alive as two eighth grade boys and the twenty-one other students arrived. One by one they marched in. She greeted them individually, introduced herself and asked each for his or her name. Then she pointed them to their assigned desks.

Tillie looked joyfully at her students. *So these were the farm kids*, she thought. *They looked like most other children she had known, except for their simple clothing. What was it Emil had said about them? Most of them had to do chores before school. They washed breakfast dishes, fed chickens, ducks and hogs. The older ones milked the cows. All that before the bus came to bring them to school. I'm sure glad I didn't have so much work before school at their age.*

Now they all sat there at five minutes after nine on this first day of the new school year. *Was that a glare from those two in the corner?* she wondered. Most of them were smiling sheepishly. *I'll bet they're wondering how this five foot, five, twenty-one-year old can possibly be their teacher. Will they accept me? Do they miss their teacher from last year? What do they know about her? Maybe they can tell me the story. Should I ask them? Not now,* she decided.

"Good morning, children. I'm happy to see that we're all here. As I said, I am Miss Tilden. My name's on the chalk board. I'm your teacher for this year. I know we're going to have a great year. Let's get started."

Things went surprisingly well that first week. The two eighth grade boys were respectful. One of the girls in grade six was very shy. The other sixth grader, a boy named Orville Switzer, looked as if he might give her a little trouble. He was nearly her height, small-boned, with a childish face, narrow lips, brown eyes, tousled brown hair and a cowlick that always needed combing. He wouldn't stay in his desk for more than ten minutes. He kept shifting around, whispering to his neighbor or trying to throw spit balls. However, by the second week, even he was beginning to settle into somewhat of a routine.

Tillie surprised herself during that second week of teaching. Her lesson plans were working. Her students had taken their first quizzes and passed, except for her curious sixth grader, Orville. What was he doing in grade six anyway? she asked herself. He hardly seemed capable of grade two work. A nice enough child. In fact, she liked him. He cooperated, but something was missing. She knew it as soon as he opened his mouth. Much of what she taught him did not somehow click. He was a slow child. He was going to be quite a challenge.

On Thursday evening of that second week Tillie sat on the edge of Eila's bed and told her about Orville. "He's really not a bad kid. He's–how can I put it, slow. I mean, really slow. He doesn't catch on. I don't think he's able to do much of anything. He's not real smart."

"Hey, Tillie, I know the Switzers. They've been to the clinic."

"Really. Tell me about them."

"Mr. Switzer is a farm hand. They're not educated. Pardon me if I sound stuck up, but they are what I meant when I talked about hicks."

"Now you sound like my mother."

"They're not stupid. They're simple people. They haven't had much experience."

"What are you talking about? Everybody has experiences."

"I mean their world is small, narrow."

"I don't suppose they've ever been any place other than around

Rosemount."

"Exactly. They have little or no education. I tried to talk to Mrs. Switzer once about how to give some cough syrup to Orville. She kept getting the instructions all mixed up. 'They're all written out on the label, on the bottle,' I said.

'Oh, dear, Nurse,' she said. 'I don't read instructions so good. I can't see 'em. I think I need glasses, but we can't afford 'em. My Hermann he ain't never learned how to read. So maybe you could just go over them instructions again.'"

Tillie shook her head. "That's how Orville acts, only he doesn't need glasses. He sees the words, but what they mean doesn't stick."

"I know what you mean. When I told Emil about the Switzers, he said trying to teach them is like pouring water down a gopher hole. Ever try that?"

"No. I've never even seen a gopher, let alone its hole."

"You're about to, kid."

They laughed together. Tillie continued, "I guess all of us teachers need to have an Orville in our classrooms. It keeps us on our toes. Funny thing, I enjoy Orville."

"Enjoy a kid who can't learn?"

"He's a challenge. He's slow or delayed, but I *am* going to teach him something, even if it kills me."

"You like challenges?"

"I do, and, maybe I can learn something about teaching in the process."

As the days went on, Tillie found that Orville was her test, but she accepted it. The teacher was being taught by her student. Orville taught her patience. He taught her how little she knew about children with limited mental capacities. He taught her to be resourceful.

Superintendent Murphy shook his head when she asked for guidance. "You won't be teaching that Switzer child anything," he said. "And sure, it doesn't matter what you do. Keep him quiet as best you can. When he gets out of grade eight, he can work with his father. There's plenty of manure to shovel on the farm."

That's it? Don't try? Face the facts? Give up? Tillie wanted to spit in Murphy's face, but what would that accomplish? *Keep your thoughts to yourself, girl. He hasn't forbidden you to try.*

She enlisted Kathy Neunaber, a bright seventh grader, to help her work with Orville. Kathy, she decided, would learn as she helped Orville. Day by day teacher and apprentice labored. Then one day Orville caught on how to read a very simple, short sentence.

"Wow," he said with his usually slow, slurred, stumbling speech. "I can read. I can read. I'm gonna show my Momma tonight. I can read."

That was the highlight of her day. No, of her week. Orville was learning, regardless of what Murphy said. I'm a teacher, she thought. Even my slowest student is learning.

District 132's Superintendent continued to show up as he had during her preparation week and the weeks following. They talked about their respective backgrounds.

"Me parents emigrated from Ireland at the beginning of this century," he said. "Sure, they were among the original settlers in this area. It is in Rosemount that I grew up and later me Da and Ma worked hard so I could attend the University of Minnesota. So for the past twenty-four years I've been teaching school in the area. For the past ten of those years I've been Superintendent of the District."

Tillie looked at his red hair, green eyes and light, freckled skin and thought, *Now there's an Irishman if I ever saw one. But he's not a young man any more. Those wrinkles around his eyes and that bulge around his middle tell me that he's seen a few years. His high pitched voice has a strange twang. Some of his speech patterns are more Irish than American. I wonder why. He grew up here. I suppose the Irish community, like the Germans, preserve their heritage and identity by the use of their peculiar language, as well as their customs.*

Murphy seemed excited about his task of supervising Tillie's teaching. "The little extra stipend from Hamline University assists me wife and me with our expenses. Don't be expecting to get rich in the teaching profession, Miss Tilden."

"I don't. That's not why I want to be a teacher."

"Good for you. There's more to it all than the money."

"I agree."

"I see by your record that you have a sister. Is she going to be a teacher too?"

"Mattie? No way. Right now all Mattie talks about is boys. Nobody knows what she plans to do with her life."

"I have two children, both grown up, they are, and moved away. It's good Catholics, they are as well. And they married within the church. Taught by the good nuns, they were and sure they graduated from St. Cecelia's school."

"Do your married children have children?"

"No, they don't, but we keep praying for them."

"I think my parents would like to see me marry and have children as well."

"'Tis a fine thing, being married, especially when a man and his wife see eye to eye. A fine thing indeed."

"I've never met your wife."

"We live in the same town, you and me. Perhaps one day you will."

"I'd like that."

"So here am I, the Super of the *public* school system. Kind of ironic, is it not? But then, it's an educator I am and there's no place for me at St. Cecelia's. That place is run by the good sisters. So I work with the public school children of 132. And sure, not all the Catholic kids go to school over there. One of your children is from a family in our parish."

Michael Murphy has his own strange ways, thought Tillie. *I wonder what he means about being married. He says nothing about his wife. He's Irish and a Catholic to the bone. Yet he says nothing about my faith. He sure has some rigid ideas about education. I wonder if he really tries to keep up with what's going on? On the other hand, he's had lots of experience. I'll bet he might be able to teach me a thing or two.*

But there's something else. What is it? He seems to enjoy (is that the word?) these supervision sessions too much. I feel a little bit uneasy on these Thursdays. He sits so close to my desk. Is it the way he looks at me? He doesn't just look at my eyes. His eyes start at the top and roam all the way to my feet and he does it every time we get together. Is it the way he talks to me? There is a sweetness, something almost seductive about his manner of talking. Maybe it's that Irish brogue. Or is it the way he held my hand that first time I met him? He didn't just hold it; he squeezed it. I don't know what it is. It's elusive. A feeling. Something.

Finally she dismissed it as part of her own nervousness and it slipped to the back of her mind.

She also decided that she would wait for an opportune time to discuss what happened to last year's teacher. Murphy had said nothing more about her. Why not? What had happened?

Chapter 5

Teacher

By the end of that second week of teaching Tillie discovered some free time for herself and was ready to accept an invitation from Eila.

"Tillie, there's a dance over at the Rosemount Community Hall this Saturday." Eila laughed. "All of us girls here at Mrs. Wilson's are going together. Lots of guys show up. We think it'll be wondrous fun. We'd like you to come along."

Tillie's eyes sparkled at the thought. Those first three weeks (counting the one before Labor Day) had been a real grind. She needed a break. "Yes. Yes, I'll come. I love to dance. Maybe I can learn how to polka."

Four girls packed themselves into Eila's little Ford and rode the two miles to the Rosemount Community Hall at the southern edge of town on the road to Farmington. The hall was a large clapboard covered frame building with a tin roof.

"As far as I can tell, nobody seems to remember when this old crate was built," said Eila. "Everybody around uses it—for town meetings, wedding receptions, auctions, you name it. Whenever it starts to rain on that old tin roof it makes so much noise you have to shout to be heard by the person standing right next to you."

As they walked up the three outside stairs, Tillie saw that the paint was fading and chipping. Inside exposed beams and unpainted walls pointed to the simplicity and economy of this country dance hall. It seemed that if the well-worn wooden floor could talk it would tell stories of thousands of happy couples.

At the far end of this rural playground stood a small stage where local bands strutted their stuff. This particular night's dance featured "The Gill Pickles," four young brothers from the same family. When Tillie commented on the corny name, Eila replied, "Face it. Like I been telling you, this is a hick town. Every brother's first name begins with a G. George plays the tuba; Gregory pounds his drums; Gilbert is the swaying accordionist and Gordon leads the Gill Pickles with his swinging clarinet. Catch those crazy blue and white striped sport coats with matching red ties. These guys are farmers, but I think they dream of becoming full time entertainers. Maybe one day somebody from some big recording studio will pop into good old Rosemount, hear them and invite the Gill Pickles to become famous. Then the whole country will start swinging and swaying to the polkas and schottisches of the good old Gill Pickles!"

All the girls laughed. The hall filled rapidly. The trills, squeaks, toots and taps of the warming up exercises of the Pickles' various instruments mixed with the cacophony of the would-be-dancers' voices.

The night was cool, but the air in the hall was warm and stuffy. The smell of freshly brewed coffee and newly tapped beer kegs drifted from the kitchen area. Outside a few young men passed around mysterious bottles wrapped in brown paper sacks.

As always, those who came as singles settled themselves on the well-worn benches and chairs along the walls. The Wilson girls joined a group of other unaccompanied young women on the far side benches. They giggled as they told one another stories about previous dances. Since they had not come as dates, each Wilson maiden hoped to be asked to dance by one of the young men on the other side of the room.

The men, of course, were searching for the courage to do just that. Many of the men stood, leaning against the wall. Some pretended to be bored. Others moved from one foot to the other, waiting for the Gill Pickles to start the first dance. They wanted to march across the room and begin the find-your-partner ritual.

In this ritual it was the custom for the young women to sit demurely and wait to be asked.

Like all the other young women, Tillie studied the lineup on the far wall. As she pondered her role, she was particularly attracted to a young farmer about her own age. She leaned over to Eila. "Who's that guy over there with the dark, wavy hair?"

"Who you talking about?"

"Gosh, you don't expect me to point, do you? He's the tall guy near the corner, just a couple feet from the kitchen, with the wavy black hair. See him?"

"Oh, him! Yeah, I know him. Even danced once or twice with him. That's Freitag, Al Freitag. He works with his dad and brother on a farm a few miles east of here. Drives a black Model-A Ford. Likes to dance too. He's pretty good at it. Nice guy. Not my type, though. I think you'd like him. Want me to introduce you?"

"Come on, Eila. I was just asking."

The first dance began. A few couples moved out on the floor. Tillie kept her eye on Freitag. She decided he must be about six feet, two inches tall, big enough to make her feel like a midget. Muscular, he had a square jaw, generous nose and beautiful black hair. She concluded his face and arms were tanned by outdoors work.

She continued to study the big farmer as he began threading his way through the dancers over to Tillie's side of the hall. Tillie's heart thumped as this tall, young farmer with the deep blue eyes came right up to her. She stood to meet him and held out her hand. She was not about to play the part of the shy wallflower.

"Hi, I'm Al," he began. "Would you like to dance?"

"Thank you," she replied with polished confidence. "I'm Tillie and yes, I'd love to dance. Only one problem. I have never danced a schottische or a polka in my entire life."

"Ah, no problem. I've danced hundreds," he replied with a twinkle in his blue eyes. "It ain't hard. I'll teach ya. It'll be fun."

As they moved out to the floor, Tillie asked, "So how do we do this?"

"What do I say?" said Al. "It's like, step, close, step, hop, real fast around the room. Just listen to the music. It has a strong upbeat. Okay? Here we go."

The next thing she knew Tillie was gasping for breath as she was swept up into the big farmer's arms and whirled around the floor to the swift beat of the Gill Pickles' music. After a few stumbles, she found her rhythm and followed Al's lead with joyful abandonment. This wild, happy dancing was a far cry from the stately waltzes she learned as a teenager. The peasants, the farmers, the common people of Poland, Czechoslovakia and Germany were loving and laughing, frolicking and having fun to this music. Now she was part of it and she loved it.

When the dance ended, Al said, "You look hot. Was it fun?"

She laughed, "Whoa. I've never danced like that before. Yes, it was fun, but let me catch my breath."

"Sure. How about a beer?"

A beer? Oh dear. Did you hear what he said, Mother? He wants me to drink a beer. Do you realize, Mother dear, I have never even tasted beer? Here I am twenty-one years old and I have never in all my life tasted beer, thanks to you, Mother! And maybe I better not tell Mrs. Wilson either. I don't want to get kicked out at the beginning of the school year.

"A beer? Yes, I think I would."

Al Freitag led Tillie to the kitchen area where a young woman sat behind a little table. On the table was a beat up cigar box with dollar bills and change in it. Beside it was a large roll of paper tickets.

Al handed her a dollar bill. "Hi Mary. How ya doing? Four tickets please."

She smiled, handed him his tickets and some change, and asked, "Who's your date, big Al?"

"This is Tillie. We just met. This was Tillie's first polka. Right Tillie?"

Tillie blushed, in spite of her resolve to remain composed. She reached out her hand to Mary. "Hi, I'm Tillie. Yup. First polka. Fun too. Good to meet you."

Al was back from the kitchen. He held out a brown bottle of Schmidts Beer. "Is a bottle Okay with you? They don't have any cups."

"A bottle is fine."

"Let's sit down," said the farmer.

They walked over to the corner where there were a couple empty wooden chairs. Al began.

"So, Tillie-first-polka, you're new around here. What do you do?"

"Well, Al-polka-teacher, I am new and I'm the new teacher for ISD 132's Rich Valley school. Do you know about it?"

"Sure do. One of my cousins went to school there. And I went to school just up the hill, at St. John's. You pass right by St. John's Lutheran Church and School on your way to your school. I know lots of things about old 132."

Lots of things? She wondered just how much he knew that she had still not been told. Maybe he knew about the former teacher.

Tillie also noted that Al sounded very much like Emil. His German accent caused him to substitute the 'th' sounds for more of a 'd' sound. It seemed typical of the German language. And the way he emphasized his gutturals seemed also typical.

She continued, "So, you went to school at St. John's?"

He laughed, "I did. Finished eight grades there and then my Pa decided he needed me on the farm. He said farmers didn't need no more school. So that was it, but I read lots. Where did you go to school, Miss Teacher?"

"Me? Oh, I went to grade school and high school in West St. Paul and I'm still enrolled as a student at Hamline University in St. Paul."

"So how can you be a teacher and a student at the same time?"

"It's a special situation; something about an emergency out here and the Depression and all. I gather that it's hard to find teachers right now. So they started asking some of us third year college students to take off a year and teach."

"Sounds good. I think that 132 is lucky to get anybody to teach out there after what happened."

"After WHAT happened?" Tillie almost shouted. A couple people nearby turned to look at her.

"They didn't tell you?"

"Tell me WHAT? NO, they did NOT tell me anything."

"Oh, sorry. I guess I said something I wasn't…"

Tillie broke in. Her face was red. She was hot, but it was not just from the dancing. "Why is everybody so darned silent about the other teacher? I don't even know her name. Nobody and I mean *nobody*, will talk about her or about whatever it was that happened!"

"Look, Tillie, I don't even know your last name yet. This isn't the place or the time to talk about this. Maybe some other time, some other place. How about another dance?"

Tears collected in Tillie's eyes. Her hands were trembling. "Not now. Later. Please excuse me. I have to go to the ladies' room."

With that she rose and walked quickly away. What was going on here? What had she gotten herself into? She had to compose herself. She was here to have a good time. Forget about school for now. She stepped into the women's restroom and found a little sink in the corner. She splashed some water on her face and dried herself with a paper towel.

When she came back out she saw Al and Eila dancing. She went back to her place on the bench and pretended to be happy. The evening was not going right. This whole thing about ISD 132 and the former teacher sat there, like Edgar Allen Poe's raven, croaking "Nevermore."

The dance ended. Al and Eila came over to where she sat.

"You okay?" asked Eila.

"Sure. Just needed a break," she replied. "I'm okay. How was the dance?"

"Eila knows how to polka all right," said Al. "It was good. How about you, Tillie; ready to try again?"

"Sure. Why not?"

Al and Tillie danced most of the dances through the evening. The Gill Pickles announced the final line dance shortly after one in the morning. As the happy dancers paraded to the final beats of the evening's music, Al turned to Tillie.

"You got a ride home? I'd be glad to take you."

"Okay. I came with Eila. I'll tell her. We all live over at Mrs. Wilson's."

"I know old lady Wilson's place. I been there once or twice." Al shouted across the room, "Eila! I'm taking Tillie home!"

Eila shouted back across a bunch of happy faces, "Okay, big guy. See that she gets home before breakfast!"

Freitag led Tillie out to his Model-A Ford and seated her on the passenger side. As he closed the door one of his buddies shouted, "Hey, Big-Al, behave yourself now. That's a proper young lady, you know."

Tillie was glad that Al could not see her blushing face in the dark of the night. He crawled in on the driver's side and started the car.

"It's not far to Mrs. Wilson's. Is it okay if we drive over to the park and talk for a little bit before I take you home?"

"Okay, talking is good. Just don't expect anything else."

Now Al was blushing. "Aw, don't pay no attention to those guys. They're always making remarks like that. It don't mean nothing. I mean, I'm not that kind of a guy."

"I believe you, Al. A young woman has to be a little cautious. Know what I mean?"

Al nodded as he put the car in gear, backed it out of its parking spot and headed toward Rosemount's little city park, a few hundred feet down the road. He turned off the motor and reached into the back seat.

"It's a little cool. Here's my jacket. Put it around your shoulders."

"Thank you. That's very thoughtful of you. Now, is a good time to pick up our conversation about the school?"

"Sure. I didn't mean to upset you back there. I mean, I didn't know. I thought they … well, I didn't know what to say and you can't talk about that stuff when everybody's around."

"Okay. What stuff are we talking about?"

"Nobody likes to talk much about it. Can we keep this between us, just you and me?"

"Sure, but maybe it depends on what it is we're discussing. I mean, I AM the new teacher, after all. And I do have to work with these kids. And she—whoever she is—worked with most of the same kids last year before something or the other happened. Did she run away? Fall in a hole? What happened?"

Al was quiet for about thirty seconds. Then he took a deep breath and began.

"It's this way. Her name was Helen Shattuck. She was the niece of Superintendent Murphy, Mrs. Murphy's sister's daughter."

Tillie broke in, "You know he's my boss, right?"

"Yah. As I understand it, Helen was about to go to college up in the Cities when the Depression hit back in '29. Her dad didn't have any savings. Some time in 1931 he lost his job, got really down in the dumps and suddenly disappeared. Nobody ever heard from him after that."

"He deserted his family?"

"Seems so. Helen ran out of money at the start of her junior year and had to drop out. Murphy was in a bind too. The lady who had been teaching in the Rich Valley school that fall got pneumonia and died just before Thanksgiving. So the way I understand it, Murphy asked the Minnesota Board of Education to grant a temporary teaching certificate to his niece. He said he'd be supervising and he couldn't find a teacher no place."

"Straighten me out. When exactly was that?"

"The fall of '31. It seems like she did pretty good too."

"I agree with you," said Tillie. "She had fine lesson plans and her students are pretty much where they're supposed to be. She was a good teacher even if she didn't finish college."

"Yah. That's what I heard too."

"So what happened after that? Why all the mystery?"

"I'm not real sure about everything, but stories go around. For a couple years nothing much happened. She actually stayed with the Murphy's.'

"In their house?"

"Right. She had her own room, lived there. Then Mrs. Wilson's husband died and she opened up her house to young ladies. That's when Helen moved over there."

"And that was a year ago last summer?"

"First of June, I think."

"That's about the same time that Eila moved in," said Tillie.

"Eila knew Helen. I'm surprised she didn't say something about her."

"She's been just as close mouthed as everybody else."

"I understand. It must have been sometime late in June that she met Bill Scheiner at a dance."

"Who's he?"

"He's a guy who grew up around here. Liked to dance, fool around, get drunk, stuff like that.

"Did you say they met here, at the Rosemount Community Dance Hall?"

"Nah. It was over at the Green Roof in Coates, where I live. I think she went with Eila and the other Wilson girls, like you did tonight."

"Coates? Where's Coates?"

"I keep forgetting that you don't know nothing about this area. Coates is ten miles east from here, on Highway 52, on the way south to Rochester. If you ever went down that road you went right through it."

"We probably did," replied Tillie, "but I don't remember going through Coates."

"Doesn't surprise me," laughed Al. "It's not much, a dance hall, a general store and a few houses. Easy to miss. Not really a town. Scheiner and her started dating. I don't want to say much about Scheiner. Like I said, he's kind of a wild guy. Gets drunk lots, drives cars fast and likes girls, if you know what I mean."

Tillie nodded. Al continued.

"Some of us couldn't figure what she saw in him, but they were together everywhere—except in church. Helen was a Catholic, of course, and her aunt and uncle made sure she went to Mass every week. She sometimes ate Sunday dinners with them. Scheiner is supposed to be a Lutheran, but he quit going to church in his teen years. He was probably too hung over most Sunday mornings anyway."

"Where is all this going, Al? I mean, so Helen and Scheiner were dating. What's the big deal?"

"I'm getting to that. Late last summer Helen and Scheiner stopped dating. She quit coming to dances. He was still around, as loud and drunk as ever. Eila says Helen stayed in her room most of the time that August. A couple times she went up to visit with her mother in Duluth, but most of that month she didn't do anything."

"Why not?"

"I don't know much about the details, only some stuff that Eila told me.

She said one night before school started, Scheiner stopped at the house to pick up Helen. They must have had a big fight or something that night, because she came back about midnight with her eyes all red and swollen. Eila said she'd been crying. She saw Helen slip into her room just as she–Eila–was coming out of the bathroom."

"What was that all about?" asked Tillie.

"Nobody knows for sure. Eila says she thinks that Helen was pregnant by Scheiner and wanted him to marry her."

"Pregnant? Wow! That would explain the tears all right!"

"That's all a guess, of course."

"A guess? Did she have a baby?"

"Let me finish. Helen started teaching that fall. Eila says she came back every day from school, all sad and depressed. She locked herself in her room and lots of time skipped supper. Mrs. Wilson got quite worried about her. I think the Murphys even got involved, but Helen wouldn't say anything."

"Murphy won't say anything about it either."

"I can see why."

"What do you mean?"

"Along about that time, Scheiner disappeared. He had been working as a hired man at one of the farms around Coates. He disappeared one night; cleaned out his clothes and snuck off in the dark. Nobody knows where he is now. One guy says he heard he's working at some bar on the north side of Minneapolis."

"Why did he leave?" asked Tillie. "Was he afraid he'd have to get married?"

"Maybe. Nobody knows. He didn't have many friends and the ones he did have shake their heads. Anyway, he was gone."

"Scheiner was gone. Helen was abandoned and depressed."

"Right. Then in early October, when the weather was turning crisp, Helen didn't come home to Mrs. Wilson's one night. Emil Wunderlich said she wasn't there when he went to pick her up."

"Like he comes to pick me up."

"Yah, only she wasn't there. So Emil drove up the hill to the St. John's parsonage to call up Mike Murphy, but he wasn't home. Mrs. Murphy said she hadn't heard from him all day. Emil told her to have him call as soon as she heard from him."

"Where was Murphy?"

"Who knows? Driving around. I don't know."

"How long did Emil have to wait?"

"He told me he waited almost an hour up there at the parsonage talking with our pastor."

"Then what?"

"Then Murphy called and Emil told him he couldn't find Helen. So Murphy came out and he and Emil went back to the school to try to figure out what happened. She wasn't in her classroom, but the school wasn't locked up either."

"She had to be somewhere around there. She didn't have a car."

"That's why old Emil said he didn't know what to say. He had been there at the usual time and she didn't come out. He called for her, but she didn't answer."

"Where did she go?"

"That's just it. Murphy and Emil were about to leave when Emil said he ought to make sure the wood-room door was locked. That's when he found her."

"Found her?" Tillie was trembling. Al's jacket was no longer keeping her warm. "What do you mean?"

"Well, she was out in the wood-room hanging from one of the rafters!"

"My heavens! Was she dead?"

"Yah. Had been for some time. It must have happened right after the children were picked up by the bus."

"Did she commit suicide?"

"Looked like it, but I don't know. Nobody does. She had some bruises on her head, like she had fallen or been hit or something. A chair was tipped over on to a pile of corn cobs. It looked like she rigged up the rope, got on the chair and then pushed it away."

Tillie's eyes were misty. "Oh Al, don't tell me it was in the wood-room. I hate that place. All the while I thought it was the spiders. Now you tell me this young woman hung herself there."

"I'm sorry, Tillie. Now you know why nobody wants to talk about it. I'm sorry. Very sorry."

Tillie was trembling. Al reached over to put his arm around her. She looked up at his blue eyes and asked quietly, "Al, did she really commit suicide?"

"There was an autopsy, of course. The county conducted an inquiry and finally ruled it a suicide, but some of us aren't so sure. It didn't fit with Helen. She was a good Catholic girl and she would believe that she'd go right to hell if she did that."

"Was she pregnant?"

"Yah, she was pregnant. About four months, they said."

"Al, are you suggesting that…"

"I don't want to say anything else. It's just talk. I know Scheiner. I don't believe he's capable of really hurting anybody. He wasn't around here when it happened. I don't know. Let's leave it at that."

"Take me home," said Tillie. "I'm getting really cold."

"Okay. I'm sorry, Tillie. So sorry we had to talk about this our very first night. I hope you understand. I mean, I really would like to see you again."

"I hear you." Tillie was quiet now. She fumbled for her hankie and blew her nose. "Please take me home."

Tillie could not sleep once she got to bed. She tossed and turned. She rose, went to the bathroom, drank some water and tried again. The house was cool, but she was sweating. Thoughts about Helen and Murphy and the wood-room churned around and around in her head. Sometime around four in the morning she fell into a restless slumber. She was awakened at six-thirty by a frightful dream about a corpse in the wood-room, with black-widow spiders crawling over it. Her heart was pounding wildly as she slipped on her bathrobe and slippers, stopped briefly at the bathroom and then appeared in the kitchen. Mrs. Wilson was humming a hymn to herself, as she prepared to scramble a couple eggs on the stove.

"Morning." She turned to Tillie. "Oh my, you don't look so good. What's wrong? You sick?"

"No. I just didn't sleep much last night."

"Something wrong?"

Tillie shuddered as she sat down at the kitchen table. She looked up at Mrs. Wilson, her forehead wrinkled. "Why didn't you tell me about Helen Shattuck?"

Mrs. Wilson put the bowl of eggs down and sat next to Tillie. She was very somber and quiet as she began. "What have you heard?"

"I was dancing with Al Freitag last night. Afterwards we stopped at the park and talked for a while. He told me all about what happened, about her hanging herself and all. Why didn't you tell me before?"

Mrs. Wilson's eyes were brimming with tears. "Oh, Tillie, I hoped to spare you all that. Eila, Emil Wunderlich, Mr. and Mrs. Murphy and lots of others would just as soon put all of that in the past. It was so painful for everyone. I'm so sorry you had to get involved."

Tillie's pain was a mixture of fear, sadness and anger. *What's with these people?* she thought. *Do they really believe that pain and sorrow will disappear if you don't talk about it?*

She looked up and said, "What can you tell me about her?"

Norma Wilson paused, glanced down at her feet and then up again. "I don't know what Freitag told you, but, yes, Helen lived here. She was a pretty girl. Young, taller than you. A little naïve, but from what I heard, she was a good teacher. The children all liked her. I know some parents of the children who went to her school. They said Helen did a good job."

"I agree. From what I see, her students are right where they should be."

"After Helen moved in here she started dating Bill Scheiner. I tried to talk to her about him. I told her nothing good would come from it, but she just laughed, said he was lots of fun and told me not to be such a mother."

"Al Freitag said Scheiner is a pretty wild sort of guy."

"I know. He has that kind of reputation, but what was I to say? I thought about talking with her uncle, but finally decided not to get involved. I didn't want the reputation of being a busy-body."

"You aren't."

"I try not to be. I figure you girls are on your own. As long as you respect my rules and don't cause any trouble, I'm not about to tell you what to do."

Tillie looked at her and in a quiet voice asked, "Did you know she was pregnant that fall?"

"Oh, no. I mean, thoughts like that go through your head, but she was a good Christian young woman. Now mind you, she got home late a few nights, but, no, I didn't know she was pregnant. She never said anything to anybody."

Tillie was lost in thought for a moment. *You didn't want to confront her, did you, Mrs. Wilson. You really didn't care enough about her to invite her into your life, to be a friend to her when she was hurting. You talk a lot about Christian love, but where was it when it came to Helen? You knew she was depressed, but you avoided it like everyone else. It sure sounds like everybody, you, Eila, Emil, the Murphy's, her priest, everybody, turned the other way when Helen was screaming out for help.*

Finally, she simply said, "No, I suppose she didn't say anything. It sounds like she was pretty depressed though. Didn't you see that?"

"We all did. She stopped dating. Stayed in her room most of the time. She hardly said a word, often skipped supper. Seemed troubled."

"Didn't anybody talk with her?"

"We tried. Didn't do no good. She kept to herself."

A hundred questions churned about in Tillie's mind. *How hard did you try, Mother Wilson? You don't want to be a busy-body, but don't you think you pushed that too far? You ignored the poor girl. You knew she was hurting. She needed somebody to love her enough to confront her and listen to her.*

Tillie looked straight into Norma Wilson's eyes and said, "And then one day she hung herself. Why did she do it, Mrs. Wilson?"

Norma Wilson dried her eyes with a hankie from her apron pocket, cleared her throat and peered down at her hands. "Like I told the coroner, I think she was too depressed by the thought of having a baby without a father. Maybe she didn't know what to do, couldn't face it. I don't know."

"Okay. Let's just leave it at that." What else was there to say. Mrs. Wilson was either unable to see her failure or refused to face it. No point in pursuing this any further. Tillie stood to return to her room. "Is there orange juice in the frig?"

"Oh, sure. Can I fix you some eggs?"

"No, I don't feel like eating. Some orange juice will be fine."

Tillie went to the refrigerator for the juice, poured out a glass and headed up the stairs. She paused, turned back and asked, "Mrs. Wilson, did all of the other girls know Helen?"

"Yes, they all knew her. I suppose that Eila knew her best. She and Helen both moved in here about the same time, right after I began boarding girls. They went to dances together. Talk with her."

Tillie stayed in her room all morning. Sleep was impossible. The idea of going to church seemed equally unfeasible. For the longest time she sat there, staring out the window, watching the fall leaves blow around in the Wilson yard. The sky was gloomy with heavy clouds that seemed to match her mood. A cold rain began to beat against her bedroom window.

Late in the morning she began to hear the sounds of the other young women out in the hall, going from their rooms to the bathroom. None of them had gone to worship either. Tillie concluded that every young woman in the house had too much dancing the night before. She decided to dress and join them for lunch.

After lunch Tillie touched Eila's arm and said, "I need to talk with you. Will you come to my room?"

The fall sky was darker than before. The rain had settled in and the cold, damp air seeped in through the windows. Eila sat on the bed as Tillie closed her door. Tillie sat down on her lone chair. Her face was as overcast as the outside sky.

"Tillie, you and Al were having a great time last night. How'd it go after the dance?"

"Fine. Al drove me home."

"And? Did he try to kiss you?"

"No, he did not." Tillie began to frown.

"What's wrong? You mad about something?" asked Eila.

"Pardon me for saying this, Eila, but I am ticked. I thought we were beginning to be friends."

"Tillie, what are you talking about? Did Freitag do something last night? I mean, if he did, I'll…"

"No, Eila, I'm not talking about Al. I'm talking about Helen Shattuck!"

Eila's face turned a deep red. Her eyes widened. She stared at Tillie and took a couple deep breaths. "He told you, didn't he! I tried to tell him. He promised to keep it to himself. Everybody thought it'd be better that way."

"Better? Better for whom? You and Mrs. Wilson and Emil, and even Murphy, all thought you'd spare me from what? For crying out loud, Eila, didn't anybody stop to think? How can something like that be brushed under the rug? Didn't you realize that some day I'd find out?"

"We hoped you wouldn't."

"So nobody talked to me – nobody! I had to learn about it from Freitag, a guy I just met! At least he was kind enough to tell me what happened!"

Tears filled Eila's eyes. "Tillie, we weren't trying to be mean. We thought you'd only be here for a year and then you'll go back to college. We really didn't think you needed to be involved with all that horrible stuff."

Tillie clenched her hands together and leaned toward Eila, "Involved? Don't you realize that I am teaching the same kids that she taught? They come to the same school where she taught them and where she committed suicide! Eila, think! Think about it!"

Tears poured from Eila's reddened eyes. She blew her nose and pushed back her hair. "I wasn't thinking about the kids," she said.

"No you were not. But I am. I sat here all morning thinking about them. My first reaction last night was to pack it up and get out of here, go back to St. Paul and to college. Then I got to thinking about those kids. Somebody has to think about them."

Eila's face was mournful as she looked at Tillie. Her shoulders were bent.

"Tillie, I'm sorry. Forgive me. You're right. I wasn't thinking; none of us were. What can I say?"

"Nothing. Tell me a little more about Bill Scheiner. What do you know about him?"

Eila blew her nose again, paused and began. "Bill is lots of fun—when he's not drunk. I was even kind of attracted to him."

"*You* were attracted to him?"

"Sure. He's always full of jokes and stories."

"But he's a drunk!"

"I know. He drinks too much, but he makes girls laugh. He doesn't like to take life so serious. There's too much gloom and doom everywhere. He said that's why they call it the Depression. Everybody's depressed. Bill says it's all a bunch of bunk. He hates being depressed. He says we need to have some fun."

"That's certainly different from what I heard from Al and from Mrs. Wilson."

"So, you're hearing it from a girl's point of view now. Bill is attractive in his own way. It's just that he gets carried away."

"Do you think he got carried away and made Helen pregnant?" countered Tillie.

"I think so. She didn't talk about it to anybody, but we all guessed it."

"You guessed it, but you never talked about it with her?"

"Couldn't. She shut us out. My guess is that Scheiner told her he wasn't ready to settle down. That's probably why he ran off. He couldn't deal with it."

"He sounds like a *very* attractive guy."

"I know what you're thinking. No matter. Helen wanted to marry the guy, have her baby, settle down."

"She said that?"

"No. I just think that's what she wanted."

"But you don't know for sure, do you?"

"No, but I think when Scheiner wouldn't marry her, she got really depressed."

"That's your theory. You think that's why she committed suicide?"

"I don't know. That's my way of looking at it."

"Your way?" asked Tillie. "Is there another way? Are you suggesting that Scheiner killed her?"

"Oh, no. I can't imagine him doing that. He's kind of crazy, but he's not that kind of a guy. I can see him running away, but I can't see him killing anybody, especially Helen. In his own way, I think he loved her."

Tillie's voice was filled with anger. "Then why in heaven's name didn't he marry her?"

"Because he's stupid; he's immature. He's still a kid, even if he's—what, twenty-four?"

"So he ran away from his responsibilities and now he's hiding out. Okay, I've met guys like him. But he's still responsible. If he pushed her to commit suicide, then he killed Helen, just as surely as if he had hung the rope over the beam himself!"

"You're right, Tillie. You're right, but there's not a thing that anybody can do about it."

"One more thing. If she didn't commit suicide and if Scheiner didn't kill her, then maybe somebody else did."

"Tillie! What are you saying?"

Tillie squinted her eyes and looked thoughtfully at Eila. "I don't know. I just don't know."

Chapter 6

Back to School

When Tillie got into Emil's truck the next morning she blurted, "Why didn't you tell me about Helen Shattuck?"

Emil's face furrowed with lines of sorrow. He struggled with his words as he spoke. "Ach, Yah! So what do you know?"

"That she was involved with Bill Scheiner, pregnant and hanged herself—in the wood-room of my school! And none of you told me about it!"

Emil looked at her with gloomy eyes. "Yah, you're right. Ach, what any of us were thinking, I do not know."

"Yes, what were you thinking?"

"That we could protect you."

"From what?"

"From getting involved with this whole thing."

"But why?"

"Because you're only here for a year."

"But I'm the teacher of these kids. They know what happened. Now that I know, I understand some of the things they've been saying."

"They talk about Helen?"

"Not directly. However, from time to time they ask me how I'm doing and if I am going to stay with them."

"Yah, I understand. I've talked to some of the parents about this."

"It's the older kids especially."

"Sure. The little ones didn't know as much. Helen left and some new teachers came. They go on."

"Right, but the older ones ask more questions."

"They ask you about her?"

"Not directly. It's just that I've been so much in the dark."

"Well, Tillie, we thought it was in the past. We wanted to put it behind us."

"I'm not sure it is over for some of them."

"Perhaps."

"What really hurts me, Emil, is that you and the others didn't trust me enough to tell me. For this year, at least, I'm entrusted with these kids."

Emil was clearly uneasy. Guilt and pain were written on his face. He kept his eyes fixed on the road before them as he said, "You are right, Tillie. We should have told you."

"When I learned about Helen this way I felt pushed out. I even thought about quitting."

"Oh, don't do that."

"I won't. I'm here for the year."

Emil pulled his Chevy pickup into the school yard, stopped and turned toward Tillie. "Good, good for you Tillie. You are a good teacher.

"Thank you, Emil. I try."

"Now that you know, it will make you an even better one."

The skies were as dark and overcast as Emil's face. "*Ach*. Another day of rain. Kind of chilly. We ought to start a fire. I'll come in, get some corn cobs and kindling from the wood room."

"I'll never go into that room without thinking of her."

"Yah. Can you keep the fire going?"

"Yes, and I'll keep school going too."

Emil started the fire. As he was leaving, the children arrived and the week began as usual.

Tillie turned to Robert Switzer, Orville's older brother, one of the two eighth grade boys. "Robert, will you see that the fire keeps burning today?" she asked.

"Yes, Ma'am," he replied and immediately went to the wood room for another bundle of wood.

Later in the morning Kathy Neunaber, her seventh grader assistant, looked up to her as they sat with Orville. "Miss Tilden," she said. "Are you feeling okay? You must be coming down with a cold."

At that moment Tillie realized that she was displaying a face as dark and somber as the cold October day outside. "Thank you for asking, Kathy. I'm not feeling real great today," she replied and said no more.

On Thursday afternoon Superintendent Murphy arrived for the usual weekly conference. Tillie spent some time going over the events of the week. She was concerned about Orville Switzer's progress. He was old enough to be a sixth grader, but could barely read on the second grade level. Murphy assured her again that she was doing the best she could and reminded her that Orville would never get much beyond the third grade level, if that.

After she gave him her lesson plans for the next week, Murphy moved his chair a little closer to Tillie's desk and asked, "Tillie, sure there's something that's bothering you. Your sparkle, sure 'tis gone. Is it something you'll be wanting to talk about?"

Tillie's feelings were mixed. Murphy was too close. His presence was invasive. He had no business being so intimate and personal. Yet she felt compassion. Now she knew of his loss and of the memories this school must evoke each time he entered it. She looked down at her folded hands for a long time. Then she slowly lifted her face.

"Mr. Murphy, please forgive me," she began. "I don't know how to say this. I learned about <u>Helen</u> this past weekend."

"What about Helen?" he asked with surprise.

"I know she was your niece. I'm so sorry about what happened."

Michael Murphy said nothing for a long time. His lower lip trembled. Tears moistened his eyes. He struggled to get hold of his emotions. His chest heaved slightly. He sniffed and wiped a tear from his right eye.

"A hard year 'tis been for Mrs. Murphy and me-self. Almost a year to the day 'tis been, since it happened. Sure I can't come here without remembering that awful day that Emil and I went into the wood-room and ... well, I guess they told you."

"They told me," she replied.

"So you know the church refused to bury her?"

"Nobody said anything about that," she said quizzically.

Michael Murphy, faithful Catholic father of two, coughed, swallowed twice and slid his chair back a foot. Tillie sensed conflict written across his face. He fought his internal battle for nearly a minute. Finally he spoke.

"Father Mulligan wouldn't have the funeral. He talked with the Bishop. She was guilty of mortal sin, they said. She killed herself and her unborn baby. No funeral mass for her could there be and she couldn't be buried in the church's cemetery."

"I don't understand," said Tillie.

"They that die in mortal sin can have no forgiveness. To bury her with rites from the church would be to deny that fact."

"So what did you do?"

"All we could do was pray by ourselves for her. The funeral director carried her body to a grave in a secular cemetery. We and her mother prayed for her. She had no rites from the church."

"Nothing?"

"Nothing. She went to hell!"

Tillie trembled at the thought. How could Murphy speak so? Was not heaven or hell in God's hands? "How can you say she went to hell?" she asked.

"Because she committed fornication. She killed herself and her unborn child. That's murder!"

This is too harsh, thought Tillie. How does Murphy or his priest or his church know what she was thinking? Was it suicide? What was Al alluding to the other night? Is there more to this than meets the eye? She started to ask more questions, but then thought better.

Murphy continued, "Oh, God have mercy on her soul! That's what we have prayed from that day to now. How can such a beautiful little girl be in hell?" Murphy paused, as if he were waiting for an angel to appear to announce that Helen had been accepted as a resident of heaven.

"That's also my question," said Tillie in a very reserved manner.

"I can't imagine it. I can't. I won't," continued Murphy. "I don't care what the church says. I can't be thinking of God doing that to Helen. She wasn't a bad girl. She got involved. That damn Scheiner! Forgive me language. She didn't know what to do!"

Tillie said nothing more. She looked at him. She hesitated and then cautiously reached out her hand as if to comfort him. He pulled back as she did so. Reaching into his back pocket for his handkerchief, he blew his nose, dried his eyes and stood.

"Forgive me, Miss Tilden. It's out of turn, me speaking like this. Who am I to question God's judgments? Who am I to question Holy Mother Church? We'll, we'll not be talking about this again ... I must be going. I have some things to do before supper and Mrs. Murphy has asked me to get some groceries. It's next week I'll be seeing you then. Goodbye for now."

With that Superintendent Murphy picked up Tillie's reports, turned toward the door, took two steps and then turned back. "We still pray for her, Tillie. Maybe you can too." With that, he disappeared into the coat room and out the front door.

Tillie sat for a long time staring at the stove. Would her Methodist minister have had a funeral for Helen? Did Helen really did go to hell? She thought about Murphy's pain and confusion. If she, herself, were Helen's aunt, would she feel this way?

She concluded that Murphy would be unable to advise her about the children. She was on her own if questions came up. She heard Emil's truck coming into the school yard. It was time to go home. Perhaps her driver-philosopher could give her more advice.

Settling down on the truck seat, Tillie turned to Emil. "Before we start, I need to ask you a couple more questions."

"Tillie, what to ask do you want?" Emil was tense. His mouth was set, his eyes fixed. He gripped the steering wheel tightly.

Tillie was also filled with apprehension. "I want to talk some more about the children."

"Yah. What about the children?"

"This is difficult. I don't know quite how to put it. What do the kids think happened to Helen? Do they think she … went to hell?"

"Tillie, Tillie." Emil paused for a long time, deep in thought. He began in a very serious voice. "Tillie, what you ask, I'm not so sure I know. I suppose you are asking why the Catholic church didn't have a funeral mass for her. Right?

"Yes. That's about it. Why would their church do that?"

"Well, Tillie, what can I say? I'm not a Catholic, so I don't know what the priest or the bishop think about funerals. I can only tell you what I think about Helen."

"I'd appreciate that."

Tillie looked into Emil's eyes. They were gentle, filled with concern. He reminded her of her Poppa. For a moment she imagined Poppa sitting beside her. Emil continued, "I drove Helen to school that fall, every day, just like I drive you. I knew her pretty good. I could tell she was sad. She seemed so, what? Like she was carrying a very heavy burden."

"That's what Eila and Mrs. Wilson say."

"Yah. Sometimes I ask her if she wants to talk. She always smiled that little smile of hers and shook her head. So nothing more I couldn't do."

"You tried, didn't you?"

"Yah. Several times. I knew she wasn't dating Bill Scheiner any more. We never talked about him."

"Never? I thought she loved him."

"Yah, but that was over in the fall."

"Okay," said Tillie cautiously. "How well do you know Bill Scheiner?"

"I know him pretty good," said Emil thoughtfully. "His family is related to mine. He is kind of a third cousin or something. He was always a wild kid, making jokes, kind of crazy. I think that appealed to Helen."

"Appealed to her?"

"Yah. She came from a mixed up family herself. Her daddy left them, you know, back when she was in college."

"Al told me a little about that. Why'd he leave?"

"*Ach.* All I know is talk; stuff gets around. Some people say he was a drunk, liked to gamble, lost all his money. He lost his job when the Depression hit. I guess, he couldn't face it. That's all I know."

"That's why Helen quit school. No more money."

"Yah. As I understand it."

"So she needed to work and ended up teaching here?"

"Yah, she needed a job."

Tillie paused, looked out at the school yard and for a second she felt as if she could see Helen standing in the door of the school. "I just had a weird thought about Helen and Scheiner. He's shiftless, irresponsible, kind of like her daddy. Maybe she wanted to help him change, become the man her daddy wasn't."

Emil had a puzzled look on his face. "Who knows Tillie? Who knows why anybody is attracted to anybody?"

"But," Tillie continued, "even if we don't know about that, what about the children? Helen was their teacher for a couple years."

"Tillie, let me put it this way. You have many children in your school. Their parents are like yours. They tell them not to question what the Catholic Church does. They don't talk about it. It's over."

That sounds so easy, thought Tillie. Push the thoughts out of your mind. Pretend it never happened. Who cares how the kids feel? Go do your chores.

"But it's not over," she persisted.

"Yah, but she's dead. Your children have a new teacher now and there's cows to milk and chickens to feed."

"I don't understand. Doesn't anybody ever ask questions about the Catholic Church?"

"Tillie, please. I say no more. These are good people, no different from Methodists and Lutherans. They love their church and their children. They do what they are told."

"But, Emil…"

"No more, Tillie. Leave it!" said Emil, with emphasis.

Tillie was flustered, obviously disturbed by this turn in the conversation. Ignoring Emil, she persisted. "I'm not a Catholic. I'm a Methodist. I learned about the Reformation in college. I know the issues. We Methodists don't swallow everything our church says and we don't let priests decide who goes to hell!"

Emil leaned toward Tillie. His eyes were tender, his voice soft. "Tillie, lots you have to learn. What you say, think about. Believe what you believe, but remember, Catholics have good reasons for believing what they believe as well."

"But I don't have to agree with those beliefs."

"No, you don't, but you have to live with these people. Together we all live here. We go to the same stores, carry our grain to the same granary. Many Catholics came to my store. I always got along with them. We respect one another."

"I don't want to start a war, Emil." Tillie fought to keep her emotions in tow. "But I feel so bad that nobody did anything for Helen. And then she killed herself!"

"Herself <u>and her baby</u>!" replied Emil. "Methodists and Lutherans believe that's a sin, the same as the Catholics. Her church dealt with it the way they thought best. Now once more, leave it!" Emil's voice had a tone of finality.

Tillie struggled. Could she push him further? She decided to continue. "But Emil, you're a Lutheran. Do Lutherans believe she went to hell?"

Emil was clearly uncomfortable. Tillie could see he wanted to start his truck, put it in gear and drive home. He was not accustomed to sharing private thoughts.

"Tillie, what do I think? I'm not God and I'm not here to judge."

Yet she persisted, putting him on the spot, driven by her own need for answers. She knew he was not a pastor, but she demanded an answer.

Emil struggled, searching for the right words. "I think God understands all about us. God loves us and He loved Helen too."

He seemed repulsed by having to talk about this. The image of Helen hanging in the wood room flashed into Tillie's mind. Emil had been with her day after day. They had been friends, sharing personal history, telling stories and laughing at one another's jokes, as she and Emil had during these past weeks. Suddenly he found her hanging lifeless from the rafter. Tillie imagined Helen, mouth contorted, eyes staring blankly, neck red and torn, arms and hands dangling like sausages at her side. The picture would not go away.

She sensed the panic Emil felt as he and Murphy cut her down, his heart pounding wildly as he put his jacket over her face. No doubt he had chided himself for being a little late. Maybe, if he had only come earlier, he might have saved her, but he had been busy that afternoon with his wood working and the time got away from him.

Emil stared, seeing nothing but the images in his mind. Finally he said, "Jesus died for Helen too."

What else could he say? thought Tillie. She knew he had prayed day after day, begging the Lord God for answers. He had struggled with her suicide. He believed God forbids anyone from taking a life, including Helen taking her own. But that was what she had done. Helen had taken her life *and* the life of her unborn child. Did Jesus understand her struggle? Would he forgive her? Tillie fervently prayed he would.

"What do I say to the children if they inquire about Helen?" asked Tillie. "Do I tell them that she's in heaven … or in hell?"

Emil had no more answers. Tillie knew they shared a belief in the love of God, a love so deep that the Father in heaven gave his only Son to die on the cross.

He spoke in a quiet voice, "If the children ask, you must remind them of Jesus. He knows our hearts and our struggles with sin. He loves us and he will do the right thing."

With that Emil started his truck. He would say no more. Tillie could see that the conversation was ended. They drove back to the Wilson house in silence. When they pulled into the driveway Tillie stepped from the truck and looked back. "Thank you, Emil. You've helped me. I appreciate it." She closed the truck door and walked slowly to the house.

Chapter 7

Getting To Know You

That evening the phone rang in Mrs. Wilson's kitchen. "Tillie," shouted Mrs. Wilson, "You have a phone call. It's Al Freitag."

Tillie flew down the stairs. "This is Tillie."

"Hello," said the man's voice. "This is your Polka-teacher. Been worried about you. How're you doing?"

Tillie was nervous and warm. She was certain Mrs. Wilson could see her face turning red. She had been waiting for this phone call all week. "Your student is doing fine," she replied in her most confidant voice, "just fine. What's up?"

"Remember how you said you didn't know where Coates was? I was thinking maybe I could show you. Now that you know how to polka I thought maybe you'd like to go to another dance."

Tillie almost could not get the words out fast enough. "Sounds good. Do you give lessons to an advanced student?"

"Sure do. Remember the Green Roof? I live just up the road. They have a dance there Saturday night. Would you like to go?"

That question lifted the heavy conversations with Murphy and Emil from her heart. A sparkle lit up her eyes. Excited, she almost giggled, "Well, teacher, I could sure use a few more lessons. Why not? What time?"

"Okay. I'll come by on Saturday about eight after we get done with the chores. See you then, Miss School Teacher."

The September air was crisp, the dark sky filled with a million stars that Saturday evening as they drove east from Rosemount in Al's black Ford. Tillie's voice was animated and excited. She turned to her handsome companion as she began, "So, Al Freitag, tell me more about your farm."

"We have a hundred and fifty acres and we rent another fifty on the other side of the railroad tracks. We raise corn, oats, potatoes. We have forty-one milk cows and a good team of horses. Takes lots of work to keep it all going."

"I bet it does. Did I tell you my Poppa was raised on a farm?"

"No kidding. I thought you was a city girl."

"I am," she said, tilting her head, blinking her eye lashes several times and shrugging her shoulders in mock refinement. "But both of my parents were raised in the country down in Iowa."

"Really. So what do you know about farming?"

"Nothing, really. I visited my Grandpa's farm in Iowa a couple times."

"Learn anything?"

"Maybe. One time we spent a two weeks' vacation down there."

A slightly sarcastic tone was in Al's voice as he replied, "Vacation? Did you go fishing at a local lake?"

"Hey," she replied with an equal dose of sarcasm. "We worked. Poppa helped Grandpa and the neighbors harvest oats and wheat and Mother, my sister and I worked with the women in the kitchen."

"How'd you like it?"

"I liked it. Two very busy weeks. When we drove back Poppa was just beaming. He said it was really good to be back on the farm."

"Your Pa likes farms."

"He does. He wanted to be a country vet."

"Is he a vet?"

"He is. Works for the government at the South St. Paul stockyards."

"How come he works in town?"

"My mother."

"Your mother?"

"She hates farm life."

Al was laughing. "Sounds like a problem."

"You got it. Poppa loves it. Mother hates it."

"I bet that makes for some interesting conversations at your house."

"All the time."

"What's your Mother got against farming?"

"The hard work. Says that all she did as a kid was work and get dirty. She hates dirt."

"It's hard work all right. And you'd better not be afraid of a little dirt."

"My mother prefers the genteel life," she said in a mocking voice, sweeping her bent wrist outward.

"Okay. But your Pa likes farming."

"He does. He's often said he'd like to have his own little farm and his own vet practice."

"So why doesn't he?"

"Mostly Mother, I think. She's very adamant about not wanting to live in the country."

Al turned his eyes toward Tillie. She was staring, her eyes uplifted, hearing countless arguments between her parents being replayed.

"What about you, Miss City Girl? What do you think about country life?"

The question interrupted her reverie. "Me? I'm having a great time. Learning tons of things. For instance, what's it like to have all those cows?"

"Kind of like being a father to forty-one girls," said Al.

Tillie tittered. "You're kidding."

"No," he responded, "I'm serious. Each one of them has her own personality, her own name. They have their own ideas. They get jealous, push and kick and butt one another. They won't obey us sometimes. They're fussy about what they eat. Get sick. They give us milk, because they know we care about them."

"Really!" Tillie was amazed. "I thought they were, well, just dumb animals."

"They're not machines, Miss Teacher. They are live animals with brains. They know lots of things. They depend on us to take care of them and we depend on them. Do you drink milk?"

"Of course, silly," she responded. "But my milk always came from bottles delivered to our door. I never really thought about it coming from a cow."

"Sometime I'll have to take you to the barn and have you try your hand at milking Wilma."

Now who's he talking about? she wondered. *Did he mean milking with* **this** *Wilma? Maybe Wilma is his sister. Surely he isn't talking about some dumb cow.*

"Who?" asked Tillie, with a very puzzled look.

"Wilma. She's the boss lady of our whole herd. We've had Wilma for about five years now. Lots of the other cows are her daughters. And they know it. She don't put up with any guff."

"You make it sound like a family," Tillie snickered.

"It is. I'm the one that sorts out family quarrels once in awhile."

"Mothers and daughters don't always see eye to eye," she said, thinking about her own family.

"Right. But there comes a day when 'mother' is gone, as in 'gone to the slaughter house'!"

Suddenly Tillie began to imagine her own mother herded into a truck and dumped into a cattle shoot at the South St. Paul stockyards. She remembered those times her Poppa had taken her and her sister to see how the cows were slaughtered. She shuddered at the thought of Mother ending up there.

"How old do cows have to be when they go to the…" She struggled with the idea. "… the slaughter house?"

"I don't know. Depends. We keep them eight, nine years. Until they quit giving milk and having calves."

Tillie hesitated again. "And then?"

"Then we turn them over to your Poppa," chuckled Al, "and they become steak and sausage."

"Wilma, too?" asked Tillie with a tinge of sadness in her voice.

"Of course. You think we're running a home for old lady cows?"

They headed south on Highway 52 toward Coates. As they drove past two farms, facing one another on opposite sides of the road, Al turned his head left. "That's the Knoedel farm. On the other side is the Wieselmanns."

"Did you say weasel, like in sneaky little animal with a long tail?"

"Yah, I did." Al chortled. "Only it's a German name. Means the same thing, but it's spelled different. Nobody knows how they got the name. By the way, Mrs. Wieselmann is auntie to a couple of your students, the Switzer kids."

"Really. And the other farm, did you say the noodles?"

"Not quite. I said 'Knoedel'. That's a dumpling in German. My Mother makes some great ones. Floats them on potato soup with ham. I can eat a hundred at a time. Another funny name, huh?"

"Mr. and Mrs. Dumpling. Sounds like some toys."

"Sort of."

"Okay. As long as we're into names, what does yours mean?"

"Simple. Means 'Friday' or to be literal, 'free-day'."

"Do you know how come Friday is called Friday?"

"Can't say I do."

"Comes from the Norse goddess Freya. She was their goddess of love! So that makes you Al the lover, right?"

Al rolled his eyes. "Only on Fridays."

"Not on Saturday?" she asked wryly.

"Maybe. Hey, here's our farm." He pointed out the window at a large barn with two stave silos in front, facing the road. Tillie could barely make them out in the dim light. At the end of a driveway leading from the road she could see some other sheds. A hundred feet further south was a large, two story farm house. "One day soon I'm going to have you over to eat Sunday dinner with us. That is, if I can convince you to come to a Lutheran Church Service first."

"Hmmm, I'll have to think about that very carefully," replied Tillie. "I don't speak German."

"We Germans worship in English too," Al replied. "But, if you'd like to go to the German church I can arrange that—and I'll even translate for you."

"I think I'll stick with English."

They were both laughing as they pulled up to the Green Roof, a quarter of a mile past the Freitag farm. Tillie noted that it was a much larger structure than the Rosemount Community Hall. Many more cars were parked in the grass alongside. The building had obviously received its name from a rounded roof covered with green shingles.

Two large red and yellow cylindrical pumps, about ten feet tall, in front of the dance hall, piqued Tillie's curiosity. Each was capped with a heavy glass jug, about the size of a couple of her Mother's wash tubs. "What are those things?" she asked.

"Gas pumps. You want gas, you drive up, pull the big handle on the side back and forth 'til you've pumped the right amount of gas up into the glass canister. See, it's marked gallon by gallon. Holds ten. Then you put the spigot at the end of that rubber hose into your tank, pull the trigger and the gas flows in by gravity. Works good."

"How old-fashioned. We've had mechanical pumps in town for several years now."

"Sorry, Miss City-Girl. We can't afford to keep up with the latest gadgets out here. There is a Depression going on, you know."

"So we've heard in St. Paul."

Al parked the car and rushed around to open Tillie's door. He reached out to take her hand and help her down. When he closed the door, he continued to hold her hand in his. Tillie felt a kind of electricity coming from his hand. It was making hers warmer by the second, but the heat felt good. She welcomed it. She felt charged and excited.

Hand in hand they climbed the two steps up to the platform in front of the Green Roof. As they were about to enter the crowded bar room, Tillie held back. She could hear her mother's voice lecturing: "Whiskey and beer are killers. Men lose control. They beat their wives. It's a curse. Alcohol is the devil's tool." Pictures from newspapers of federal agents breaking up stills of whiskey came to mind. Stories of gang wars in Chicago flashed before her. Prohibition was over. So what? What was she doing here? What would Mother think?

The air was heady with the smells of cigar and cigarette smoke, beer, whiskey and sweaty people. The heavy smoke made it hard to breathe in some parts of the room.

Clusters of men and women stood everywhere. The noise of their conversations made it impossible for Tillie and Al to understand anything except their own voices. Many, with mugs of beer and or shots of hard liquor in their hands, faced the back wall, leaning on a fifteen-foot-long, oak-colored bar. Three white-shirted bar tenders with rolled up sleeves were busy serving. Sounds of a polka band in the dance hall beyond seeped through the doors.

As they entered, Tillie began a sardonic inward conversation with her Mother. *Here's a den of iniquity, Mother, the devil's front room. All these young men and women are on a short journey to hell and they don't even know it. They're laughing, dancing—and getting drunk, right? Not a single one believes in God. And your daughter is here. Oh, but, don't worry. I'll be a good girl. Demon rum has not captured me—yet. All we're doing is dancing. No harm in that, is there? Or is dancing also sinful, Mother?*

As they made their way through the crowd various men and women greeted Al. He introduced Tillie to so many that she couldn't keep track of who was who. He was no stranger to this *devil's-den*. This was his community ... And she liked it.

Al led her through double doors to the dance floor. About forty couples were crowded together, leaping, swaying and jumping to the happy sounds of Whoopee John's Polka Band. Along the sides were benches and small tables and chairs filled with dancers resting from the vigorous exercise. The band came to the end of one polka and segued immediately into the next.

"Let's dance," shouted Al as he grabbed her into his arms. She was immediately pulled into a tangle of couples that crammed the floor. The happy sounds of the polka filled her ears and she was lost in a sea of rhythmic circling and skipping.

Several hours later Tillie and Al were standing on the edge of the crowd, filing out to the parking lot. "Getting late," said Al. "We got to get you back to Rosemount."

Suddenly, they heard some shouting outside. Turning to one of the young men nearby, Al asked, "Hey, Art, what's going on?"

"Same old, same old. Some hot heads can't hold their liquor and got into a fight out in the parking lot."

"Too bad Scheiner ain't here," shouted Al.

"Right on," said Art. "He likes a good fight. Where's he been? I ain't seen him in over a year."

"Made himself scarce after the Shattuck girl got in trouble."

"You really think Bill had anything to do with that?"

"Who can say? We was talking about it the other day. Everybody knows Scheiner likes a good time," said Al.

"I thought once he got her in trouble, he'd do the right thing."

"You mean marry her?"

"Yah. The Scheiners are decent folk. His Ma would have insisted on a wedding, but I guess Bill ain't like the rest of the family."

The crowd moved rapidly out the door, spilling into the parking lot to form a circle around a half dozen young men, punching and thrashing about. Shouts, jeers and laughter filled the chilled night air. Suddenly one came flying right toward Al and Tillie. Al caught him, gave him a shove and sent him back into the makeshift arena. Tillie wondered if her tall, powerful escort would also jump into the melee. Soon the six combatants were joined by several others. The shouts turned into screaming as one of them pulled a switchblade from his pocket.

"Come on," said Al, grabbing Tillie's arm. "We're getting out of here."

"I'm for that," she said.

Al slipped a reassuring arm over her shoulders. He shook his head and smiled at her. "I'm with the prettiest girl in the place. Things are getting too rough. As deputy sheriff, I should be in there, settling them down, but tonight I'm not on duty, so I'll let my brother and the other deputies around here handle it. Right now, I'm taking you home."

Sheltering Tillie with his body, he led her around the noisy crowd to his car, parked at the far end of the lot. Tillie noticed that many of the girls were enjoying the fight as much as the men. Nothing like this had ever happened to her at dances. The fighting men looked wild and dangerous. In spite of the warmth of Al's protective arm, she shivered.

"Don't you be afraid, *Liebchen*. Nothing's going to happen to you."

"It's awful! They're like animals. I'm glad you didn't get involved."

"Some guys forget how much they scare their dates. Maybe some girls like to see men show off how tough they are. Stupid. There's enough trouble around without that. Sometimes a guy has to fight to take care of his family, but a brawl is not my idea of fun."

He opened the car door and waited until Tillie was settled before he slammed it shut. Tillie thought about what he had said. She hadn't realized that her farmer was also a sheriff's deputy. Sometime she'd have to ask him to explain about that. For now, she knew she could trust him to do the right thing. He made her feel special, cherished. Who would have thought a thoroughly modern girl would enjoy such an old-fashioned feeling?

Al got in the car and started the engine. Tillie wondered if he would kiss her goodnight. She suspected a kiss from Al would be something special. She was looking forward to it.

When they arrived at Rosemount, Tillie's heart was glowing with a strange, happy feeling she had never known before. The sounds of the polka band were still ringing in her ears as they drove up to the Wilson house. The smells of the dance hall's smoke and sweat clung to her clothing. A smile was on her face as Al took her in his arms and pressed his lips to hers. Tillie pressed back as they held one another in the darkness of the Wilson porch.

"Tillie, I'm so happy you said yes."

"So am I, big Al. So am I."

Al's heart was filled with excitement as he drove away from the Wilson house. *She kissed me. She really kissed me. She meant it. I know she did. She likes me. How amazing! A college educated woman actually allowed me, a dumb farmer, to kiss her. Wow! Is this love?*

He crawled into bed as the downstairs mantle clock chimed two a.m. He could not get to sleep. All he could think about was the warmth of their embrace. He began to fantasize about her next to him. He could still smell the sweetness of her closeness, feel her breasts pressing against his chest, her arms around his neck. He wanted to reach out again to press her lips to his and hold her through the night. The last thing he remembered was the clock chiming two-thirty. The next thing he heard was ...

"Albert. Albert. ALBERT!"

"Yah, Ma," he said in a groggy voice.

"Albert, get up! Pa told me to call you at six. He said he was letting you sleep a little longer since you got home so late."

Slowly, very slowly, Al pulled his legs over the side of the bed and sat there, his head in his hands. He was about to fall back on the bed when Ma called again, "Albert! Are you up?"

"Coming, Ma. Coming."

Later that Sunday morning, after the cows were milked, Al sat in the pew with his family at St. John's Lutheran Church. He remembered hearing Pastor Dornfeld announce his sermon text. The next thing he knew a sharp elbow jabbed his left side and Pa Freitag whispered loudly, "Albert, wake up! Sleep all afternoon, not in church."

Sleep is what he did that Sunday afternoon, all afternoon. His older brother, Werner, was quick to pick up Al's weariness as they milked the cows that evening. "Some date, little brother. The new school teacher wore you plumb out."

"It was worth it," replied Al. "You should be so lucky."

The next Thursday afternoon Al called Emil at his Rosemount residence. "Emil, don't bother picking up Tillie today. I'll be over there before school lets out. I'll bring her home."

"*Ach*, yah, that sounds good. Such a nice young woman. Albert, you be good to her."

It was fifteen minutes before the end of the school day when Al drove up to the Rich Valley schoolhouse. Tillie flushed as Al slipped into the one empty desk in the back of the room, but quickly regained her composure. "Children, we have a visitor with us today. Some of you know him. Please welcome Mr. Freitag."

In chorus the children shouted, "Good afternoon, Mr. Freitag." They laughed and giggled.

Robert Switzer, Orville's brother, one of the two eighth grade boys, raised his hand.

"Yes, Robert," said Tillie.

"Miss Tilden, will Mr. Freitag be joining our eighth grade class?"

"No, Robert," she replied, "he'll have to pass the seventh grade first."

At that the whole classroom broke out in a wave of hilarity and talking. It took Tillie about five minutes to calm them down. When they finally did, she reminded them of their homework assignments and excused them for the day.

After the last student had climbed on the school bus, Tillie turned to Al. "What a surprise. I sure didn't expect you today."

"I suppose not. It's just that that if you're not real busy, I'd like to introduce you to Wilma."

"Excuse me. Wilma?"

"You mean you forgot already?"

"The cow, right?"

"I'm serious. I want you to meet Wilma." He motioned toward his car.

"I'm not milking some cow."

"Oh, come on. She won't hurt you."

"Not on your life, buddy."

"But I told Emil I'd bring you home."

Tillie wrinkled her nose, but gathered her books and papers anyway and climbed into Al's Model A. "I suppose you're the only ride I've got."

"I want you to meet Wilma."

"Okay. You got me. Take me to Wilma, but remember, I'm not going to milk her."

Fifteen minutes later Al drove the car into the Freitag farm driveway. "We're here. Come on. I'll introduce you to Wilma."

Tillie was laughing. "The grand old lady of your dairy herd."

"Come on into the barn. Wilma, her sisters and daughters are just parading in from the pasture."

Al took her hand and led her into the meticulously clean cow barn. The floors were swept and white lime had been spread everywhere. At first, the smell of the barn seemed overwhelming. It was a mixture of hay, straw, grain, silage, manure, and animal body odor. Her first impulse was to run out into the clean air, but suppressing it, she soon adjusted and the smell drifted to the back of her consciousness.

As she entered, Pa Freitag walked up to her and held out his hand. He was in his late fifties, several inches shorter than his son, with fine features, weathered face and strong hands. "Good evening, Miss Tilden. Albert has been telling us about you. Welcome to our farm."

"Thank you," she replied, smiling broadly. "Call me Tillie."

"Good. Tillie it is." Gesturing toward an imposing young man with dark brown hair, he said, "This is Werner, Albert's older brother."

Werner, a couple inches shorter in stature than his brother, was equally as handsome and muscular as Al. Tillie compared the two in her mind, deciding that she still favored Al's curly black hair and deep blue eyes to Werner's straight hair and hazel eyes. Nevertheless, if she and Al ever did get married, she thought, Werner would be a fine brother-in-law.

Werner also reached out his hand. "Good to meet you, Miss ... Tillie," he said, smiling engagingly.

Tillie's small hand disappeared in his giant, calloused paw. She knew he had the strength to crush hers, but he was very gentle, squeezing it, she supposed, as he did the teats on the bags of the cows.

Looking out the back doors, Tillie saw forty-one Holstein cows slowly walking toward the barnyard from an adjoining pasture.

"They know when its time to come in," said Al. "There's Wilma at the head." He pointed to a large black and white Holstein with deep brown eyes. Her belly was round and her pink colored bag swayed back and forth beneath her hind legs. She paraded slowly and majestically toward the barn. "Wilma is always out in front and no other sister had better try to take her place."

"She's bigger than I imagined."

"She gives lots of milk. We start milking in about a half hour."

"You're not expecting me to do anything, are you?"

"Naw. Just watch. When we're done, Ma, Pa, Werner and I would be honored if you'd join us for supper. Then I'll drive you back to Rosemount."

Tillie laughed again. "Fine. By the way, what do I say to such a fine old lady?"

"She don't care what you say, as long as she gets her hay. She won't mind if you scratch her forehead or her ears. Just be careful her big nose doesn't get slurp all over you. That could gunk up your dress real good."

Tillie watched with amazement when Al opened the doors to the barn. Each cow knew exactly where to go. Each had her own stall. Each went to it immediately and began to munch contentedly on the oats, cracked corn and hay awaiting her. None of the animals objected when Al closed a stanchion on her neck. They swished their tails at an endless cotillion of huge black flies dancing up and down their backs, but otherwise were content to have the men wash their bags and hook up the milking machines.

"Would you believe," asked Al, "that we had to do all this by hand when we first started milking cows? Now we do all our milking with these machines."

"How do they work?" she asked.

"By air pressure. Put two of your fingers in here."

Tillie put her fingers into one of four aluminum cylindrical devices, lined with smooth rubber tubes and attached to a sealed pail that hung by a strap under the cow's belly. Al turned on the machine and she felt the rubber liner pulse, alternately compressing and releasing her fingers with a gentle whooshing sound.

"We slide these over the four teats of the cow and the machines gently squeeze out her milk into the pail."

"Still looks to me like a lot of work," replied Tillie.

"It is. We have to milk each cow every morning and every evening, seven days a week."

When the milk had all been gathered, strained and placed into covered, steel milk cans they carted them to a large cooling tank in the milk house, opposite the barn.

"We have to get the milk cooled down in the water as quick as possible, so it don't sour," Al explained. "The water comes out of our well. We keep circulating fresh, cold water over the cans all night long. The dairy truck picks them up about seven-thirty in the morning, after our morning milking."

When the milking was completed and the cans were all in the cold water holding tank, Al invited Tillie to help him clean up the machines and pails. "I bet we keep this place cleaner than most women keep their kitchens," he continued.

"You don't know my mother," she replied.

When they were finished, he led her into the house and introduced her to Ma Freitag. Ma was a modest woman. Her dress was plain and practical and her hair was pulled back in a bun. She was not a woman given to the vanities of powder and makeup. She wore dark brown stockings and flat heeled shoes. Her hands gave evidence of hard work, both indoors and out. A reserved woman, she customarily expressed herself best with her cooking and the loving care of her family. Her greeting was a quiet, monosyllabic 'lo' and a gesture to Tillie to be seated.

Assisting her was Al's sister, Irene. Irene was equally modest, a young teenager dressed in a plain smock and nearly the same height as Tillie. She bore a strong family resemblance to Al, except that her black hair was straight like Werner's and she wore it in a page cut. She smiled shyly when Al introduced her and then went silently back to her work.

"Excuse me," said Tillie. "Could I use your telephone?"

"Yah," said Ma. "It's there on the wall."

Tillie lifted the phone from its hook and asked the operator for Norma Wilson's home in Rosemount. When Norma answered, she apologized for not calling earlier.

"We knew where you were," said Mrs. Wilson. Emil told me Al Freitag was picking you up after school, so I figured you'd be eating with them tonight. Enjoy a good farm meal."

Ma's eyes twinkled with delight as she invited all the members of her family to take their places. She served a supper of fried pork chops and potatoes with baked beans and sweet corn. When she offered Tillie a piece of apple pie at the end of the meal, Tillie asked, "Everything tastes so good, but do you eat like this at every meal?"

"Sure," said Al. "Farming's hard work. Takes lots of good food to keep us going."

"Teaching is hard work too," replied Tillie, "but if I ate like this every day I'd get so big I wouldn't be able to squeeze through the door into my classroom."

Pa Freitag laughed. "Well, Miss Tillie, I think if you spent a summer working with Ma here, she'd work all that off in a hurry."

"My mother has often told me how hard the work on a farm is," commented Tillie.

"It is," continued Pa, "but did she tell you how much fun it is?"

"No. That I had to hear from my Poppa."

"Good. Then you learned something from each of your parents."

"I suppose I did."

Nearly every weekend that fall Tillie and Al had a Saturday night date. They continued to attend the Green Roof dances. They went out to eat at O'Hara's Café in Rosemount. They went to a moving picture theatre in St. Paul, a real dress up affair. Tillie wore her best dress and hat. Al put on his only white shirt and a suit in which he felt quite uncomfortable.

One Saturday Tillie coaxed Al to a choir concert at Hamline University. Al was reluctant to attend.

"I'm just a farmer" he said. "I know how to plant corn and milk cows. I don't know nothing about colleges and concerts and stuff like that."

"Well," she replied, "you took me to your barn. Now I'm taking you to mine."

"They don't have barns at Hamline, do they?"

"No, silly. I'm talking about the campus, the office workers, staff, profs and students. Let's pretend that they're a big herd, just like yours."

"Okay," he said, with a quizzical look on his face.

"I've been hanging around this herd for these past three years. We have 'bossy cows' around here too."

"Bet they wouldn't want them to hear you call them cows."

"Maybe not, but some of those 'old cows' in the registrar's office can be just as pushy as your Wilma."

"Do they look like her too?"

"Maybe I'd better not go there. Yet, on second thought, I can think of a couple that kind of do."

"Them I'd like to meet."

"No you wouldn't. My point is that our 'cows' push their weight around just like yours."

"I think I'm more interested in the 'calves' than the old cows!"

"Well, big guy, if you start letting your eye roam when I'm with you, I should remind you that we have a few good looking bulls as well!"

Al fell asleep during the concert.

The next weekend they had a great evening at a vaudeville show in South St. Paul. It was a little theater near the stockyards. The dancers were second rate and the wise cracks were ridiculous. The magician for the night was a local talent from Minneapolis. His assistant forgot to put the rabbit in his hat and he had to make a poor joke when he discovered the mistake.

One evening in late October, Tillie was talking with Eila about her dates with Al. "You two been going pretty steady since that night at the Rosemount dance."

"You're right. And it's been fun."

"Hey, lady. What's your mother think about you dating Mister Tall-dark-and-handsome-farmer?"

"She's giving me a hard time."

"But what are you thinking about it?"

"I'm getting pretty good at the schottische."

"And at kissing and hugging."

Tillie felt her face getting warm at Eila's remark, but her heart was warm as well. "I won't deny that," she said.

"You two are getting pretty serious, if I read you right."

"Sort of, but I've got some really mixed feelings."

"Like?"

"Like what if Mother is right?

"You mean about the hard work and the lack of culture?"

"I suppose. I mean, I know how to work, but I don't know a thing about planting a garden or feeding chickens."

"You could learn."

"Sure, but do I want to? Do I give up my love for literature and poetry and music?"

"Come on, Till, there's a *few* of us with some education out here too."

"You know what I mean."

"Sure. Raising a big family and a big garden doesn't leave much time left for literary societies and symphony concerts."

"Something like that. I never dreamed about marrying a farmer. Poppa always talks about how much he loves country life, but when it gets right down to it, I'm a city girl. That's all I've ever known."

"So what does your heart tell you?"

"I'm afraid to answer. Remember how I told you that coming out here was like crossing a bridge, leaving my childhood behind?"

"I remember."

"This side of the bridge is wonderful and scary, both at the same time."

"What are you scared of?"

"I'm scared that if he asks me to marry him, I'll say yes!"

Chapter 8

Relatives

The next weekend Tillie's scary night arrived. Parked again in the little city park in Rosemount, Al took her in his arms and said, "Tillie, I love you very much. I want you to be my wife."

Tillie's eyes were brimming with tears of joy and confusion as she replied, "Al, I don't know what to say. I care for you so very much."

A huge smile broke out on Al's face. "Then it's yes?"

Tillie pulled back from the embrace until she could see Al's eyes clearly. "My dear Al, my sweet Al. This is so hard for me."

"What's hard? I love you, Tillie." Al spoke softly, enunciating each word with emphasis, "<u>I want you to be my wife</u>!"

Tillie kept her eyes fastened on him. "But do we really know one another well enough?"

"I know enough about you, my dear, to ask you to spend the rest of your life with me."

Tillie spoke with hesitation. "It's … it's…"

"It's what?" he asked.

"You're a farmer. Your life is so different from everything I've ever known."

"You can learn." A little uncertainty crept into Al's voice. His body was tense.

"I know I can," she said. "It's just that I have so many things to think about."

"You're not saying no then?"

"No, my darling Al. I'm not saying no. I need time to think."

Al relaxed and pulled her back into his arms. With his cheek pressed to hers he whispered, "Then take all the time you need. I'll wait forever." He pressed his lips to hers in a long and passionate kiss.

A few moments later he continued, "Remember how I said that to know me, you're going to have to meet all of my family?"

Tillie shook her head.

"You've met my parents, my brother and sister. But you haven't met my aunts and uncles and cousins. We're a big family. We all go to the same church. Come with me next Sunday and meet them. Let them meet you."

"What are they going to say?"

"Good morning!" Al laughed. "Nobody bites."

"I know that. But I'm from the city. I'm not a German or a Lutheran. My people came from England and I'm a Methodist."

"Yah. I see." Al emphasized his German accent. "*Und da last time vee had an English Metodist mit us vee all tuk up stones und trew dem at her*!"

Now Tillie was laughing. "Okay. You made your point."

"Great," said Al. "I'll pick you up next Sunday."

At nine-thirty the following Sunday morning the sun was bright, the weather crisp, the temperature in the thirties, the ditch water coated with a thin layer of ice. Herds of contented cows in the pastures munched on their cuds, puffs of vapor drifting from their nostrils. A few dry leaves hung yet on some of the trees, but the fields were barren, covered with stubble left from the fall corn harvest.

As they neared Rich Valley, Al talked about his church. "We're about a hundred families, all living around the church."

"How long has your church been there?" asked Tillie.

"About twenty-five years. We're a daughter congregation of Trinity Church of Lone Oak, about ten or twelve miles north."

"How'd it get started?"

"My Ma and Pa and some other families were living out here in Rich Valley. They decided to start St. John's. Ma and Pa and the others put together enough money to buy the land. They borrowed enough to build the sanctuary and the school. They themselves did the building."

"I'm impressed."

"I'm proud of them."

"How big is your church?"

"Seats about a hundred fifty, including the balcony. We have a little pipe organ up there. Our school teacher plays it and the boys of the church turn a handle that pumps the air."

"You pumped it when you were in grade-school?"

"All of us older boys had our turn."

"Your school building is bigger than mine."

"Doubles as a fellowship hall and has a second room."

"What for?"

"It's where the seventh and eighth graders meet every school day to study catechism with the pastor."

"Your students sure get lots of religion."

"It's a part of everything we do."

"I do some of that in my school, too."

"At St. John's school, every day starts with prayer and every student studies Bible stories and memorizes Bible and hymn verses."

"We start every day with prayer at '132' and we pledge allegiance to the flag."

"You need to meet our school teacher, Mr. Hartung. Been with us for about twenty years. Most of our kids have been taught by him."

"Is he a good teacher?"

"Not easy."

"Made you work, eh?"

"Strict."

"So how'd you do?" asked Tillie.

"Okay," Al replied, "I studied Catechism in German and memorized a bunch of Bible verses and hymns, but I forgot a bunch, too."

"Sounds normal," laughed Tillie, "but why German? This is not the fatherland."

"Yah, but lots of our people—and some pastors—believe that God's native language is German and everybody will have to talk it when they get to heaven."

"Yeah, right," chided Tillie. "We Methodists will have to build a wall there to protect ourselves from such nonsense."

They joined a small caravan of cars and farm trucks entering the church parking area at that point. Slowly they made their way through the gravel covered lot to a parking space toward the rear. They stepped from Al's Model

A across from a red brick church building with stained glass windows, topped by a thirty feet high bell tower. A large concrete platform in front of the church was filled with farm families, busily talking, shaking hands and hugging one another.

Behind them, at the south end of the parking lot, stood the parish school building with its first floor raised high enough to accommodate a fellowship hall in the basement beneath. On the other side of the school, beyond a grove of oak trees Tillie could see a graveyard. Another grove of trees on the north side of the church surrounded a modest, white-framed two-story house, the home of the pastor. Behind the house was a small garage and what looked like a chicken barn. The total complex occupied about five acres.

Noticing the chicken barn, Tillie asked, "Does your pastor raise chickens?"

"Sure. He and his Missus have a big garden too. We keep them and their kids well supplied with meat and vegetables. It might be the Depression, but they don't starve. We farmers raise lots of stuff and our Pastor gets his share."

Observing people coming out of the church, Tillie asked, "Are those the German Service people?"

"That's them. Mostly older folks. When they die off we'll probably drop the German Service, but that's not going to happen very soon."

"Too bad we didn't go."

"Some day I'll teach you some German. The language is pretty important to these older people. They're getting ready for heaven, right?"

"Sure, Krauts on one side of the New Jerusalem talking German and English-speaking Methodists on the other," said Tillie, with a slight rise of her eyebrow.

"Hey, there's Ma and Pa, next to the Schwanzes and the Wechslers. Come on. I want you to meet my relatives."

They approached the crowd of farmers gathered in front of the church. The men wore a variety of dark brown or blue woolen suits, starched white shirts, dark ties and a variety of caps and hats. Some wore clean bib-overalls, with a shirt and tie beneath an aged woolen suit jacket. Their Sunday clothes may have been old or dated, but no one cared.

The women wore plain ankle length dresses beneath their woolen coats. Not surprisingly, a few of the coats had visible patches. Their heads were covered with a variety of simple hats or kerchiefs tied at the chin. Many of the coats and hats were outmoded as well. The girls were dressed in calf length dresses similar in fashion to their mothers, including hats. In contrast to the city girls, Tillie realized that these young women probably knew nothing about the latest fashions. All of the boys, including the teenagers, wore bib-overalls.

Pa Freitag started beaming when he saw Tillie approaching. Turning to the man next to him, he said in a voice loud enough for Tillie to hear, "Look, there's Albert's Tillie. Now if I was only his age again I'd give him a run for his money ... Ah, Tillie, good little Tillie. We're so glad to have you here. How are you?"

The young couple was immediately surrounded. Al introduced his relatives and friends. Tillie recognized the Switzers, Orville and Robert's parents. Were they relatives also? she wondered. She recognized Kathy Neunaber and her parents. Obviously, not all the children of the congregation went to the parochial school.

Friendly people, thought Tillie. *The women seem a bit shy. Maybe they don't know what to do with this Methodist girl from the Twin Cities. I only hope I'm not too much of a city girl.*

At about ten-twenty the German Service people began to go to their cars and the English Service members started drifting into the sanctuary. As they went up the stairs to the crowded narthex, Al explained to Tillie how the seating worked. "All the women sit on the right side and the men on the other. You'll sit with Ma and Irene."

A slight frown crossed Tillie's forehead. For a moment she rolled her eyes. *Men on one side and women on the other?* she thought. *What's that all about? We Methodists gave up on that idea a long time ago. Looks like changes come very slowly out here.*

"An usher will give you a little black hymn book," he continued, "All you do is follow along."

Ma Freitag was waiting for her as they entered the worship area. She smiled as Tillie approached and motioned for her to follow. They found a pew in the middle of the sanctuary among the other women. Tillie felt the eyes of many women and men focused on her. They probably don't have many visitors, she thought. In the corner of her eye she caught Al, on the men's side, looking at her with a big smile. She was tempted to wave at him, but restrained herself.

The Service was formal, with a variety of responses quite unfamiliar to Tillie. The hymns had many more verses and were sung at a much slower tempo than in Methodist services. She noted, however, that congregation members, even those who sang off key, sang with gusto. The pastor's sermon was well over a half hour in length. It was based upon the Gospel reading for the day. His applications were related to farm life and the difficulties farmers were facing in the Depression. The Service ended close to noon.

After they left the building the worshippers continued to stand around talking, catching up on events of their families and friends. Tillie met more relatives and friends and promptly forgot most of the names. Many of the children ran over to swing in the school yard or play games of tag while they waited for their parents.

The late fall air was still crisp. The sun shone brightly on the little congregation. Tillie pondered a few memorized lines by the English poet John's Keats:

To one who has been long in city pent,
'Tis very sweet to look into the fair
And open face of heaven – to breathe a prayer
Full in the smile of the blue firmament.

As they entered the back door of the Freitag farm house, Tillie could immediately smell a pork roast baking in the oven of Ma's wood-burning kitchen stove.

"Mmm, that really smells good," she said.

"It should be almost done," Ma Freitag explained, "I've had it roasting all morning."

Al led Tillie past the large round kitchen table, covered with the dishes and pans Ma used to prepare the Sunday feast, into the dining room. He pulled out a chair for her to sit at the table, loaded with Ma Freitag's gold edged china.

Tillie picked up one of the cups and said, "This is the most beautiful china I've ever seen."

"Thank you," said Ma. "It came with my parents from Germany. It's called Bavarian china. They brought the silverware, too."

When all members of the family were seated, Pa bowed his head and folded his hands. The rest of the family followed suit. He prayed reverently, his words carrying a heavy German accent and reflecting the common usage of the King James' English Version of the Bible.

"Father in heaven, we thank Thee for this food. Even in these hard times Thou dost pour it generously into our hands. We begin another week in Thy name. Bless us in all we do. We thank Thee for bringing Tillie to be with us again and we ask for Thy continued blessing on all her work with the children of her school. And now Father, as we have invited Thee, so we invite Thy Son among us as we say together (at this point everyone joined in except Tillie, who did not know the prayer), Come Lord Jesus, be our guest and let Thy gifts to us be blessed. Amen."

As bowls of mashed potatoes, boiled carrots, corn and pork roast were passed, the entire family broke out into happy conversation. "I heard that the price of cattle has dropped again," said Al.

"Not again," said Werner, his brother.

"Yah, it's getting very bad," Pa remarked. "The Wechslers had some cows go dry last week. When Harold took them to the stockyards, he said he got practically nothing for them. He's not sure he'll have enough money to buy a couple to replace them."

As at supper the previous week, Tillie did her best to eat a plate full of generous helpings. Nevertheless, she heard Ma say, "Come, Tillie, have some more. You eat like a little bird."

"Hey, Ma," said Al, "remember what she said last week. She's worried about her figure. And I like it the way it is."

Tillie blushed. She did her best to reject the bowls pressed upon her, while the others took second and third helpings.

As she looked upon this happy, well-fed family she felt these farmers were among the few citizens in the country who did not have to be concerned about food. She remembered newspaper accounts of people starving in Kansas, Oklahoma and Texas, even on farms. Huge droughts and dust storms were blowing away good dirt, forcing farmers to abandon their homesteads to wander the country in search of work.

When it seemed that no one could possibly eat any more, Ma and Irene carried the dishes into the kitchen. Tillie offered to help, but they insisted she keep her seat, because she was their guest. Then Ma produced an apple pie. She filled their coffee cups from a large and very ornate coffee server and the meal continued.

Tillie wondered how any one person could eat so much food. She struggled to eat her piece of pie and settled back in her chair feeling as stuffed as a Thanksgiving Day turkey. In her own family, she recalled, her mother always carefully limited servings and preserved leftovers for some upcoming meal.

When the meal was completed Tillie joined Ma and Irene in the kitchen to wash the dishes. Al, Werner and Pa settled in the front room for a time to talk about farming, but Pa, as usual, soon fell asleep in his easy chair, so Al and Werner took a walk outside to carry on their conversation.

By the time the women were finished with dish washing, storing the dishes and sweeping the kitchen, Pa was awake, yawning and stretching. Ma and Tillie joined him in the living room. Irene excused herself and retreated upstairs to her room. Ma settled into her favorite chair to began crocheting. She invited Tillie to take her place on the couch.

"Well, little Tillie," Pa began, "how goes school teaching?"

With some amusement, Tillie noted his continued use of the diminutive, but also realized from previous conversations that it was a phrase of affection. She smiled as she replied. "Great, Mr. Freitag. I was nervous the first six weeks, but I've got a pretty good handle on the job now."

"Good."

Pa's German accent was much stronger than Al's. His 'good' rhymed with hoot.

"Yah, and all those German Lutherans that you met today, what do you think?" he continued.

"Really great people, but I can't remember all their names."

"Yah, that takes a while. We're all one big family around here. Lots of family, cousins, aunts, uncles."

"That's what so great. Most of my relatives live in Iowa. We don't get to see them more than once or twice a year. Some we never see."

"Yah, and some of our relatives we never see. We didn't always live on this farm. Did you know I didn't grow up here?"

"No, I didn't," she replied. "Tell me more."

At this point Ma looked up from her crocheting. "Pa, don't bore the poor girl to death with all your stories."

"No, no," said Tillie, "I'd love to hear more. I really would."

Pa's eyes lighted up. He pulled himself up in his horse hair chair and leaned toward Tillie.

"My Papa and Momma came with their parents to the United States when they was in their teens about eighty years ago. They settled on farms in the south part of Indiana."

"Why'd they leave Germany?"

"To be free to worship as they wished. The government tried to force everybody into one church. They were Lutherans and didn't agree with the teachings of that German state church."

"They moved to the United States for religious freedom?"

"Yah, and the chance to homestead good farm land. They were just going good on their farm when the Civil War broke out."

"Was there fighting in Indiana?" asked Tillie.

"No, but my Papa fought in the war. He said God made all men the same, black or white. So he fought for the freedom of the Negroes. He served in the 74th Indiana Regiment. He was only twenty-one when he was wounded in his left leg. He limped for the rest of his life."

"One of my great uncles was killed in the battle of Bull Run," said Tillie.

Pa's eyes were sad. "It was a bad time for our country."

"But some good things came out of it."

"Yah, I suppose so. Always so much fighting. When I was a boy, comes the World War. Not a good time for the German people then either."

"I've only read about it."

"Now I hear some more bad things. Hard times in Germany. Some of our relatives write letters about Adolph Hitler and the Nazi party. They wonder if the Nazis will lead them to better times. This Depression touches every country."

"I don't know much about that," replied Tillie. "I read the newspapers, but…" She paused, because she wanted Pa to get back to his story. "Anyway, what happened to your folks after the Civil War?"

"After Poppa and Momma got married they homesteaded a good farm, about forty miles south of Fort Wayne. That's where I grew up." A big smile crossed his weathered face. "And that's also where I met my Ida."

Ma looked up again. "Now Henry, do you have to get into that?"

"No, really," countered Tillie. "What happened? How did you two meet?"

Ma was blushing. Pa continued. "It was at a funeral."

"Really," asked Tillie. "A funeral?"

"Pa!" Ma seemed a bit irritated. "Have some respect."

"Ida, nothing wrong with that." He turned back to Tillie. "We are third cousins, me and Ida. That's how we both ended up at the same funeral. Afterwards, at the family's house for lunch, we got to talking. I found out she lived about ten miles closer to Fort Wayne than we did, but we had never met. So I asked her if I could see her again sometime. She said I'd have to ask her Pa and Ma. So I did."

"Henry, please!" Ma was looking quite uneasy. It was obvious that she was uncomfortable talking about their romance. To her it was a very private matter and she was a very private person. "Why don't you tell her what color your socks were while you're at it."

Pa was thoroughly enjoying the retelling of his tale. "Okay, Ida. I won't go into the whole story. We got to know one another better over the next year. I took her to a couple dances. Finally, I asked her parents for her hand in marriage and we were married there at Zion Lutheran Church in Decatur, Indiana. We were both in our early twenties."

"That's a wonderful story," laughed Tillie. "Did you move to Minnesota then?"

"Yah. Not much good land left anymore in Indiana. With our poppas and mammas, a long time we talked. What should we do? We wanted our own place."

"Most of the good farms were already taken?"

"Yah, so one day in German newspaper we read about Minnesota. Lots of German people to Minnesota was coming. Good land still to be homesteaded, the paper said."

"But how to move, right?"

"Right. We had a couple cousins who had moved up here. So we wrote a letter to them and about a month later we got one back. They said we should come. There was still some good land to be homesteaded and they would help us."

"It sounds scary to pack up and leave everybody back in Indiana and set out for a new, strange place," said Tillie. She was thinking about her own adventure in the country.

"Yah, we were scared, but it was exciting too. We were young and full of life. Don't forget, Tillie, my Poppa and Momma had come all the way over the ocean from Germany when they was young. They never saw their folks again. I never knew my Gross-papa and Gross-mama."

"I bet you'd like to," she replied, thinking about her own grandparents in Iowa.

"Yah, but our Lord has a plan for everyone … So we prayed and he brought us here."

"How long did it take to get here?"

"We rode in the train to Chicago and slept in the train station. Early the next morning we rode to St. Paul. Our cousins met us and we stayed with them for a month while we looked for land."

"That's how you found this farm, right?"

"No, first we moved to Rich Valley, up the road about four miles north from where your school stands. It was the last homestead available then, but it was ours and we were excited about it."

"Did you build a house and a barn then?"

"Ach, yah. There was nothing but woods, hills and some pretty rocky ground. Those first years was hard, very hard for both of us. Right Ida?" He looked at Ma and their eyes connected in the memories. Pa continued.

"But we had some help from our cousins and from the neighbors and it went okay."

"We buried two babies." Ma's voice quivered. "And we had two fine boys and a girl."

At that point Pa picked up a large tattered, leather-covered German Bible lying on a little table next to his chair and opened it. Just inside the front cover he had pasted a brown-tinted photograph. It was a picture of Al and Werner when they were little boys, sitting cross-legged in front of Ma and Pa on the grass, with their Rich Valley farm house in the background. Ma was seated in a chair and Pa was standing next to her. Everyone looked quite sober. Posing for a photograph was apparently very serious business.

"I keep this picture in my Bible and one day I will give it to my grandchildren and tell them the story."

Tillie pointed to the picture. "Is that little Al sitting on the ground?"

"Yah. Those were good days. Our children were all born there. We lived there for fifteen years. Then we had the chance to buy this place. The land here is much better and so is the pasture. So we sold the old place, took out a mortgage and moved. We still miss the old place."

He looked off into the distance, as if he were seeing the house and barn he had built. Tillie imagined the sounds of the windmill creaking in the wind. She watched him walking in the summer up the hills to the woods to bring a newborn calf back to the barn. For a time she said nothing. She was also imagining what it must have been like for his parents to sail across the Atlantic, knowing they would never see their parents again. She wondered if she could ever make such a journey herself.

Finally, Pa blinked his eyes, stood up, stretched and said, "Yah, well, time to milk the cows. Thanks for listening, Tillie. Jesus loves us and leads us all."

Chapter 9

Uptown Visit

Tillie and Al continued to date through the long Minnesota winter. They went to a couple more dances at the Green Roof and to Hamline one Saturday evening to join the students to laugh at a special showing of Buster Keaton's silent film, *The Boat*. They had dinner at O'Hara's in Rosemount three times. They shared dreams about their futures, held hands, hugged, kissed and controlled their deeper desires with great difficulty.

Al arrived in his Model-A at Mrs. Wilson's two weeks before Easter. "I know how to get to West St. Paul," he said, once Tillie was seated, "but after that you need to show me where to go."

"You nervous, sweetie?" asked Tillie.

"A little. Not sure I know how to get along with all those 'up-town' people."

The weather was clear, a relief after several days of constant rain had produced puddles of standing water everywhere. The soggy fields gave no promise of early cultivation by area farmers. Newly arrived robins, hopping about in search of breakfast worms, gave hints of a rapidly approaching spring. Some of the trees and lilac bushes were budding out.

"Really nice day. My kids have been arguing with their parents about when to take off their heavy winter underwear," laughed Tillie.

"Been there. Done that," Al chuckled.

Tillie guided them through the West St. Paul streets to St. Paul Methodist Church. They arrived a few minutes before the eleven o'clock worship service. "Look," she said. "Mother and Poppa are waiting for us."

Al parked the Ford around the corner from the large, red brick building. "Welcome to St. Paul's," said Poppa to Al. "Ever been to a Methodist church before?"

"No sir. Anything special I need to know?"

"Not at all," laughed Dr. Tilden. "We'll help you through it."

They joined about five hundred worshippers to sit in oaken pews, stained dark mahogany, like the wood paneling. A large rose-type stained glass window portraying Christ with the children looked down upon the sanctuary from the front wall.

Dr. Morris Dueworthy, teaching elder and pastor, sat directly behind the pulpit, robed in a red chevron-striped, black academic robe. In his early fifties, he was a tall, stately figure, with carefully combed hair and a pleasing face. He rose as the organ played softly.

"Won't you join me in prayer," he intoned. Congregation members bowed their heads. After completing his Call to Worship, he looked up and said, "We join together to sing John Wesley's great eighteenth century hymn, *Jesus, Lover of My Soul*."

As the congregation rose, the organist played a brisk introduction, filled with emotional crescendos, held the final chord for a moment, broke and then, with most of the organ's stops pulled open, played Joseph Parry's familiar tune. The people joined to sing Wesley's words with great fervor.

Jesus, lover of my soul,
Let me to thy mercy fly
While the nearer waters roll,
While the tempest still is high ...

Al had never been inside a Methodist church in his life. He simply stood beside Tillie, the congregation all around him, hymnbook in hand, mouth open, unable to say a word or join in the singing. He had heard the hymn, but never played or sung in the fashion now reverberating through the sanctuary. Since birth he had only attended Lutheran churches in rural Dakota County. The way this hymn was played was strange to him. This music was so moving, so emotional. He felt the stark contrast to the somber chorales of his Lutheran experience. He wondered if his pastor would approve of such a display of feeling.

The service following the hymn was not at all like the liturgical worship he had always known. There were no responses from the congregation and there was no chanting by the pastor.

With both hands held out, Dr. Dueworthy motioned the people to be seated. "Please follow along," he said in cultured tones, "as we read from the Gospel of Saint Matthew, chapter twenty-five, verses thirty-one and following, the parable of the sheep and the goats."

When he had completed the reading, he smiled upon his congregation and said, "This, my beloved people, is the Word from our Savior for this day. Now our music director, Dr. Langston, will lead our choir in a special rendition of John's Newton's oh so-familiar hymn, *Amazing Grace*."

The choir's singing emulated the emotional style of the earlier music. Their rendition of the familiar eighteenth century song, set to the early nineteenth century melody, *Virginia Harmony*, was flawlessly performed. When they sat down, their faces were filled with smiles of satisfaction. Al thought about the tiny choir at his church and their sometimes pitiful attempts at harmony.

Following the choir anthem, Dr. Dueworthy stood to begin his exposition of Jesus' parable. As Al listened, he felt awkward and uncomfortable in his dark blue, seldom-worn Sunday suit and starched white shirt. He wondered what he had gotten himself into. How did he end up in this foreign land? Did Methodists and Lutherans worship the same God? He supposed they did, but why did they do it in such different ways? The pastor's sermon was interesting, filled with good stories and important applications. It wasn't the preaching; it was the whole experience. What was he, a farmer and a Lutheran, doing up here with all these citified Methodists?

After worship, Al drove Tillie to her parents' house. His hands were so damp with perspiration they stuck to the steering wheel, despite the forty degree temperature outside. His armpits were drenched with sweat and he couldn't stop blinking his eyes.

What do I say? he asked himself. *How do I talk to somebody with a doctor's degree? I haven't even attended high school. How can they consider me a suitable candidate to marry Tillie?*

By the time they reached the house, he had talked himself into a near panic. He thought of simply dropping Tillie off and driving out of her life as rapidly as his Model-A would take him, but he knew he couldn't. This was Tillie. He loved her and these were her parents. Then a sense of firm resolve arose. One way or another, he *was* going to have her for his wife. He believed she loved him and they were going to marry, but God help him, he didn't know how he was going to make it happen.

Tillie could see his nervousness. "Hey, big Al, what's going on? You afraid of my folks or something?"

"Me? No. What's to be scared of?" he lied.

"It's just that you look a little tense. Don't be! Poppa likes you. I know it. I can tell it by his eyes. He's a farmer in his heart. Always has been."

"And your Ma? What about her?" Al asked. He could feel the sweat pouring down his back.

"Well, she's going to like you too—because, well, because I do! Okay?"

Al, unaccustomed to sharing his inmost feelings, fumbled for words. "Thanks. I think you know what you mean to me."

"I'm sure I do, my dear, sweet man. Don't let Mother scare you. I know she has a big speech waiting for me, but I can handle her. Just relax. We'll get through this just fine."

Dr. Tilden greeted them at the front door, held out his hand to Al and smiled warmly. Al was certain Dr. Tilden would feel his sweaty palm. He wiped it again on his trousers before offering it. As they shook hands, Al smiled weakly and prayed to God for courage. Poppa gave Tillie a big hug and invited them to be seated. Tillie immediately excused herself to join Mother and Mattie in the kitchen.

"Tell me all about your farm," Dr. Tilden began, as they settled into the living room chairs. "I grew up on a farm in Iowa. I love farming and animals. I love to go back home, walk into the barn and take a deep breath. That smell is perfume to my nose. That's why I'm a veterinarian."

Al began to feel at ease. His anxiety began to melt like April's snow. He knew Tillie's Poppa was a farm boy and a vet. The problem was, he had never been to a vet's house for dinner. His farm vet treated their cows' infected udders and helped their sows deliver piglets. They relied upon him, but he wasn't a personal friend. How could he be? He knew all that stuff about animals and medicines and shots. They simply weren't equals. Yet here was a vet talking with him as an equal, wanting to know his ideas and plans about planting corn and mowing hay. He seemed so down to earth. He knew farmer talk. This was more than a vet; this was a person, Tillie's father. Perhaps they really could get to know one another.

So they talked. They discussed the price of milk and the use of new cattle food supplements. They talked about the falling prices of grain, meat and dairy products. They worried together about the depressed economy. An increase in efficiency and in the amount of land being farmed around the world had certainly driven prices down. They mutually wondered why President Hoover's administration had failed farmers so miserably.

"We tried to raise more corn and oats, but the prices keep going down," complained Al.

"It's Hoover's farm program," said Dr. Tilden. "That Agricultural Marketing Act back in '29, was supposed to help farmers, but they didn't build in any production controls."

"I know," said Al, wrinkling his forehead. "Until a couple years ago, wheat prices were okay. We still made a little money, but last year everything went haywire. The government funds were gone, and the Farm Board warehouses were full. Crop prices fell through the floor."

"So what do you think President Roosevelt will do?" asked Dr. Tilden. "After all, we need you farmers. Do you think he can rescue the agricultural economy?"

"Lots of us are counting on him," responded Al.

As they talked, Tillie was busy in the kitchen, helping Mother and Mattie with Sunday dinner.

"He's a real handsome guy," giggled Mattie. "I love that wavy black hair and those big shoulders."

"Me, too," said Tillie. "That's the first thing I noticed when I met him at that dance in Rosemount."

"I bet he's a good kisser, too."

"Mattie! What a thing to say," snapped Mother.

"What do you think about him, Mother?" asked Tillie.

Mother was clearly nervous, agitated. She busied herself with the dinner preparations and said nothing.

"Mother?"

"He's a farmer. Do I have to say anything else?"

"So? You knew that before you agreed to invite him for dinner."

"Yes, I knew. I did it because you asked me. He's still a farmer."

"What are you trying to say?"

"I'm saying that you really need to think about this before you go any further."

"Any further with what?"

Mother put down a plate and turned toward Tillie, her eyes flashing. "Don't play games with me. You two have been talking marriage. Otherwise you wouldn't have brought him up here."

"That part's true."

Mother raised her voice. "You know very well how I feel about farming."

"You've never hidden that."

Tillie pushed shut the swinging door to the kitchen and prepared for the worst. "What if I told you I loved him?"

"So? I loved your father when we got married." Mother's face was getting red. "We still ended up on that miserable farm. What did my love get me? Hard work and loneliness! We struggle with the farm thing to this very day."

"Mother, please. I'm not you!"

Mother put her hands on Tillie's shoulders and looked straight into her eyes. "I know that. You have something I never will have. You have a college education. You're a gifted teacher. You have your whole life in front of you. Please! Don't throw it all away by becoming a farmer's wife."

Tillie struggled with her feelings. Finally she put her head on her mother's shoulder and held her tightly in her arms. "I know you love me, Mother. But I love Al, too. All I can tell you is that I haven't said yes–yet."

"Hey, you two, dinner is getting cold," said Mattie.

Mother stepped back from Tillie. "You know what I mean," she said. She turned, picked up a dish of mashed potatoes and carried them to the dining room. Turning toward Poppa and Al, she said, "Time to eat."

As Al drove them back to the country later that evening, he asked, "So, how do you think it went?"

"Better than I expected."

"Your Pa is real easy to talk to."

"So I noticed."

"We solved all the problems with the Depression."

"Great. I'm sure President Roosevelt will be happy to hear from you."

"Your Mother didn't cut my head off."

"She thought about it."

"She's a pretty good cook."

"She learned on a farm."

"You three were doing a lot of talking in the kitchen before dinner. Did she say anything about me?"

"A little. I've told you how she feels about farmers."

"So what do you think?"

"About?"

"Her feelings?"

"Let's give it some time."

Tillie decided the Sunday dinner was a limited success. Poppa felt Al was an intelligent, progressive farmer, in spite of his lack of formal education. Poppa even said he was going to visit Al's farm the next Saturday when he came out to pick her up for the Easter vacation.

Mother? Well, she was more than a little cool. Yet she warmed up a little when Al complimented her on the meal.

Yes, all things considered, it was a good meal and a good Sunday. But where was this all going? If she only knew. If she only knew.

Chapter 10

Orville and the Manure Spreader

The week after Easter, the last Saturday in April, Tillie was in the basement of the Wilson house running her freshly washed bed linens through the wringer at around ten in the morning.

Mrs. Wilson shouted down the basement stairs, "Tillie! I think you'd better come up here. Eila's on the phone. She's calling from the clinic. She sounds scared!"

Tillie dropped the wet sheet in a wicker basket and scampered up the stairs. She lifted the earphone to her ear and began.

"Eila, it's me. What's up?"

"Oh, Tillie, thank God. The Switzers called. Robert's been hurt real bad. Dr. Wagner and I are going out to their farm. We'd like you to come along. Maybe you can help Orville while we work with Robert."

"Pick me up on your way," said Tillie without a moment's hesitation. "You can fill me in on the details while we're driving."

She hung up and turned to her landlady standing in the kitchen next to the stove. A sense of panic began to rise within her chest. Her voice quivered as she spoke. "Eila says Robert Switzer's been hurt. She's on her way to pick me up. Since I'm his teacher she thinks I can help with his brother Orville."

"Of course. I'll finish your wash. Anything else I can do?" asked Mrs. Wilson.

"I'm running upstairs for my coat. When she gets here tell her I'll be right down. I need to get a book from my room. By the way, do you have a couple chocolate candy bars around?"

Mrs. Wilson looked at her quizzically. "I, I think so, but why do you ask?"

"Orville loves chocolate," smiled Tillie. "Maybe it'll help."

Five minutes later Eila and Dr. Wagner were at the boarding house. Dr. Wagner was a young man in his late thirties, of average height and slight build. He had light brown hair and an engaging smile. The one thing Tillie noticed about him when she first met him was his hands. They were strong, but tender, the kind of hands a physician should have.

Tillie climbed into Wagner's car. He turned around to her from the front seat and put one of those wonderful hands on her shoulder. "Thank you for coming, Tillie. You will be a great help, I'm sure."

"I'm glad to do whatever I can," she responded, with a weak smile. "What happened?"

"I got to work about eight," said Eila. "We got things straightened up and started seeing patients when the phone rang. It was Mrs. Switzer. She was screaming and sobbing. 'You got to come,' she yelled. 'You got to come. Robert … You got to come.'

"I tried to get her to calm down, but it was no good. She kept saying something about Robert and me and Dr. Wagner coming."

"What happened to Robert?"

"Oh my God, Tillie, I hate this! Let me finish. I just hate this!"

"What? What are you talking about?" Anxiety spread across Tillie's face like a disease.

"I'm not sure. Something about a manure spreader. Have you ever been to the Switzers?"

"No," answered Tillie. "Now that you mention it, I know they live less than a mile north of my school."

"Right," said Dr. Wagner. "They live in a little, old, beat-up house on the Wechsler farm. Orville's dad's a hired hand there."

"I know," responded Tillie very slowly. "What about it?"

"We'll soon find out. Mrs. Switzer was pretty shook up. We couldn't make much sense out of what she was saying. It sounds like Robert's been hurt pretty bad, however. We'll know more in a few minutes."

When they arrived at the Wechsler farm, Robert's father and the Wechslers were waiting for them. They led them into the house to their bedroom.

Robert lay on the bed. His clothing and the bed sheets were soaked in blood. His arms, face and upper torso were a mass of gashes and wounds. His breath was coming in short gasps. He was barely alive. Dr. Wagner and Eila went to him and immediately began to remove the shredded clothing so they might attend to the wounds.

Tillie turned to the Switzers. Her face was ashen. Her heart was beating wildly, her head light. She braced herself with one hand on the wall as she asked, "What happened?"

"He was hurt early this morning," said Harold Wechsler. Wechsler, a typical farmer, in his late forties, with strong muscles toned by years of hard labor, was normally a reserved man. He did not show his feelings easily. But this time tears filled his eyes and his chin quivered. "Hermann and Robert had finished loading manure into the spreader," he continued, his voice about to break from the emotional strain. "Then Hermann told Robert to drive the tractor and pull the spreader out to the field in back of the barn."

Tillie broke in, "Forgive me, but what's a manure spreader?"

"It's a kind of a wagon with chains with cross arms and a bunch of beaters on the back end. The chains move as the wagon goes along, pulling the manure back into the beaters. There's a power take-off from the tractor that makes the beater arms go around. The beaters are jagged wheels that break up the manure and spread it out into the field. Get the picture?"

"Kind of. What happened?"

"Robert took Orville along with him when he drove the tractor pulling the manure spreader. They got out into the field and everything was going along fine until something got stuck in the beaters and they had to stop."

"I told him not to take the dummy. I told him!" shouted Hermann Switzer. Switzer, his ragged overalls covered with his son's blood, his graying hair disheveled, paced back and forth across the room, clenching and unclenching his fists. "He said it would be all right. And I believed him. I let him take the dummy along! Damn it! Why didn't I stop him?"

Harold Wechsler tried to ignore Switzer as he continued. "Robert put the tractor out of gear and crawled back by the beaters to try to pull a clod loose. Orville was up in front sitting on the tractor. I guess he started fooling around with the levers or something."

Switzer continued to shout, "The damn dummy! That damn dummy! I told him not to take the dummy!"

Wechsler's frown deepened. Now his voice cracked as he said, "Anyway, Orville must have gotten the power take-off in gear just as Robert got the stuff out of the beaters. It yanked him right in!"

"That's when I heard him screaming!" Switzer kept shouting. "But the damn beaters kept going and going. I ran as fast as I could from the barn out to him, but by the time I got there Robert was … was all ground into the beaters. And the damn dummy was jumping up and down and screaming and yelling as loud as he could. He didn't even know how to turn the damn tractor off. After I stopped it, I pulled Robert out and carried him to the house. He was bleeding something terrible. And the damn dummy came along, yelling at the top of his voice."

"Is–is Robert going to be okay?" asked Tillie, looking at Eila.

"No, Tillie, he's not," said Eila. "There isn't much we can do. Dr. Wagner is going to bandage him. We'll wash the wounds and try to stop the bleeding, but there's too many cuts on his face, shoulders, arms and upper body. He's lost so much blood. Too much!"

Hermann Switzer kept pacing back and forth across the bedroom. His gaunt, unshaven face was contorted with pain and anger. He normally stood less than five feet eight inches in height, but looked like the weight of these events had crushed him down to less than five feet four. Over and over he shouted, "The damn dummy! The damn dummy!"

Tillie's knees were trembling. Her face drained of color, she stared out at the walls and said nothing. Her breath came in short gasps. Her eyes were red, filled with tears. Finally she asked, "Where's Orville?"

"I think I saw him running toward the barn," said Mrs. Wechsler.

"We have to find him," said Tillie.

"Come with me," said Mrs. Wechsler. Willa Wechsler was dressed in a cotton print dress with her hair covered by a red bandana. A short, sturdy woman with striking brown eyes and hair, she was as familiar with the barn as with her own kitchen. She led Tillie out of the house down to the barn.

After a brief search in several rooms, they found Orville hiding back in a dark corner, behind a pile of hay, holding his arms around his knees, rocking and sobbing. His eyes were shut. Over and over he kept repeating, "I hurt Robert. I hurt Robert. I hurt Robert."

Tillie folded her legs under her and sat on the straw in front of him. She began to speak softly. Mrs. Wechsler stood, watching, both hands on her mouth, tears pouring from her eyes.

"Orville. Orville, can you hear me?" asked Tillie. "Orville, it's me, Miss Tilden. Open your eyes Orville. Open your eyes. I'm here to help you."

Orville continued to rock and repeat, "No! No! No! I hurt Robert. I hurt

Robert."

Tillie continued to repeat his name. She touched him gently on his shoulder. "Orville, please open your eyes. Please, Orville, please."

After about five minutes the boy stopped chanting, slowly opened his eyes and looked at Tillie. She smiled at him and held out her hands.

"Would you like to come sit by me?"

He shook his head no.

"Its all right, Orville. I'm not here to hurt you. I thought maybe we could read a little from your book. Would you like to do that? What do you think? How about it? Want to come and read a little?"

Orville made a small nod.

"Come on then, sweetie," she continued. "Scoot on over here and read with me."

Carefully, cautiously, Orville took his arms away from his knees. He kept his eyes focused upon Tillie. She continued to smile and did not move.

"Come on. I'm here. Come sit next to me."

Slowly he moved and took his place next to her, looking up to her like a child of three. She put one arm around him and with the other held the second grade reader.

"Let's read together," she said. They joined voices as they began the story.

"Billy lives in a white house. He has a sister. Billy's sister is Mary. Mary lives in the white house too. Billy and Mary have a dog. Their dog's name is Spot."

They paused and Tillie whispered quietly in Orville's ear. "Do you have a dog, Orville?"

"Yes, Miss Tilden."

"What's your dog's name, Orville?"

"Wooly."

Tillie's voice had a twinkle in it. "I saw Wooly outside. That's a nice name. Why did you name him Wooly?"

"'Cause he has lots of hair. It hangs down over his eyes and sometimes I wonder how he can see."

"But he can, right?" asked Tillie.

"Oh, sure. He can see real good. He likes to fetch sticks. Me and Robert throw him sticks and..."

Suddenly Orville began to cry again. There was a sound of despair in his words. "Robert's dead! Robert's dead. Orville killed him! Robert's dead! Orville killed him!"

Tillie gathered him into her arms and hugged him as he laid his head upon her chest and continued to cry.

"Oh, Orville, I know, I know," she said, "but you didn't kill him, honey. It was an accident."

"My daddy said I killed him. He said I'm dumb. He said I turned the tractor on and killed him. He said he's gonna kill me."

"No, he's not. He's hurting and confused. He doesn't know what to say. He loves you, and so does your Mommy."

What can I possibly say that will help this child? she thought. *How can he comprehend?*

Orville turned his tear-stained face up at Tillie, as he said, "No they don't, Miss Tilden They think I'm dumb and they think I killed Robert."

"You're not dumb, Orville," she said. *But he is slow,* she thought, *so slow to catch on. His mind doesn't work like the other children's. He needs to realize he is still important. How can I help him? Perhaps his reading.* "You can read, right? We just read from the book, didn't we, Orville?"

"Yes, Miss Tilden."

"Okay. So remember that, Orville. Remember that you didn't kill Robert. It was a mistake, a terrible accident. You didn't know that those levers would turn on the manure spreader, did you?" Tillie struggled with her own emotions. For a moment she was certain she would begin sobbing just like Orville, but she must not. For Orville's sake she must remain calm. Somehow she managed to control herself.

Orville sniffed and replied, "No, Miss Tilden. I didn't know. I didn't want to hurt Robert. Me and Robert played with Wooly."

"That's right, Orville. You and Robert played with Wooly."

Orville was a bit more relaxed now. Tillie put the book on the floor as Orville wiped his eyes with his sleeve. She handed him her hankie and he blew his nose.

"Orville," she began with a smile, "would you like to have a candy bar? I have a chocolate bar."

"Yes, Miss Tilden," said Orville as he looked at her with sad eyes.

"Okay," she said, "good. It's right here in my pocket. Let's stand up now and I'll give it to you."

Tillie helped Orville up, gave him the candy, took his hand and led him slowly out of the barn. Willa Wechsler had been watching. Unable to say a word, she picked up the reader and followed. Tears streamed down her face as she slowly walked toward the Switzer house. She wiped them with her free hand.

Orville ate the chocolate and clung to Tillie's hand. "Thank you, Miss Tilden. I love you, Miss Tilden."

"I know you do, Orville. I love you too. Orville, honey, what do you think about staying at my house tonight? Nurse Stricklund and I live at the same house. If it's all right with your mommy and daddy you can sleep in my bed and I can sleep with Nurse Stricklund. Would that be okay?"

"Yes, Miss Tilden. I can sleep in your bed ... Miss Tilden."

"Yes, Orville."

"Will Robert be coming home soon after he gets better?"

A deep sadness filled Tillie's heart. Again she nearly began to weep. Tears flowed down her cheeks. Orville didn't understand. He didn't know that death was the end. What could she say?

"No, Orville, Robert won't be coming home. Robert is dead."

"I know, Miss Tilden, but he's gonna get better and then he'll come home and we'll play with Woolly."

"We'll see, honey. We'll see. Finish your candy bar. I need to talk with Nurse Stricklund. I'll be right back." She turned to Mrs. Wechsler. "Look after him for a few minutes."

Willa Wechsler nodded and put her arms around Orville as Tillie hurried back toward the house.

Suddenly Orville began to cry again, "I hurt Robert," he continued. "I hurt Robert. My daddy says I'm a dummy. I hurt Robert. My Daddy's going to kill me." Willa drew him to herself. They sobbed and clung to one another.

Tillie paused, came back and wrapped her arms around them both. "It's going to be okay, Orville. It's going to be okay."

A moment later she broke away and went into the house to explain her plan to Eila. Returning, she took Orville's hand and led him to Dr. Wagner's car where she held him on her lap in the rear seat. Mrs. Wechsler returned to the Switzer house.

"Orville, sweetie, it wasn't your fault," Tillie continued. "You didn't know what you were doing. You were just fooling around, having fun, like you always do."

Orville calmed. Tillie smoothed out his hair and dried his eyes. She looked up to see Eila standing on the front porch, motioning her to come.

"Orville, stay here in the car. I'll be right back," she said.

When she reached the porch, Eila took her hands and said quietly, "Robert just passed away. There was nothing we could do." She reached out to take

Tillie in her arms.

As they embraced on the porch they could hear Hermann Switzer's shouting increase in volume. His voice was high pitched, filled with an intense anger. "Where's the damn dummy? I'll kill the stupid idiot," he screamed. Then a door slammed and they heard a couple chairs being thrown to the floor. Suddenly he was on the porch. His eyes were red, his mouth contorted with hate. "Where's the damn dummy?" he screamed.

Harold Wechsler came through the porch door after him. "Hermann!" he shouted, "you gotta get hold of yourself." Then he grabbed Switzer from behind and held him. For a moment Hermann Switzer struggled to break loose from Wechsler's strong grip, but then gave in and collapsed to the floor of the porch. Dangling his legs off the side, he held his head in his arms and began to sob. Wechsler sat beside him, his arm on Switzer's shoulder, his own face tearful.

Tillie and Eila stood, hand in hand, watching the two men. Eila turned to Tillie. "You go back to the car. Look after Orville. Dr. Wagner and I will tend to Robert. Mrs. Wechsler will help Mrs. Switzer." She turned and disappeared into the house as Tillie walked over to join Orville again.

About a half hour later Dr. Wagner came out and followed Mrs. Wechsler to her house. Eila came toward the car and Tillie stepped out to meet her. Eila whispered, "He's calling up the funeral director in Rosemount. They'll come out, pick up the body and get everything ready. Dr. Wagner gave Mrs. Switzer a sedative. She's resting."

"What about Mr. Switzer?"

"I think Wechsler will stay with him."

"He sounds like he wants to kill Orville."

"I know. Dr. Wagner and I talked about that. We think your plan to bring Orville into town with us is best for now. Mrs. Wechsler says Switzer has a real bad temper and he never cared for Orville. She's afraid he'll do something really bad."

"Orville and I already talked about that."

Tillie climbed back into the car to sit beside Orville on the back seat. "Orville, honey," she said, "you're going to Rosemount with me, like we talked about. Okay?"

Orville nodded, his eyes downcast and his mouth drooping.

"There's not much more we can do out here," continued Eila. "Mrs. Switzer will sleep for at least a couple hours. Mrs. Wechsler will stay in the house with her. As soon as Dr. Wagner finishes his phone call we'll head back to town."

Eila explained to Mrs. Wechsler that she and Tillie were taking Orville to spend the night with them in town. "He'll need some clean clothes," said Willa Wechsler. Without another word she disappeared into the Switzer house. In a couple minutes she returned and handed Tillie a paper sack stuffed with a clean shirt, overalls, socks and underwear. "You take good care of him," she said. "He's had a real bad day."

Dr. Wagner climbed in and started the car. "Thank you, Mrs. Wechsler," he said. "We'll be in touch. Call my office if you have any other questions." He turned the car around and drove off, with Tillie and Orville in the back seat.

When they arrived at the small clinic in Rosemount, Eila made another phone call to the Wechsler farm. Tillie and Orville waited for her in one of the three examining rooms. In a few minutes she appeared.

"I called Mrs. Wechsler," she began. "She said that Mrs. Switzer is still resting. Mr. Switzer is sitting on their back porch steps just staring. Mrs. Wechsler has some more pills from Dr. Wagner for Mrs. Switzer and she's going to see that Mrs. Switzer sleeps through the night. She still agrees it's best if Orville stays with us. I talked with Dr. Wagner. He said he'll give me a very mild sedative for Orville just in case we have any trouble with him tonight. I also talked with Mrs. Wilson and she says it'll be just fine with her whatever we do."

"Okay, it's agreed then. I'll take Orville to the house. When are you finished here?"

"We close up at about one o'clock on Saturdays and it's past that now. Mrs. Wilson's coming over to pick you up. You two go on back there with her and I'll follow, soon as we wrap things up here."

Tillie turned to Orville. "Orville, would you like another candy bar?"

"No, thank you, Miss Tilden."

"Okay. We're going over to my place now. Okay?"

"Yes, Miss Tilden."

Tillie took Orville's hand and they walked to the waiting room where Mrs. Wilson greeted them. They followed her to her car and she drove them back to the house.

Chapter 11

Funeral

As Tillie and Orville entered the kitchen, Mrs. Wilson began, "You haven't had any lunch. How about I fix you and Orville a sandwich?"

"I couldn't eat anything," said Tillie weakly, "but Orville is probably hungry." She turned to Orville. "Orville, honey, are you hungry? Would you like Mrs. Wilson to make you a baloney sandwich?"

"Yes, Miss Tilden, I'd like that," replied Orville as he sat down by the kitchen table.

"Good," said Mrs. Wilson. "I'll have one ready in a minute."

The telephone rang.

"Three shorts and a long," said Mrs. Wilson. "That'll be for me." She picked up the earphone from its hanger and answered, "Hello. This is Norma Wilson … Oh, hello Al. Yes, she's here." She handed the earphone to Tillie, "It's Al Freitag. He says it's very important that he talk with you."

"Hi, did you hear about Robert?" asked Tillie.

"Yah. With these party lines the news has gotten to everybody. Awful for you. I'm sorry you had to be involved."

"It's not been a picnic," replied Tillie. "Orville is here with us at Mrs. Wilson's. He's eating a sandwich right now."

Tillie wanted to tell Al what she was feeling. She really wanted to cry. She wanted to pour out her pain and tell him how incapable she felt. Nothing in her experience or college training had prepared her for what had just happened. Grief counseling was not what a teacher was supposed to do. On top of that, she was protecting a dull witted little boy from his father's anger. She could understand Switzer's pain, but the intensity of his hate frightened her.

"Good. I'm calling about Orville," said Al. "Do you remember the people just up the road from where we live, the Wieselmanns?"

"How could I forget a name like that?" She tried to laugh, but it didn't come out that way.

"They're relatives of the Switzers," Al continued. "Erma Wieselmann is Sally Switzer's sister. They don't have a phone, so when I heard about it I drove over to their place to tell her about Robert. She's pretty shook up. She cried for a while and then she asked about Orville."

"What did you tell her?"

"I told her I heard that you took him back home with you. She said she'd like to have Orville come stay with her for a few days. So I said I'd call you and Eila."

"Eila's still over at the clinic," said Tillie, as she struggled to sound normal, composed. In fact, she wanted to run away to some tropical island where she wouldn't have to figure out how to comfort a little boy who had just killed his brother.

"I know. I called there first and she told me all about you and Orville and your plans. I think it'd be best if he stayed with his aunt. He knows her and her kids. He'll be better off with his relatives."

Tillie stood there. She could hear Al talking, but somehow she couldn't concentrate on his words. Her mind was racing back and forth with a hundred questions: *What is best for Orville? What can anyone do with a child like him? How can you explain to him that Robert is never coming back? How can you help him understand about death? What about his father? Will he calm down? What if Orville goes back home in a few days and he decides to take out his pain and anger on him? How do we help Orville? There's so much he can't grasp. How can I help him? How can I protect him? What will the children say to him? Some of them may blame him for what happened. What can I say to them?*

"Tillie? Tillie? Are you there?" It was Al.

"Yes, Al, I'm here," she mumbled. She was in a fog. She knew he was out there somewhere, but she couldn't find him. Everything was getting dark.

"I was asking if I should come over and pick you and Orville up," Al continued. "I said, I think we should take him over to the Wieselmanns."

"Yes, yes, Al, that'll be here," she muttered in a distracted voice. "I mean, yes, that'll be fine. I'll be worrying for you. I mean, I'll be waiting for you. I'll explain to Orville."

"Honey, are you okay?"

"Yes, I'm not. I mean, no I'm … Just come."

Tillie clung desperately to consciousness. She was dizzy. The blood was rushing from her head. She struggled to stand and nearly dropped the ear piece before she hung up. Mrs. Wilson noticed her swaying and rushed over. Taking Tillie in her arms, she helped her to a kitchen chair. "Sit here," she said. "Hold your head down. I'll get some aspirin."

Tillie slumped to the chair and held her head on her knees. Even at that she nearly fell from the chair before Norma Wilson came back. "Here. Take these aspirin," she said.

Tillie was shaking so much that she nearly dropped the aspirin and spilled the glass of water. After she swallowed the aspirin with the water, Mrs. Wilson put the glass on the table and held her for a minute, waiting for the aspirin to take effect.

Finally Tillie looked up at her and spoke in a quiet voice, "Thank you. I'll be okay now." Then she turned to Orville. "Your Aunt Emma wants you to stay with her for a few days."

Orville asked, "Does that mean I'm not gonna stay with you, Miss Tilden?"

"That's right, Orville. You're not going to stay with me. Your Auntie thinks it'll be better if you stayed there. I hear that you have some cousins who live there, too."

"Yes, Miss Tilden," replied Orville. "Wilbur and Walter live there. Wilbur is bigger than me and Walter is littler."

"Good. Then you … can … play with them this weekend."

Tillie's face was white, her eyes glazed. She was swaying on her chair again.

"Tillie, I think you should lie down for a little bit," said Mrs. Wilson. Her forehead was creased with worry. "Come into the living room, lie down on the couch. I'll get you a pillow. I'll look after Orville until Al gets here."

Tillie rose on weak knees. Mrs. Wilson helped her to the living room, covered her with a blanket and closed the door as she went back into the kitchen. "Now, Orville," she said, "how about an oatmeal cookie? Since you're going to visit your Auntie, how about going into the bathroom. You can wash your face and arms and put on the clean clothes Mrs. Wechsler got for you."

Orville ate the cookie and walked slowly to the bathroom. Mrs. Wilson filled the basin with water and handed him a wash rag and towel. In about fifteen minutes he emerged, wearing his clean clothes.

Al arrived about an hour later. "How's Tillie?" he asked.

"I'm better," said a weak voice behind the living room door.

"Let's see how she's doing," said Mrs. Wilson, as she led Al into where Tillie was now sitting up.

"I'm ready to go," Tillie continued. "I just needed a little rest."

"You sure?" asked Al.

"Yes, I'm sure." Turning to Mrs. Wilson, she said, "Thank you. I guess it all got to me."

Norma Wilson smiled sadly. "I know."

Erma Wieselmann stepped from the back porch of her small house to greet them. A slight woman in her late thirties, she wore a battered blue sweater over her simple cotton print dress. Her dark brown hair fell to her shoulders, partly hiding plain features and dark eyes.

She tried to smile as Orville got out of the car. She held out her arms to him and said, "Hello, Orville. Come here and let your Auntie give you a big hug."

Orville walked to her. She embraced him for a long moment and spoke in a quivering voice, "Now go out to the barn, Orville. Little Walter is feeding the ducks and he wants you to help him."

Then turning, she sniffed a couple times, wiped tears with one hand, reached out to take Tillie's hand in the other and said quietly, "Thank you, Miss Tilden. Thank you for helping Orville. He's slow, but he's a sweet child. Thank you for helping."

All Tillie could say, as she struggled with her own feelings, was, "You're welcome. I am glad I was able to help."

The funeral service was held at St. John's Lutheran Church on the following Monday morning. Since St. John's was just up the hill from her school Tillie arranged for Emil Wunderlich to drive her to the church after she checked to make certain that none of her students had come to school, unaware of the Saturday accident and the Monday funeral.

The little red brick church was filled to overflowing. The Freitag women motioned for Tillie to sit with them as she appeared in the door to the sanctuary. She sat beside Irene and looked up at the simple wooden casket, draped with a white funeral pall, in front of the altar. The Switzer and Wieselmann families were sitting together on the two front pews on the men's side. Everyone else sat according to custom, men and boys on the left and women and girls on the right.

Pastor Dornfeld, a slight man in his forties, clean shaven, with thinning brown hair barely covering his balding head, spoke from his pulpit with the warmth of a man intimately acquainted with these members of his flock.

"Sally, Herman, Orville, Auntie Erma, Uncle Reinhold, Wilbur, Walter and all of you who loved Robert, yes, all of you gathered here today. What can we say in a time like this? Where can we go? We must go to the Word of God, for we have nowhere else. Listen to what our dear Jesus says about this lamb of his in the Gospel of St. John, chapter ten:

I am the good shepherd, and know my sheep, and am known of mine. As the Father knoweth me, even so know I the Father: and I lay down my life for the sheep.

"Just two weeks ago, on Palm Sunday, most of us were here in this place. On that day Robert sat on a chair in front of us to be confirmed. Robert and his four classmates together confessed their faith in Jesus. In the past couple years I spent some individual time with Robert, since he was not a part of our school. He had a real love for his Savior and he knew most of his catechism very well.

"Now Jesus has called this young sheep of his to come with him to the Father's house.

"Why did it happen? Should you blame yourself, Herman, that you didn't see it coming?"

Then turning to Harold Wechsler, seated in the pew behind the mourners, he continued, "And you, Harold, should you blame yourself for allowing Robert to drive your tractor?

"No, no! None of you must blame yourself. You are not guilty of anything. You were only doing your work, caring for your families, doing the best you could.

"Little Orville, please do not be sad. You didn't know what those levers did. You didn't want to hurt your brother. You loved him.

"But for reasons not known to us, Jesus called Robert to himself last Saturday. We know that he is safe. He is in the arms of his shepherd. He is safe in the Father's house."

Tillie sat beside Ma Freitag and Irene, listening to the sermon, with pain in her heart. *What is Pastor Dornfeld saying?* she thought. *Is he saying that Jesus is a loving shepherd who lets things like this occur? Doesn't Jesus care? Why did he let this happen? If he is so all knowing, why does he let Orville go through this? And these poor people, why must they have more suffering? Look at them. They don't even have any decent clothes to wear to their son's funeral. They have so little and now they have lost even more. Why? I don't understand. I really do not understand.*

After the funeral service ended, the mourners went in procession to the graveyard on the south side of the church property. Led by their pastor, the pall bearers carried the small wooden casket and placed it gently beside the grave. Once again Pastor Dornfeld led them in prayer, placing Robert into the hands of their Savior in the sure and certain hope of the resurrection. They prayed the Lord's Prayer once more and slowly, reluctantly, walked back to the school's fellowship hall for lunch.

As they approached the school building, Al turned to Tillie and said, "I have two little brothers buried here in this graveyard. All my relatives are buried here, too."

"I know. Your mother told me about it that time I came to your place for dinner. She still hurts when she talks about it."

"Yah, she does. She puts flowers on their graves in the summertime."

"Al, I don't know how mothers can do it. How can you bury your own child? I was only Robert's teacher and I feel so much pain. How does a mother stand it?"

"I don't know. I never knew my little brothers. It's hard for Ma, but what else can you do? You got to believe Jesus loves you even when your kids die. Isn't that what Pastor Dornfeld said? Jesus knows about death and suffering. He went through it and he came back from the dead. Now he walks with us in our pain."

Tillie breathed deeply and squeezed Al's big hand as she looked up at him. "It's so hard to understand," she said. "So hard. What's going to happen to Orville?"

Together they walked down the basement stairs of the school building to join the others in the fellowship hall.

The children of grades six, seven and eight, together with their parents, filled plates with potato salad, beans and fried chicken served by the women of the congregation. Tillie walked among them, hugging the children, shaking hands with the parents.

The Wechslers and Switzers were at a table by themselves. Many others stood around them, touching, expressing condolences. Tillie embraced Sally Switzer. "I'm so very sorry, so very sorry."

"Thank you for coming to the farm," whispered Sally. Her eyes were red, swollen and her cheeks streaked with tears. Her hands shook as Tillie held them.

Hermann Switzer said nothing. His eyes were hard, his expression grim. He sipped coffee from his cup and looked straight ahead. When Tillie touched him on his shoulder he winced. She walked slowly away and joined the Freitag family.

Tillie said nothing as Al drove her back to Rosemount. "Are you okay?" he asked.

"I don't know." She began to cry.

"How about I pull into the city park for a little while so we can talk?" He parked the car. The air was cool, the sky clouded. Tillie shivered and wrung her hands. Al reached over to put his arm around her shoulders. She leaned on him.

"I don't think I can go back to school tomorrow. I don't know how to begin the day. Do we talk about Robert?"

"I think you should start like every other day. Life has to go on."

"What do I say to Orville?"

"Nothing. Give him a hug. He'll understand."

"Will he? He doesn't understand death. He believes that Robert will come back somehow."

Al squeezed her shoulders. "Nothing you can do about that for now. It takes time."

"Another thing." Tillie looked up with a worried expression on her face. "Did you see Mr. Switzer? I'm afraid of what he'll do to Orville."

"Nothing you can do about that either," said Al in a soft voice. "Harold and Willa are there. Orville will be okay."

Tillie pulled away, sat straight in her seat and gazed out the window at the gloomy sky. "Right now I'm not sure I want to be a teacher. It's too hard. I'm not ready for all this hurt. I'm just not."

Al drove her back to the Wilson house. "Thanks," she whispered and walked silently to the front porch.

Chapter 12

Deputy Sheriffs of Coates

Al's brother Werner was sleeping soundly in his upstairs bedroom. Pa Freitag stumbled up the stairs to his son's room and began pounding on the door. "Werner! Werner, wake up! Wake up! Grady's store has been broken into. They want you now to come."

Werner mumbled something, rolled over and said no more. When he heard no movement, Pa began pounding on the door again. "Werner, wake up. You are the deputy. They need you now to come. Wake up!"

Werner slowly pulled his six-foot frame out of the warm bed covers and put his feet on the cold wooden floor. "Yah, Pa, I'm awake. I'm coming." He yawned loudly. "I'm coming." Pulling on his shirt, overalls, socks and shoes, he scratched his dark brown hair, yawned and headed down the stairs.

Pa, dressed only in his long legged underwear and untied shoes, was waiting for him in the kitchen. "Grady says somebody broke into the store. They got some groceries and tools and drove away."

"Pa, what time is it?" asked Werner, yawning again.

"About half past twelve, I think."

Pulling open the hall closet door, Werner took his coat and hat from a hook and pulled them on. Reaching down to the corner, he picked up a double-barreled shotgun pocketed a half dozen shells from a box on the shelf and headed out the door. "Wake up Al," he said as he headed down the back entryway stairs. "I may need him. I'll call from Grady's."

As Werner drove out the yard in his Ford farm truck, Al came stumbling down the stairs into the kitchen, like Pa, dressed only in his long legged underwear and socks. "Pa, what's going on? I heard you shouting at Werner."

"It's the Grady's. Broken into a while ago. They called here. Wanted Werner to come. He said he might need you."

Al stretched out his long arms and yawned. "Man, I hope not. I put in a long day on the tractor. I'm bushed. Who in the world would bust into Grady's store? We don't have thieves around here, except maybe a few of those gypsies."

"That's not quite true, Albert. There's lots of people riding the rails these days, bums who can't find no work. You know that. All the time they come by. Ma gives them a sandwich, makes them chop some wood. Maybe it was one of them."

Al yawned again as he slumped into a kitchen chair. "I guess so. I was just thinking about gypsies yesterday. A wagonload came by last week. I swear, Pa, it must have been them that broke into the chicken house in the middle of the night, woke everybody up."

"Yah, lots of people hungry. Farmers are blessed. We got food. Lots of people got nothing. I suppose that's the way with gypsies and bums. Work is hard to find. We can spare a couple chickens."

Al rubbed his eyes and yawned a third time. "I can't wake up. I'm going back to bed. If Werner calls let me know."

Al stumbled back down the dark hallway to the front of the house and climbed the stairs to his second floor bedroom. He crawled into his bed and was almost asleep again when the downstairs telephone rang. After some brief conversation he heard Pa shouting up the stairs, "Al come on. Werner says he needs you right away. Put your clothes on and get down to Grady's."

Al muttered something under his breath, dressed and banged down the stairs again. He grabbed his coat and hat from the hall closet and turned to Pa. "Am I supposed to take a gun?"

"Yah, Werner says to take his deer rifle. It's down in the basement in the closet under the stairs."

Al grumbled, "Why did Werner take on this stupid job? Now I'm the deputy's deputy."

"Albert, we don't got no sheriff except over in Hastings, twelve miles from here. Somebody around here we need. You know that. Werner thinks it's important. So should you. Now go with him and…" Pa paused. His voice was quiet as he continued, "and be careful. May the Lord watch over you boys."

Al found the deer rifle in the basement closet. He loaded it, put a handful of shells in his pocket and went out to his Model-A. In five minutes he was down the road at Grady's General Store. Werner was waiting in front as he drove up.

"What's going on?" asked Al as he stepped from his car.

"Somebody busted in the back door. Come on. I'll show you."

The two brothers walked around to the rear of the store and entered. Werner had a kerosene lantern in his hand. Mike Grady, the storeowner, was inside, walking from room to room.

"You can see how they broke the light back here and then pried off the padlock on the door with a crowbar or something," said Werner. "It didn't take much. Mike says he never had anybody try to get in before, so he never paid a whole lot of attention to what kind of locks he had."

Mike Grady was a middle-aged man of Irish descent, with dark hair, graying around the temples, and a paunch that hung over his belted waist. Smaller than the two farmer-deputies, he looked worried and tired.

"I locked up the store about six and went home as usual," Mike began. "Then that big storm came through a little after eleven. I was worried about it, so when it was over, I came down to make sure everything was okay. That's when I saw the door ripped open. So I called you, Werner."

"What storm?" asked Al.

"Man, you are dense!" laughed Werner. "Didn't you hear anything? It rained and thundered around for about a half hour."

"No." Al laughed. "When I hit the sack around ten I died. I didn't hear no storm."

Turning toward Mike, Werner continued, "What'd they take? Can you tell?"

"Not real sure yet. Far as I can tell," replied Mike, "they took some clothes, some groceries, beer and maybe a shovel. I stock shotgun shells. It looks like they took some of them too."

"Any money?" asked Al.

"No, the safe is still locked. You'd have to be some kind of an expert to get into that thing."

"Okay, we'll look around outside some more," said Werner. "See if we can see anything. Do what you can to lock the place up for tonight. We'll call a report in to Hastings when we're done here."

114

Werner led the way outside, shining his kerosene lantern around the back of the store. A large trash barrel stood off to one side beside a loading dock. Aside from that the small parking lot was empty.

"Look over there!" shouted Werner. "See that puddle by the dock. There's some tire tracks coming right out of it. It looks like they drove out on the road and turned right. With all that rain you can still see where they went."

Led by Werner's lantern, the deputies followed the tracks out to the gravel road that ran alongside the store.

"See, the tracks cross the highway," said Al. "The mud from the tires is all over the place. It goes right on toward the train tracks. Hey, do you think we still might be able to catch 'em?"

"Let's try," said Werner. "Get in the truck."

Werner drove them across the highway to an old country gravel road on the other side of the railroad tracks. The night was very dark. Rain clouds drifted above, shutting out any light from the stars and moon. The two deputies could barely make out muddy tracks in the road ahead of them by the light of the old Ford's headlamps.

"Why didn't they head on down the highway?" asked Al.

"Who knows?" replied Werner. "Maybe they figured on hiding out someplace around here."

"But there ain't no place to hide out this way. This old road leads past the Reichenbach and Wildemuth farms."

"Well, maybe they were low on gas and were afraid to break down on the highway," said Werner.

They continued bumping along on the road, peering into the darkness ahead of the headlights. After they had gone about two miles, Al shouted, "Over there! A car on the side of the road."

Werner pulled up behind the car. With the truck's headlights still on and the motor running, he reached for his shotgun and motioned for Al to take his rifle. Cautiously they stepped out and moved toward the parked vehicle.

"Empty," said Werner. "Nobody here. Where do you suppose they went?"

Al walked slowly around the abandoned car. "Looks like there were only two of them," he said. "There's some footprints heading toward the Reichenbach farm and another set goes into the ditch toward those woods."

Werner thought for a moment and then said, "I'm turning off the truck. You take the kerosene lantern and see if you can make out where those tracks lead toward the woods. I'll try to follow these other ones down toward the Reichenbachs. Be careful. We don't know what kind of guys these are."

"How you gonna see those tracks in the dark?" asked Al.

"I got a flashlight in the truck," said Werner. "I think the batteries still got some power."

"I hope so. It's awful dark out here," said Al as he slid down into the ditch and moved toward the adjoining barbwire fence. Climbing through the fence, he held his lantern out in front of him in one hand and gripped the deer rifle in the other. Slowly, he picked his way through the muddy field, made ready for planting by recent plowing and disking. His shoes began to cake with mud. As he walked, they became heavier and heavier. In the middle of the field he paused to knock off mud with the butt of his rifle, unaware of the figure watching him in the shadows of the woods before him.

When he reached the edge of the field he lifted the lantern to eye level and peered out into the darkness. He began to mutter to himself, "Stupid job. Walking around in mud out here in the middle of the night."

Here's the woods, he thought. *Can't follow no prints into the woods. It'd be dumb to try.*

As he stood there puzzling about what to do next he heard a man's voice coming from the edge of the woods. "Drop the rifle, Al. I can see you and you can't see me. Drop it, man. I got a shotgun and it's loaded."

Al turned toward the voice with the lantern still in his left hand. "Hey, I know that voice. Is that you, Scheiner?"

"So what if it is?" replied a trembling voice.

"Don't be dumb, Scheiner. You're in enough trouble already."

"Shut up Freitag! Shut up!"

"Come on, Bill. Don't make it worse."

"You go to hell!" yelled Scheiner. "I told you I got a double-barreled shotgun here and if I have to, I'll blow you away."

Al lowered the lantern to the ground. "Okay, Bill. Take it easy," he said. "Take it easy." With that he kicked the lantern with his right foot. It flew about three feet, shattering the glass. The light sputtered for a moment and then it was dark.

"Okay, Scheiner," continued Al. "Now we're both in the dark. You can't see me any more than I can see you. So give it your best shot man, 'cause if you miss I'm aiming right at where your shot comes from and you're dead."

"Shut up, Freitag! I know where you are. I'll shoot, I swear it!"

Al said nothing. Holding his rifle in his right hand, he moved quietly to his left and forward toward Scheiner's voice. The heavily overcast sky made it impossible to see more than a foot ahead. He waited, listening intently for any noise. Then Scheiner spoke again.

"Damn it, Freitag! Where the hell are you? I'm gonna shoot, man. I really am."

Al still said nothing. As he continued to move toward the voice, he could hear the slight squish of his shoes in the mud and hoped that Scheiner was so preoccupied that he could not. Suddenly there were two blasts of a double-barreled shotgun toward where he had first been standing. Now he could see that Scheiner was only about four feet ahead.

Al ran the final two steps and leaped upon Scheiner. Bill Scheiner was a much smaller man and when Al's six-foot two frame hit him the shotgun flew from his hands and he fell back into the brush where he had been standing. The fall knocked the air out of him. Before Scheiner could catch his breath, Al caught him hard on the side of his face with his fist and Scheiner passed out.

It was so dark that Al had to feel his way. Crawling off the unconscious man beneath him, he felt around until he located Scheiner's belt. Pulling the belt out of the pant loops he turned the man on his chest, jerked his arms behind his body and secured them tightly. Then rolling Scheiner over on his back again, he grabbed his coat collar and wrenched him to his knees. Slowly Scheiner began to regain consciousness. Al slapped him several times until he was wide awake.

"Okay, smart guy, wake up! Wake up and get on your feet!" he shouted as he tugged on Scheiner's shirt with his left hand and slapped him several more times with his right. Then reaching down, he picked up his rifle and continued to tug on his prisoner's coat.

Scheiner, pulled by Al's powerful grip, struggled to his feet. Al stepped behind him, pushed the rifle into his back and shouted, "Move it! We're going right back where you came from. Go!"

Prodded by Al, Scheiner stumbled across the muddy plowed field, back toward his abandoned car. As they approached, Al could hear his brother shouting, "Al, Al, is that you. Talk to me, man. 'Cause if it ain't you, I swear I'm gonna shoot whoever you are!"

"It's me. It's all right!" Al shouted back. "I got me a prisoner. It's that idiot Scheiner!"

"Good. Come on in. I'm waiting," answered Werner. "I got a prisoner, too."

Al pushed Scheiner toward Werner's flashlight. They struggled through the barbwire fence, down through the ditch and onto the dirt road. When they got near Werner asked, "What in the name of heaven went on out there? I heard a couple shotgun blasts. Man, I was scared. I thought maybe you were dead."

"Nah, not this time. This dumbbell tried, but he couldn't see nothing. I jumped him in the dark and here we are. What happened to you?"

"I went on down the road to the Reichenbachs. Woke them up. They helped me look through their buildings and we found this kid hiding in the back of their machine shed."

Werner pointed to a teenager in the bed of his truck leaning against the cab with both hands and feet firmly tied with rope. He was thin, small in stature. His clothes were caked with mud. He said nothing.

Al led Scheiner to the truck bed, pushed him up and forced him up to the front to sit against the cab as well. Then he took some rope from the floor and secured Scheiner's feet. "I'll ride back here with these guys. You drive us to Grady's," he said.

Werner nodded, got the truck started and drove about a hundred feet further down the road to the Reichenbach farm driveway. Turning the truck around, he drove them to Grady's store. When they arrived Grady was pounding the last nail into the boards he was using to secure his back door.

As they pulled up, Werner shouted out, "We got the creeps! They were down the road. Open up the store so we can call Hastings."

Grady opened the store's front door. While Werner made the call, Al pushed the prisoners into a back room and forced them to sit on the floor. The teenager wept and Bill Scheiner scowled. Al looked down at him and asked, "What are you doing out here, Scheiner? I heard you was living out on the other side of Minneapolis."

"You go to hell, Freitag! You don't know shit!" said Scheiner in a bravado voice.

"Don't get smart with me," said Al evenly. "You ain't in no position to make wisecracks. I asked you a question and you'd better answer me or so help me, you get another black eye. I asked you what you're doing back out here."

"Okay, man. Take it easy," whimpered Scheiner. His blond hair was caked with mud and filled with pieces of grass and wood from his fall. The whole side of his face where Al had hit him was swollen and bruised blue. He was clearly in agony. "Me and this kid come out here," he continued, "because we was hungry. Ain't no work in town. I was working at a bar on the other side of Minneapolis and sleeping in one of their little upstairs rooms, but I got into a fight and they threw me out. After that I met this kid. We didn't have no money. There's no jobs. So we started stealing. We broke into a hardware store and got the shotgun. Then we stole the car and started driving."

"But why out here?" asked Al.

"Man, how do I know?" said Scheiner. "I don't know no other places. I ain't never been nowhere. Shit! I guess we kinda figured we could break in a couple more places like Grady's and hide someplace. I don't know. We didn't really have a plan. We started running out of gas and nothin' is open at night, so we split."

"You are one stupid piece of cow manure," said Al. "All you know how to do is get yourself into trouble."

Scheiner hung his head and said no more. The kid continued to weep. At this point Werner stepped into the room. "The sheriff said he'd send a squad car over with a couple deputies to pick up our prisoners. They'll be here in about a half hour."

About three in the morning two uniformed deputies arrived from Hastings. They seated the prisoners in the back of their car, locked the doors and took down the information about the robbery, the car, the shotgun and the capture from the Freitag brothers. They assured Grady that they would be sending him a report so he could file his insurance claims. Then one of them turned to Werner and Al and said, "Good work, men. We'll be back later to pick up that car and locate the shotgun out in the field. There's plenty break-ins going on these days. Lots of men roaming the roads, riding the rails. Keep your eyes open. This may not be the last one."

Turning to Grady, he continued, "You sir, get the best locks you can on your doors. Desperate people are looking for what you got in there."

Turning back to the farmer-deputies, he said, "Once again, good work men. Sergeant Gates will be very pleased with what you did. I'm including it in my report to him. There'll probably be a hearing in about a week. The trial usually comes in less than a month. You may be called as witnesses. Bye for now."

With that he slid down into the car and headed east toward Hastings. As he drove off, Al turned to Werner. "Man, let's go home. I wasn't cut out for this dumb sheriff stuff in the middle of the night. Next time make sure we get to do our chasing in the daylight."

Chapter 13

Diary

The temperature is cold for early May, thought Tillie, as she stepped from Emil Wunderlich's truck. *I'll sure be glad to see this school year end. Only a couple more weeks to go. I can't get Orville out of my mind. And every time I come here I think about Helen and what happened to her. And my superintendent. I'll be so glad to get away from him. He gives me the creeps.*

Emil noticed Tillie shivering. "Cold today," he said. "Maybe I should make a little fire. What you think?"

"I think it'll warm up, Emil. I'll keep my coat on for the first hour. We'll be fine," she replied as she walked up the front steps to unlock the door.

As Emil drove away, she began to have second thoughts. The sun was not coming out from behind the clouded sky and the whole building had a chill. Finally she decided to go back to the wood room, gather up some corn cobs and kindling and start a fire on her own.

Looks like we need summer to come, she thought, as she looked at the remaining cobs and kindling. Not much left out here anymore.

A pile of corn cobs in a far corner were all that remained of a formerly large heap. As she scooped them into her bucket, her hand struck a wooden crate with a hinged cover. The crate was old and weathered, with some faded lettering on the outside that she could no longer read. The cover's hinges were rusty, but workable. A heavy wire spring fit through a hole on the top to secure it. Tillie grabbed one of the handle holes on the side of the box, pulled it out from under the remaining cobs and dragged it off to the backside of her classroom wall.

Never noticed this before, she thought. *What's an old crate like this doing out here? Might be useful yet. Wonder if anything is in it?*

She pushed on the spring and pulled the lid open. There was nothing in it, except a dust covered book. She picked it up and blew off the dust.

What's this? she wondered. *Why it's a diary of some sort. What's going on?*

She was about to open it when she heard the voices of the children coming into the classroom. She stuffed the diary into her coat pocket, picked up her bucket of cobs and kindling and stepped out of the wood room to greet her students.

"Who wants to help me get a fire going this morning?" she asked. Several stepped up to assist and the day began.

All through the day Tillie's mind kept wandering to the diary in her coat pocket. By ten that morning the classroom was warm and she hung her coat on the rack beside the bookcase. She noticed the bulge in her pocket, but none of the students paid any attention to it.

As soon as everyone was gone that afternoon, she gathered the day's papers together into a file folder so she could grade them that evening. Then, making sure the fire was out and the windows were secure, she picked up her coat and stepped on the front landing to wait for Emil. Prompt as usual, he pulled into the school yard at about a quarter to four. As they drove back to Mrs. Wilson's, Tillie could feel the book in her coat pocket.

"Did you start a fire after all?" asked Emil.

"Yes," she replied. "After you were gone I decided the place was a little too chilly. So I got one going. I'm getting good, Emil. I can start my own fire now."

"Yah, Miss City Girl, you have learned a couple things at school, I think. Pretty soon you become a country girl," chuckled Emil.

Tillie laughed along. "If you mean country girls can start fires, then that's me. Learned lots of things this year. It's been quite a year, quite a year."

She said nothing about her discovery. For some reason she felt she wanted to look at the diary first before telling anyone. It was her own secret for the moment. Maybe later she would tell somebody. It all depended on whose it was and what was in it. Who would put a diary in a box under the corn cobs anyway? Strange. Really strange. The thought that maybe it was Helen's flitted across her mind.

Waving goodbye to Emil, she vaulted up the front porch steps and went into the Wilson house.

"Have a good day, Tillie?" asked Mrs. Wilson.

"Sure did. I keep thinking how fast this year has gone," replied Tillie as she hurried up the steps. "See you at supper."

She closed the door of her room, pulled the diary from her coat pocket, dropped her coat on the bed and deposited her file of papers on her little desk. Seated at her desk she opened the book to the title page and stared in disbelief. That fleeting thought was true. Written in a careful script were these words,

MY PERSONAL DIARY
BY
Helen Shattuck
September, 1932

With a trembling hand Tillie turned the page. The first entry was dated Monday, September 16, 1932.

Dear Diary,

I've decided to write about my life from time to time. Everything seems to be in such a mess. My daddy left us. He got drunk, lost his job and ran away. Mommy is all torn up. We don't have any money and I had to quit college. Here I am out in Rosemount, living with Uncle Michael and Auntie Mary. Uncle Michael has been so good to me. He got me this job teaching at one of his schools. He gives me lots of help with my lesson plans and tells me all about what to do. Without him I don't think I could do this. Mr. Wunderlich drives me to school and he will be here soon. I'm going to hide this diary here at school, because I don't want anyone else to read it. I don't have much privacy at Uncle Michael's house. So, dear diary, I hope you don't mind being hidden in this old crate under the corn cobs.

Tillie turned the page. The next entry was dated the end of that week, September 19, Thursday:

Dear Diary,

Uncle Michael was just here. We went over the lessons for this first week. We talked about the children and what is to happen in the next several weeks.

But, the strangest feeling came over me. I don't know how to put it. It was
something about the way he looked at me. He sat very close. At the end of the
hour he picked up my hands and said, "Helen, I'm so sorry about how things
have gone for you and your mother. I want you to know that I am here for you.
I'm here to help."

He didn't invite me to ride home tonight. He said he wasn't going back to
the house right away. Mr. Wunderlich will take me home like always. I can't
get over the feeling though.

Tillie continued to read the next pages. As she did so she began to feel like
she was trespassing on private property. What am I doing reading this? This
isn't my diary. It belongs to Helen and now it belongs to her family. I should
not be reading this. And yet, I keep thinking about how she died. Why did she
commit suicide? Is there something here?

With that thought, she set aside her compunctions and decided to read on.
The next months' entries were quite mundane. Helen wrote about the
children, about the weather, about problems with completing her lessons as
planned and about her mother. But then Tillie came to an entry dated
Wednesday, May 17, 1933:

Oh Diary,

I'm so confused. Uncle Michael came into my room after I had gone to bed
last night. I think I smelled alcohol on his breath. Where did he get it? It's
against the law. Anyway, Diary, I was in bed reading. He must have seen the
light shining under the door. He didn't even knock. He just opened the door,
stepped in and then closed it very quietly. Then he came over to the bed and
sat down right next to me. That feeling came over me again. I wanted to ask
him what he was doing in my room, but I was scared. He and Aunt Mary have
done so much for me.

Anyway, Diary, he sat there right next to me and told me how happy he
was that I was living in his house. He said he knew we could talk about
important things and he was proud of how well I had been teaching the
children. Then he said, "Helen, you are so wonderful. I love you, Helen."

And—oh Diary, how do I write this—he put my face between his hands
and reached down and kissed me right on the lips! Then he got up and said,
"Good night, my dearest little Helen," and walked out.

Oh, Diary, I couldn't sleep after that. I kept asking myself why he did that.
Why, Uncle Michael, did you come into my bedroom and kiss me? I'm so

confused. I am so afraid.

Tillie read the entry again. Then she sat at her desk, looking out the window as the gloom of the evening turned into the dark of night. What's going on? she wondered. I've had similar feelings when Michael Murphy is around. It's his eyes, I think. The way he looks at me. Sometimes I feel like, like he's undressing me in his head. I hate that, especially when we're all alone in that classroom.

Suddenly she was pulled from her reverie by the sound of Mrs. Wilson's voice. "Tillie! Tillie! Time for supper. Everyone else is down here."

"Coming, Mrs. Wilson," she shouted back. "I'll be right down."

After the evening meal Tillie and Eila were sitting on the dark green divan in the living room, talking. "Won't be long now, will it?" asked Eila. "What do you have, three more weeks?"

"Right. Three weeks and I'm done with the school year. Hard to believe. I keep saying that, but really, where did it go?"

"Then what? Heading back to the city?"

"Probably. Can't stay here. Got to finish college."

Eila looked at her with a playful smile on her lips and asked, "What about you and Al? Any plans? Has he asked you to marry him yet?"

Tillie blushed. "Eila! Stop it!" Then in a whisper, "I can't talk here. Come up to my room."

When they both arrived at Tillie's room, Eila kicked off her shoes, flopped on the bed, crossed her legs and put her arms behind her head as she leaned on a pillow propped against the headboard. "Okay, so what's the good word?"

Tillie sat on the single small desk chair facing Eila with her hands folded on her lap. After a moment she looked at Eila and sighed. "It's not that he hasn't asked me. He's asked me at least once a week ever since we ate dinner with my folks. Poppa asked me about it when he came out to take me home last weekend. Al made quite a hit with him."

"So?" giggled Eila. "When's the wedding?"

"I haven't said yes." Tillie was frowning as she clenched her hands together. "I want to. He's such a handsome, sweet, fun guy and I love him. I really do. We've had lots of fun together, but…"

"But what?" Eila was now sitting at the side of the bed, looking at Tillie. "He's steady. He's honest. He's handsome. He's a Christian. What do you want, kid? What more could you want? Why the 'but'?"

"We're from two different worlds, Eila, that's the 'but'. All he knows, all he has ever known is the farm and Rosemount and Coates. Eila, he's never even been to Iowa or Wisconsin. He has only an eighth grade education."

"Aren't you the high and mighty one!" sneered Eila.

"No, really, Eila. You've been to college. You know what I mean. A whole world opened up to me when I went to Hamline. I love teaching and kids, but I also love music and poetry. I want to travel and see things, go places. I want more than polkas and Holsteins and selling milk in South St. Paul."

Eila leaned toward her until she was just a foot away. She took Tillie's hands and said, "So what are you going to do, Tillie? Break it off? He's not going to sit around waiting for an answer forever. There's lots of other chickees around here who'd give their eye teeth to marry that guy."

"I know." Tillie was quiet as she looked back at her friend. "I know. I'm torn up inside. One day I want to say yes and the next day I want to run away. Maybe I'll have an answer by the end of the school year."

With that Tillie pulled her hands from Eila's, sat up on her chair, lifted her right eyebrow, wrinkled her forehead and said in a serious voice, "There's something else I need to talk about with you, something that scares me to death!" Turning around to her desk, she picked up Helen Shattuck's diary. "Do you know what this is?"

"Offhand, I'd say it is some kind of diary," replied Helen as she peered at the little black bound notebook in Tillie's hand.

"Right, but I'll bet you'll never in all the world guess whose it is."

"Well, I'm certain it isn't yours, lady. If it isn't, then what are *you* doing with it?"

"Eila!" Tillie spoke very slowly and deliberately. "This is Helen Shattuck's diary! I found it in the wood room at the school."

"You've got to be kidding!"

"No, I'm dead serious. Look at the first page."

Tillie opened to the first page. Eila read it. "I don't believe it," she said in astonishment. "What's in it?"

"It's all about her stay with the Murphy's and teaching that first year. I read about half of it." Turning the pages, Tillie found the entry about the kiss, held out the book to Eila and said, "Read this."

After Eila had read the page she looked up. "You know, this doesn't surprise me. I don't know the guy very well, but, well, this doesn't surprise me. Have you read any more?"

"No. I just got this far before supper. You knew her. I thought maybe we could read the rest together."

Tillie moved over to the bed to sit beside Eila. Eila put her feet on the floor beside Tillie and they both began to turn the pages and read. "Look here," said Eila. "This is just before Mrs. Wilson started her boarding house and Helen and I moved in, May 29, 1933. See those splotches all over the page. It looks like she spilled some water on it—or she was crying and those were tears!"

Dear Diary,

Oh how can I write this down? No one must ever read this. Diary dear, I'm going to have to keep you in the box forever. Aunt Mary went to spend a week with her mother, Great Aunt Elizabeth, in Minneapolis. Aunt Elizabeth has been very ill. They're afraid she's going to die. And I wish I were dead too!

No one was in the house last Saturday night except Uncle Michael and me. He was down in the basement for about an hour. I thought he was working down there in his shop. When he came upstairs he was humming to himself. I was listening to the radio and he came and sat down right next to me. I could smell his breath. It had alcohol on it, just like that other night when he kissed me.

Then he put his arm around me and started saying things like how much he loved me and how he knew I loved him too. I started to cry and he said, "Now Helen, don't cry. I love you, Helen and I need you."

Oh dear Jesus! Then he started putting his hand on my leg and the next thing I knew he was pulling up my skirt. I told him to stop, but he wouldn't. He wouldn't stop. He pulled down my panties and pushed me down. And before I knew it, he was on top of me right on the couch and then he was in me.

Oh it hurt so bad. Nobody had ever been in me before! When he was done he got up and staggered around for a while. I was crying I know. I think he said something like, "There, that was kind of fun now wasn't it?"

Then he stumbled down the hall to his room, went inside and slammed the door.

I don't know how long I laid there. I was so confused and I hurt so bad. Sometime during the night I got up and went to my room. I could hear him back in his room. He was snoring really loud.

The next morning he didn't say anything. He just yelled through my bedroom door and told me to get dressed for Mass. How could he do that? I told him I was sick and I couldn't go. He got real mad and shouted some more. He opened my door and said that if I ever told anybody what happened last night he'd kill me. He walked out and went to church. Oh God, he went to church!

Eila and Tillie said nothing to one another. They stared at the tear-blotched page. Finally Eila said, "I think there's more." She turned to the next entry. It was dated June 2, 1933.

Dear Diary,
School ended today and I said goodbye to the children. They were so nice. We wished one another a happy summer.
Uncle Michael stopped in after school yesterday like he often does. He didn't have much to say and he wouldn't look at me. He told me that Mrs. Wilson's boarding home is all set for me to move there and I should start getting my stuff together. He and Aunt Mary already paid the first month's rent like we talked about last Monday and they'll be helping me to move. That's all he said. I wanted to ask him some questions, but I couldn't. So I guess I'll be moving. I'll be glad to get out of his house. I wish I never had to see him again. Oh, Diary, I hate him. I hate him so.

Tillie looked at Eila with a deep frown on her face. "Is that when you moved in here?" she asked.

"Yes. We both arrived the first part of June that year. I had just finished my nurse's training and was starting my first job over at the clinic.

"I remember trying to talk with Helen, but she was always so shy. She stayed in her room most of the time. A couple of us were worried about her and we kept bugging her to do some things with us, but she always turned us down."

"Eila, you told me she dated Bill Scheiner that summer. How did she meet him if she was always in her room?"

"It was this one Saturday, about the end of June," said Eila. "We kept after her to come with us to the Community Hall to a dance. Finally she agreed, but she said she didn't feel much like dancing.

"And that's when she met Scheiner?" asked Tillie.

"Right. Bill was there and was his usual crazy self. He flirted with every skirt in sight. He had never seen Helen before, so when he spotted her sitting against the wall he went right over and asked her to dance. She, of course, said no. But he wouldn't back off. He literally pulled her out on the dance floor. The next thing you know he had her laughing and dancing and having fun.

"So then they started dating, right?"

"Right. He really got her out of herself. They'd go out every week; sometimes two times a week all through the summer.

"That's when she started drinking. Bill always knew where to find booze, legal or not. Lots of time he'd come to dances three sheets to the wind. The next thing you know, Helen began stumbling up the stairs after her dates with him. I told her that if Mrs. Wilson ever caught her she'd be thrown out on her ear."

"Did she stop?" asked Tillie.

"No, but she was more careful. Most of us girls knew she was drinking. It amazes me Mrs. Wilson never picked up on it."

"So they dated all through the summer?"

"Yup, almost up to the time school was about to start except for those trips she made to Duluth to visit her mother."

"Did her mother know about Scheiner?"

"I doubt it. Helen never said anything about telling her mother. I think she was scared her mother wouldn't approve."

"Way back last fall Al told me you told him that Helen and Scheiner had a fight and you saw her come in after the blow up."

"Sure, I remember that," continued Eila. "Helen wouldn't talk about it. A little while later Bill left the area and Helen started teaching school again."

"Let's see if she writes anything about that," said Tillie. They turned another page of the diary. It was dated August 31, 1933.

Dear Diary,

Next week school starts. I haven't written in you all summer. I wanted to, but I couldn't find a way to come over here. Anyway, so much is happening and I don't know what to do. Oh, I don't know what to do.

My period didn't come in June and I started to get worried. I started to wonder if I was pregnant from that horrible night when Uncle Michael came to me. Then it didn't come in July and I really got scared.

It was about the end of June that I met Bill Scheiner. He's a crazy guy, lots of fun, but really crazy. He helped me forget about my troubles. He got me started drinking booze with him. I don't think that's good if I'm really carrying a baby, but I'm so scared and the booze helps me forget.

One night the first part of July I got really drunk and so did he. We had sex in the back of his car. I didn't care what he did. I decided I was going to hell anyway. After that we had sex a lot.

128

Last week I told him I was pregnant. He got all panicked. He wanted to know if I was carrying his baby and I told him I was, but I wanted him to marry me. He told me I was crazy and started shouting at me and calling me all kinds of dirty names. I started to cry. That's when he drove me back to Mrs. Wilson's and pushed me out of his car. I haven't seen him since. I think he left town.

Oh, holy Mother of God, pray for me. What am I going to do? You know what it is like to carry a child. You were once pregnant and they thought you were a whore. O blessed Mother, I know you understand. I don't know what to do. Oh, Mother, pray for me. Ask the Father in heaven to show me what to do. I'm so scared, so scared.

Tillie turned to Eila. "That means she was carrying…"

Eila broke in to complete the sentence. Her voice was filled with sarcasm. "Michael Murphy's child! That creep! That good for nothing, drunken creep!"

"There's a couple more pages left," said Tillie. She turned to the next entry. It was dated September 14, 1933.

Uncle Michael comes every week on Thursday like he always did. He pretends nothing ever happened. We talk about the school and the lessons. I have to tell him I'm pregnant, but I don't know what he will say. I don't know what he will do. He has such a bad temper. I'm really afraid of him.

"There's just one more entry," said Tillie as she turned to the page dated September 29, 1933.

Dear Diary,

I'm so depressed. I wanted to write these past couple weeks, but I just couldn't put it into words. I can't keep my mind on the children. I'm doing a terrible job teaching. Discipline is terrible too. Everything's a mess.

I met with Uncle Michael yesterday and I decided I had to tell him I was pregnant. He got so mad. He started calling me a whore and a bitch and accused me of sleeping with Bill Scheiner. I started screaming too. Then I told him it was his baby. He lost it. He broke a desk and threw the wastebasket against the wall. He grabbed my wrists and threatened me again. He said I was crazy. He said if I tried to tell anybody he'd raped me, he would deny it and tell them it was Scheiner. Who would believe Scheiner anyway? Who would believe me? He said he'd tell everybody I was an ungrateful niece and they'd believe him. He said I didn't have any proof it was his baby. He said I should get an abortion!

Oh Mother of God now what do I do? How can he tell me to kill my baby? I know I'm a sinner, but I didn't do this. He did it to me and now he wants me to kill my baby. Oh dear Mother Mary, what will I do? What will I do?

"And that's it?" asked Eila. "That's where it ends?"

"I guess so," replied Tillie. "That's the last entry. When did they find her in the wood shed?"

"Let's see. It had to be the very next week after this entry, the first week in October."

"So what happened?" Tillie was thinking out loud. "Helen got so depressed by the whole thing that she finally hung herself in the wood shed?"

"That's the story that's been circulating. Everybody knows she was pregnant. That came out in the autopsy. Everybody believes it was Scheiner's baby."

"But what if," countered Tillie, "what if she told Murphy that she wasn't going to have an abortion, that she was going to carry the child to term? What if he got so panicked that he hit her and she was knocked unconscious?"

"Tillie," said Eila. "I think I know where you're going. Don't!"

"No, hear me out," continued Tillie. "What if Murphy saw her lying there and this plan came into his head to hang her in the wood shed and make it look like a suicide?"

"Tillie! Do you realize what you're saying? You're saying that Michael Murphy murdered his own niece! He's her uncle. He's a married man and a father. He's a respected man in this community. And he's *your* supervisor!"

"I know, Eila, I know, but I'm thinking he did it. The thing is, how can we prove it? The diary leaves it hanging. There's no real proof that he did anything other than rape her."

"As if that was nothing! But, wait! The Diary does prove that she was carrying Murphy's baby or at least Helen thought she was. If that comes out it will ruin him. That will show that he had a motive for murder, won't it?"

"Right. But how can we get him to admit that he did it?" asked Tillie.

"You'd have to trick him somehow. You can't do it by yourself. You're going to need help."

"I'm calling Al," said Tillie with some confusion in her voice. "Maybe he'll know what to do. But until we talk, don't tell a soul. I'm putting the diary back in the woodshed box."

"Tillie!" It was Mrs. Wilson's voice.

Tillie shouted through the door. "Yes, what do you want?"

"You have a phone call from Al Freitag."

"Tell him I'll be right down."

Tillie turned to Eila. "Shall I tell him?" she whispered.

"Not over the phone. Mrs. Wilson will hear."

Tillie shoved the diary back into a drawer of her desk and hurried down to the kitchen. Her mind raced and her heart beat rapidly. Straining to control her excitement, she spoke into the phone. "Hi. Glad you called."

"Tillie. I got to talk with you. Last night me and Werner caught Scheiner stealing from Grady's. I need to ask you and Eila some questions. There's going to be a trial. Could the three of us get together tomorrow night?"

"I think so."

Now what? Tillie asked herself and then said, "Come over to school about three thirty. I meet with Murphy then. Since school is nearly over, we don't have much to do."

"Sure you want me to come at three-thirty?"

"That would be best," said Tillie, as she watched Mrs. Wilson busying herself in the kitchen, but listening to Tillie's every word. "Okay. I'll see you right after school tomorrow. Bye." With a flourish she hung up the phone.

Turning to Mrs. Wilson, she smiled and said, "That Al, always looking for an excuse to get together. I love him for it."

Tillie hurried up the stairs. Eila was still sitting on the bed. Tillie closed the door to her room. "Eila, Al says he and Werner caught Bill Scheiner stealing from Grady's last night. I don't know what in all the world he means by that. Couldn't ask any questions. Mrs. Wilson was right there."

"Caught Scheiner?" Eila looked at her with a puzzled expression. "What happened?"

"I don't know. Can you get off a little early and drive over to the school, say by around three-thirty? I'll tell Emil I have a ride home. Al says he needs to talk with the two of us and we sure need to talk with him. School will be private."

"I think so," said Eila. "Thursday shouldn't be a very busy day."

The next afternoon Tillie was waving goodbye to the last two children as Michael Murphy drove into the schoolyard. She stood in the doorway looking at his familiar smiling face and her heart began to pound. *Be calm,* she said to herself. *He doesn't know a thing about the diary. As far as he's concerned nothing has changed. Just smile like you always do. And above all, be calm. Be calm.*

"Hi, Mr. Murphy," she said, forcing herself to be cheerful and composed. "Only a couple weeks to go. Come on in."

"Yes, only a couple weeks. We're going to miss you, Miss Tilden. In fact, after all this time I was wondering if we could be dropping the formalities. May I call you Tillie?"

"Sure. Fine with me, as long as you don't expect me to call you Mike." She chuckled. "I'm not comfortable with that."

"Sure and I understand," said Murphy as they settled into chairs at Tillie's desk. Tillie noticed that he was sitting very close to her and looking intently into her eyes.

"And what do we be having today?"

Tillie was finding it very difficult to remain objective. *Man, I hate this guy and what he did, she thought. I didn't like him much before. I can't stand the creep now. That sick smile, that smooth talk, that brogue, that carrot hair. The dirty, filthy slime ball! To think what he did to Helen. To think that he might have killed her. What if he sees I'm nervous and suspects something? Where are you, Al? Show up quickly. I need you.*

"Well, there's the final tests I have to give," she said. "I've prepared them for all the subjects and all the grades. I'd like to go over them with you." She handed him a stack of papers.

Murphy smiled. "I'll just be flipping through them. There are no standard tests from the state yet. Some of us think there should be," he said as he turned the pages. "Ah, but these look fine." His smile was broad, benevolent.

Murphy worked through the pages. Tillie felt a bead of sweat on her forehead. Her hands were sweating as well. "Does it seem warm in here to you? I guess summer is coming. I'm going to open the window a little."

She jumped up from her desk and walked to the window. *Where are you Al? You're supposed to be here. You said three-thirty. Is Murphy watching me? What's he thinking? Al, where are you?*

She reached down and pulled the window open several inches and returned to her desk.

Murphy had his fingers on the papers. He was pointing. "Tillie, this geography question. Are you sure this is what you are intending to ask?"

Tillie took the paper from him. She could smell his breath. It had the faint scent of mint. She could detect no alcohol. He continued to smile.

"I—I see what you mean," she stammered. "No, I meant the capitol of Maine, not Massachusetts. I'll change it. Thank you."

"Good," he said as she handed the paper back to him. He put his hand on hers. "You do fine work, Tillie. 'Tis a very fine teacher, you'll be."

"Thank you, sir," she replied as she pulled her hand from his and reached for a pencil.

Where are you, Al? Why aren't you here?

Her heart was pounding so strongly she was certain Murphy could hear it.

At that moment she heard the sound of Al's Model-A coming into the schoolyard. "It's Al Freitag," she almost shouted, as she jumped up. "He called me last night. Said he was coming by this afternoon to drive me home."

"I see." There was a coolness in Murphy's voice. "You'll have to be telling him we're working."

"I will. He's used to sitting in the back of the room. I've trained him to be quiet." Tillie walked to the door. Her voice was calmer now, more relaxed.

Al bounded up the stairs and through the cloakroom. He poked his head in the door and said nonchalantly, "Hi Tillie, Mr. Murphy. Don't mind me. I'll just sit back here 'til you're done."

Tillie gave him a hug, beamed and returned to her chair at the desk. Murphy grunted and nodded with a slight frown on his face.

Tillie and Murphy continued their conference. She went over a few more test papers. Then the conversation turned to end of year arrangements for graduating the one eighth grader. "Is there any kind of ceremony?" she asked.

"Not ordinarily," replied Murphy in his most professional voice. "Just see that he completes all his work and you sign this certificate of graduation." He handed her a form. "That pretty well wraps it up for today," he said curtly. He picked up his briefcase and rose. "Unless there's something else you'll be wanting to discuss, I'll be going."

"No, I'm fine," said Tillie, "I suppose we'll be getting together next week? It's the last week. We have to talk about my evaluations and reports to the university."

"To be sure, Miss Tilden. To be sure, but make it Friday. I'll be visiting all the schools that last day, to congratulate everyone. I'll be here a few minutes before the children leave."

Murphy walked over to Al. Al stood and held out his hand in greeting. Murphy shook it perfunctorily and said, "Nice to be seeing you, Freitag." He hurried out to his car. In a few seconds he was gone.

Tillie rushed to Al's arms and hugged him tightly. Then she reached up and kissed him long and hard.

"Wow! I'm gonna show up every week from now on!" he said as their lips parted. "What's going on?"

"There's a lot to tell you," she replied. "Come over here. I've something to show you."

Al sat on the chair Murphy had occupied. Tillie reached into her desk's drawer and produced Helen's diary. "Look at this," she said. "It is <u>Helen Shattuck's diary</u>! I found it yesterday in an old wooden crate out in the wood room."

Al picked it up and held it as if it were his mother's prized Bavarian china. "Helen Shattuck's diary? Unbelievable," he said, as he opened to the first page and read her name.

"I have book-marked several pages I want you to read," said Tillie.

Al read the pages about the rape and Helen's encounters with Scheiner and Murphy. As he read, his mouth hung open wider and wider. He looked up and stared at Tillie with his wide blue eyes. His forehead was wrinkled. "Remember when we first met? I told you I suspected something? It was just a gut feeling. You're thinking Murphy murdered his own niece, aren't you?"

"I don't know. It sure looks like he might have. On the other hand, Scheiner had a motive as well."

"Yah, but Scheiner wasn't around when it happened. He was gone. Anyway, Scheiner ain't got the guts. He's too stupid."

"If you say so," replied Tillie. "I don't know him. As far as I'm concerned, I keep thinking it was Murphy. That's why I was so scared today. I was ready to explode before you got here."

"Well, your hero arrived just in time!"

"Speaking of Scheiner, what was all that about him stealing and you catching him?"

Al laughed. "He's one dumb rooster. Me and Werner caught him and some kid he hooked up with in a plowed field a couple miles from Coates in the middle of the night."

Al described what happened. He was getting to the fight in the dark when Eila stepped into the room.

"Eila!" shouted Tillie. "You surprised me. I didn't hear you drive up."

"Course not, silly. You and Al were so wrapped up in one another you couldn't hear a tornado coming. Hey, big guy, what's happening?"

"Come sit with us," said Al, pulling up another chair next to Tillie's desk.

"I was telling Tillie how I caught Bill Scheiner night before last."

"This I got to hear," said Eila, settling down.

Al back tracked to the midnight call from Grady and brought Eila up to where Scheiner shot at him. "Then I jumped him," he continued. "I hit him a good punch right on the side of his face and he lost his gun. He went out like a light. Then I tied him up with his belt. After I got him awake, I pushed him back across the mud to Werner's truck."

Al enjoyed the retelling of his heroic adventure. His audience was hushed, attentive and wide-eyed.

"I dumped him into Werner's truck and we drove him and that kid back to Grady's. Some uniformed deputies came to pick up the two of them."

"Will there be a trial?" asked Eila.

"Sure. The trial is set for two weeks from now, in Hastings. It's pretty much an open and shut case. The sheriff says they're getting so many robberies these days the jails are getting filled to over flowing. That's why the judges are moving these cases through the courts fast."

"But you said you caught him red handed," said Tillie. "What's the need for a trial?"

"I don't know. Maybe there won't be a trial. Scheiner might plead guilty and throw himself on the mercy of the court."

"Al, do you think this diary will change the charges against Scheiner? Maybe the district attorney will open up an investigation about Helen's death and charge Scheiner with murder!"

"I really don't know how all that works. All I can do is take the diary to our supervisor in Hastings and let him, the sheriff and the D.A. decide what they want to do. It seems to me charges need to be brought against Murphy rather than that dumbbell."

"I agree," chimed in Eila, "but I'll bet they won't do that. All they'll have is this diary. Murphy will say Helen made it up, claim she was crazy and that everybody knows she was sleeping with Scheiner. She even says so in her diary. She did tell Scheiner it was his child."

"Yes, she wrote that," countered Tillie, "but if you believe that then you have to believe the stuff about Murphy too."

"One thing is sure," said Al. "She was pregnant and she wasn't no virgin!"

"So what do we do?" asked Eila.

"We take the diary to Hastings and let the fur fly," said Al.

"Right," said Tillie. "That's what has to happen. Maybe Murphy will get so shook up by the whole thing he'll be forced into admitting that he raped her."

"I wouldn't count on that." Eila was frowning and squeezing her eyes. She turned to Tillie. "I think he's a very dangerous man. Who knows what he'll do once he hears you found the diary and turned it over to the D.A.? He might even come after you."

"I've thought about that," replied Tillie. "But I can't run. Next week is the end of the school year. Murphy's coming next Friday to complete my evaluation and send it back to Hamline. I need that stuff to finish college."

Eila turned to Al. "When did you say the trial was?"

"Week after next. They have to assemble a jury and all."

"So, you take the diary to the sheriff and tell him Tillie and I will be witnesses if he decides to charge Scheiner with murdering Helen, as well as trying to kill you and rob Grady's store?" Then turning to Tillie, "How's that sound to you?"

"I'm scared," she replied. "What if word gets back to Murphy?"

"I'll convince the sheriff and the D.A. to keep it quiet until the trial," said Al.

"Wait a minute. If they decide to bring charges against Scheiner, he'll know about it." asked Tillie. "Who knows what he'll say, even in jail."

"He won't dare talk about it," said Eila. "He'll be charged with murder. His lawyer will make it clear he has to keep quiet before the trial. His life will be on the line, you know."

"It's risky," said Al. "We're all involved, but I think you're right, Eila. I don't know nothing about courts and trials and stuff, but I think you're right."

Tillie smiled stiffly. "We're agreed then. The diary goes to the sheriff and we trust the D.A. and Scheiner's lawyer to keep it quiet."

They rose together from their chairs. Tillie turned toward the wood room. "I hated that room from the first time I ever saw it."

Chapter 14

Important News

As Eila and Tillie were about to drive back to Rosemount, Al looked down at Tillie seated in the car. "This is really hard on you, sweetie. From now on I'm watching out for you. I'm not letting anything happen. Now, how about tomorrow night? I got something real important to tell you. Are we still on?"

"Sure, we're on. What is it?"

"It's got to wait. I'll pick you up about 7:30. We can go to O'Hara's for a steak. I'll tell you all about it then."

Al picked Tillie up at the Wilson boarding home as promised on Friday evening. He had on a new blue shirt and a new pair of overalls. He had put on his Sunday shoes. Tillie dressed simply in a tweed skirt and white blouse.

They drove the two blocks to O'Hara's Café on Main Street and parked in front. Hand in hand they walked into the small restaurant, its name in gold blocked, arched letters, pasted on a large, plate glass window. White lace curtains hung across the window's bottom. Al stepped under the faded blue and white canopy and pulled open the main entry door.

They walked to one of three booths lining each of the side walls and sat down. A variety of washed-out, black and white pictures of the old country pointed to the owner's Irish ancestry.

Tillie turned to Al. "How many times have we been here over the past year?"

"I don't know. Maybe eight or ten."

"Nothing ever changes, does it? Same old booths, same old pictures, same old tables, same old waitress."

"Anything wrong with that?"

"No. I like it. So many things are changing. This year has been filled with changes for me. Some things need to stay the same."

A middle-aged woman in her late forties, overweight, with graying hair pulled back in a pony-tail and a smile that betrayed the loss of one front tooth, served them.

"What can my five bucks get for us tonight, Doris?" asked Al.

"Hey, farmer, your five bucks can get you a couple steaks and leave ya some dough left over. We got some good T-bones."

"Bring us a couple," said Al. "Tonight I'm a big spender. Medium well and leave lots of fat. Me and Tillie got things to talk about."

"Same for you, Missy?"

"Same for me," laughed Tillie.

"Comin' right up," Doris snickered and sauntered off toward the kitchen.

Tillie turned to Al with a puzzled smile on her face. "What's the big secret?"

"This is going to take some time," said Al. He looked very serious. "Farming is always a tough business. I guess you kind of picked up on that during this past year. We're not making much money. Just barely getting by. Milk prices have dropped to almost nothing since this depression set in. Hundreds of farms like ours down in Kansas, Nebraska and Oklahoma have gone under in the past couple years."

"I read about it in the papers and hear it on the radio."

"You've heard about droughts and dust storms all over the south last year. We ain't really had enough rain around here this spring, even though we had a bunch before Easter and that little shower before we caught Scheiner."

"Mrs. Wilson's lawn looks dry. She's always complaining about having to water it."

"The ground's got just enough moisture in it to get the crops in. We almost didn't get any corn last summer because it was so dry. Everybody's really worried. Nobody knows what's going on."

"What do you think?"

"I think we can't control the weather. Every farmer knows that farming is always a kind of gamble."

"No, I'm talking about the economy, farm prices and all that stuff."

"We're in a depression. That's for sure. President Roosevelt and the congress are making some changes, but will it really help us?"

"Help you?"

"Pa's worried about keeping the farm. You know he bought it twelve years ago. When he did, he had to take out a big mortgage. Up to this year we been making the payments, but right now we're not going to be able to make any more unless we get a pretty good crop."

"That sounds pretty serious."

"It is. Maybe we're okay now that the federal government has set up that bankruptcy act to keep the banks from throwing us out on our ears."

Tillie frowned. "Are you saying that your farm is on the verge of bankruptcy?"

"We don't know. Right now me and Pa and Werner are pretty worried. For the time being we're probably okay. It depends a lot on how the crops turn out and how much we get for milk this year. We don't have many savings and we still got a dozen years to go on that mortgage."

"From what I'm hearing," said Tillie, "you're in the same boat as everybody else."

"Right. At least for the time being, things are going along. Pa and Werner and me are keeping busy and we got lots of food to eat. Once in awhile I even find five bucks to take my girl out to eat at a *fancy* restaurant!"

"Last of the big spenders," laughed Tillie.

Al swept his hand toward the room. "Only the best for my Tillie."

"So that's the big secret? Your farm is not going bankrupt?"

"Nope. That's not it. It's something else I got to tell you."

"So tell me."

At this moment Doris appeared with bread, butter and their salads. As she plopped them on the table she asked, "You folks want some coffee while you're waiting?"

"Sure," said Al. "I can always use a cup of coffee, Doris, as long as I know *you* didn't make it. How about you Tillie?"

"Yes, I'd like some, too. Bring a little cream and I'd like some sugar as well."

Doris disappeared again into the kitchen. As Tillie's eyes followed her, she noticed that the five remaining booths and two of the tables were now filled with couples, all involved in noisy conversations. She turned back to

Al. "I'm waiting," she said as she cocked her head with a wry smile on her lips.

"Last fall, just before we met, I was up at the Minnesota State Fair. I had a booth all my own."

"Really?" Tillie looked at him, now more puzzled than ever. "What were you showing? Cows?"

"No, silly. You don't show cows in booths. I was showing my invention, seeing if I could get some people interested in buying it."

"Your what? What invention? You never mentioned anything about an invention before."

"I didn't know if it would amount to anything, so I didn't say nothing."

"What is it?"

"A milk strainer."

"A what?"

Al sighed. He wanted to tell Tillie that she knew nothing about the dairy business. It seemed obvious to him that milk would need to be strained. He wanted to ask her why she hadn't thought about it, but he controlled himself.

"When the milk comes from the cows it gets all sorts of dirt and straw and stuff in it, so it has to be strained before we put it into the cans. We never found a strainer that worked real good, so I drew up something I thought would work and had a machinist make me one. Pa was skeptical at first. He said we didn't have no money for such foolishness, but I told him I'd use the little money I saved and do it myself. I even got a patent on it from the United States Patent Office."

"Oh, that's impressive. Not another like it, huh?"

"Only one around. To make a long story short, I had to have some kind of cotton pads for the milk to strain through. I didn't know nothing about that so I went up to Minnesota Mining and Manufacturing, started talking with them about my problem. They said they're always interested in new business ideas. So they developed some pads for me."

"I'm awed," said Tillie. "That took lots of initiative on your part."

"Yah. Pretty good for a dumb farmer, huh? Anyway, that's how I got this booth at the State Fair. The 3-M Corporation financed me and helped me to print up some literature. With their help I also found somebody to manufacture the machines. Plenty of people stopped in at the booth during the fair. Lots of dairy farmers. When I talked about my problems I found dairy farmers all around the area have the same problems and they want a better strainer. So that's how I got me a little side business going now."

"You're kidding! Wow! That's great!"

"Yah, we've sold about two hundred so far, all over the state."

"Two hundred! Rolling in the bucks now, right?"

"Sorry. It don't work that way. I've had to give everything right back to 3-M. They put up the money to get it started, no profits for me yet. It's going to take a long time before I can pay back the 3-M loan and start making any money on this thing."

"Oh," sighed Tillie. "I'm pretty dumb when it comes to business stuff. So that was the big secret." She smiled. "Wonderful! Congratulations!"

"No. There's more. This is all background stuff. I needed to tell you about this, but the really surprising thing is this..."

Suddenly Doris stood before them again. "Here ya go, kiddos," she said, as she plunked two large plates of steaks, boiled carrots and mashed potatoes with brown gravy on the table "I think you'll like these. I made sure they was done just the way you asked, Tillie. Yours, Freitag, is burned. Would either of youse like any ketchup or steak sauce?"

"Not me," giggled Tillie.

"I'll take some ketchup," said Al. "I like it on my steaks. Covers up your cook's mis-steaks."

"I'll tell the cook how much you love him," said Doris as she turned to wind her way back through the crowded, noisy room to the counter. Retrieving a large bottle of Heinz ketchup from a shelf, she brought it back to the young couple. "Okay, sweeties. If youse need anything else, just holler. I'll bring some fresh coffee in a minute."

After Doris had left, Tillie looked to Al. "I'm still waiting."

"Sure," said Al. "It's this. The 3-M people said they're looking for young people who would like to become designers and draftsmen to work with their engineers. I've been talking with them. They're telling me that if I can get my high school degree, they'll hire me and help me to get a degree from Dunwoody Institute in Minneapolis."

"But you're a farmer."

"I am, but I been thinking. Maybe I can do something else besides farming."

A thousand butterflies began floating around inside Tillie. She felt like they were lifting her off her chair. This farmer wanted to go back to school. That might change everything. Excitement filled her voice as she asked, "How long would it take to get the Dunwoody degree?"

"It's a two year program. I could work and go to school at the same time.

I could probably complete it in three years or so. Then I could always go on to the University and get a degree in engineering."

"Become an engineer? Wow! That is an ambitious goal."

"I know, but I'm thinking about it. I think my new invention will eventually make me a little money."

Tillie stared at Al. "I don't know what to say. I thought you were a farmer, end of discussion."

"I *am* a farmer, but I've always loved to work with machines. I enjoy trying out new ideas. It's like an adventure. I just never knew how my invention could become anything. Then along came this thing. It surprised me."

"Taught you that you can turn your ideas into something real."

"Right. Opened up a whole world for me."

"I'm excited for you," said Tillie, beaming with a wide smile.

"Me, too. But there's more. It has to do with us."

"With us?"

"Yah. With us. I know you've been struggling with the idea of being a farmer's wife. You know how I feel about you … and you know I want you to be my wife." Al reached across the table and took hold of Tillie's hands. He looked into her eyes and smiled as he continued.

"We've had lots of fun together these past months. And, well, talking with you about college and stuff has helped me too. I've started to think that…" Al looked down at his hands holding hers and struggled to find the words. "…that maybe I could do something with my ideas, more than I have been able to do here on the farm. If I get my degree from Dunwoody, well, maybe you'll give me a chance and say yes."

He looked up at Tillie. Tears filled her eyes. "You're crying," he said. "Did I say something that hurt you? I don't want to hurt you, Tillie. You mean so much to me."

Tillie looked across the table at her suitor's deep blue eyes and squeezed his big, rough hands with hers. "No, you didn't say anything that hurt me. I'm crying because I'm happy. I'm crying because I'm so proud of you. I'm crying because I believe you can do this."

"What about my question? Do I have a chance?"

"Of course, you dumb ox. You've given me tons of things to think about. Now I need some time. Let me dry my eyes and blow my nose. Our steaks are getting cold."

Chapter 15

Visit with the Sheriff

As agreed, Al picked Tillie up the following Monday, immediately after school was out. She had Helen Shattuck's diary tucked in her purse.

"I got my training as a deputy sheriff at the courthouse," said Al, as they drove east from Coates toward Hastings, a town of some ten thousand on the banks of the Mississippi River. "It was really Werner's idea. He's always pushing stuff like that. I told him I wasn't no sheriff and I didn't want to be one, but he kept pushing."

Tillie smiled, "Now I get to see the famous courthouse where you trained."

"Of course. I'm a sheriff's deputy and I get to carry this badge in the breast pocket of my overalls."

"How come you guys didn't get uniforms?" asked Tillie.

"The sheriff says it's a community relations thing. He thinks farmers dressed as farmers can relate better. I don't want no dumb uniform anyway."

"Uniform or not," said Tillie with a smile, "I'll bet you feel pretty good about catching Scheiner."

"Yah, I got to admit. That was my first arrest and it does feel good, even though I'm a little bit sorry for the dope."

"First or not, I know I'm safe riding with you."

As they entered the town, Tillie looked with interest at Hastings' renowned Spiral Bridge. Its entrance ramp spiraled up from the main downtown street and out over the river.

"So there's the famous bridge," she said. "I've heard about it all my life. I'm kind of a bridge nut, especially since I grew up in West St. Paul right next to the High Bridge. Do you realize how long has this one been around?"

"Nope, never thought about it."

"Well, let me fill you in. The Hastings Spiral Bridge was built toward the end of the last century for horses and wagons. It was the only way they knew to get up high enough to cross the river."

"No horses and wagons spiraling across it now," laughed Al. "Just cars and trucks."

"Do you know who built it?" asked Tillie.

"Haven't heard that either," replied Al.

"Lots of claims. No proof. Seems it was a project of local businesses. Records are cloudy."

"Okay, Miss College Historian, let me ask you when the courthouse was built."

"Oh, dear. I only study bridges."

"Well, this is the oldest courthouse in Minnesota, built just a few years after the Civil War."

"Really. Where'd you learn that?"

"Read the plaque next to the front door when I was going for training."

"Wow! You can read."

Al parked his Ford in front of the stately red granite courthouse.

"This is a marvelous building," said Tillie. "The columns and dome remind me of ancient Greek temples."

"Don't know nothing much about Greeks," said Al. "All I know is it looks old."

Al led Tillie to the back where he located the entrance door to the Sheriff's office. He walked to the desk, greeted the duty officer, showed his badge and asked if the sheriff was available. He said he had a special report to make about a current case.

The officer smiled knowingly and remarked, "You're supposed to file your reports with your supervisor, Freitag. You know that."

"Yah, I know," replied Al. "It's just that this is important. I think the sheriff himself will want to see it."

"Well, I can't disturb him. He's a busy man. I'll check with your sergeant. If he says it's okay, then he can take you back himself."

"Right. Whatever you say. Work it out. We'll sit here."

Al motioned to Tillie to join him on the hardwood bench along the opposite wall. He turned to her and whispered, "That's why I don't make much of a deputy. Too much like the army. Everybody has to salute and say yes sir and all that junk. We'll wait."

Tillie was amused. She sat with her hands folded in her lap and a smile on her lips. "Who's this supervisor he's talking about?" she asked.

"Sergeant Gates. He's had been a deputy in Dakota County for about thirty years, I think. He and Sheriff Raymond Wahlberg are personal friends. I think that's why the Sheriff appointed him to supervise us special duty farmer-deputies. He's also a farmer, works a hundred acres in his off hours. That's another reason. Wahlberg believes he needs somebody who thinks like we do."

The duty officer spoke into his phone, "George, one of your farmer-deputies is here. Says he has something special the sheriff should see. You better talk to him yourself." He paused, listened, and turned to Al. "Freitag, George says come on back to his office."

Both Al and Tillie rose and started to move down the adjoining hall. The officer interrupted them with a wave of his hand. "Sorry, Miss. You have to wait out here until Officer Freitag returns. That's the rule."

"No way, Frank," said Al, a growl was in his voice. "She's part of my report. I need her. She discovered the evidence."

Frank scowled back. "Well, farmer, you should-a said so. Let me call George again."

Al opened his mouth, but he felt the firm pressure of Tillie's hand on his. She looked up and smiled widely, holding her finger to her mouth. He said no more.

Frank spoke briefly with George again and then turned back with a frown on his face, "George says you both can come on back."

As they walked down the hall, Tillie whispered, "What's bugging him?"

Al lowered his big voice. "Werner says some of the uniforms think it's really dumb to hire us farmers. They figure we're all a bunch of hicks who'll mess things up, maybe even hurt a pile of people. No love lost between some of the uniforms and us farmers."

"Then why'd they hire you guys?" she asked.

"Too many drifters and bums running around. Regular deputies can't keep up with it all. And we're cheaper. The county budget is tight."

They reached an office door with the title "Special Deputies Supervisor" printed across its glass panel in black letters. Al knocked and a voice said, "Come on in!" Al motioned for Tillie, followed her in and closed the door behind them.

Deputies Supervisor Sergeant George Gates sat in his small office behind a large oak desk with his back to a window that looked out on the courthouse lawn. On either side of the window were his framed credentials, awards and photos. Against the left wall were two black, three drawer file cabinets piled high with papers and books. On the right was a glass covered bookcase filled with ringed notebooks and professional journals. On top were several photos of the sergeant's wife and family.

Gates was a tall man in his late fifties with a receding hairline of light brown hair and bushy eyebrows. He put his pipe in a rack alongside four others and motioned for his guests to be seated. The sweet smell of tobacco smoke filled the room. Al and Tillie settled into two of the four oak chairs sitting in front of the desk.

"Morning, Sergeant. This is my very dear friend Tillie Tilden," Al began. "She has discovered some evidence in connection with the Scheiner robbery case out in Coates. I believe this'll be of great interest to you and the Sheriff."

Al respected his sergeant and was confident that Gates respected his special farmer-deputies, despite the grouchy attitude of some of his uniformed peers.

"So, Al, I hear you and Werner did some important work last week. I want to extend my personal congratulations to you both. The sheriff is quite pleased. We've noted it in your file."

"Thank you, sir," replied Al. "Bill Scheiner did a dumb thing when he robbed the Grady's store over in Coates. He wasn't that hard to catch."

"No, I've seen the report. But he did try to shoot you, didn't he?"

"Yes sir, he did. That's the kind of the dumb stuff he's always done. I've known him since we was kids."

"I can believe that. Now, what have you and Miss Tilden brought us?"

"I'm going to let Tillie explain, sir. She's the one who found the diary."

Tillie reached into her purse and pulled out Helen's diary. She put it on the desk before the sergeant and began.

"I was out in the wood room of my school a week ago."

"Your school?" asked the sergeant.

"Oh, I forgot. I'm the teacher out at ISD 132 in Rich Valley."

"Really. You seem so young, like you'd be still in college. No offence intended, Miss Tilden."

"None taken, Sergeant. I accept it as a compliment. I *am* a college student. I'll be a senior next year—at Hamline. This is a special one-year assignment."

"I see. Then you're working for Superintendent Murphy, out of Rosemount."

"Yes sir, that is correct. Mr. Murphy is my boss and that's what makes this so difficult."

"Hmmm. Explain," said the sergeant. He sat very straight in his chair, his face lined with concern. "Please continue."

"Excuse me, Sergeant," Al broke in. "May I ask you a question?"

"Go ahead."

"Sir, how well do you know Superintendent Murphy?"

"We've talked a few times. There have been several break-ins to three or four of his schools over the past couple years, drifters looking for shelter, things like that. He's also had a little difficulty at the high school. A fight broke out at a football game last fall. I've supervised those cases. He's been in to see me. I'm not sure what you're getting at."

"It's just that I was wondering if you knew him personally, sir," replied Al.

"No, not personally. Only professionally. Please continue, Miss Tilden."

"Sir," Tillie said with some reservation, "what I'm about to tell you is deeply personal and we believe it will seriously affect the career and life of Mr. Murphy."

Gates said nothing. He continued to gaze intently at Tillie with his elbows resting on the arms of his desk chair, his hands folded and his two index fingers resting on his lips, just below his nose.

"This is the diary of Mr. Murphy's niece, Helen Shattuck, the young woman who was found hung from a rafter a year ago last fall, in the wood room of my school. I found this diary there in an old wooden crate under some corn cobs. I didn't know what it was, so I took the liberty of reading it. I also let my good friend Eila Stricklund read it. She's a nurse at the clinic in Rosemount. We talked about it and decided to show it to Al. At the time we didn't even know about Al catching Bill Scheiner."

"That's how I came to know about it," said Al, breaking in. "Last Thursday the three of us met at Tillie's school to talk it over. We all decided the first thing we needed to do was bring the diary here."

Sergeant Gates put his folded hands across his abdomen and lifted his chin slightly. "What does this diary say, Miss Tilden?"

"It describes Helen's life with the Murphy's and some things about her first year in school."

"Are you certain this is Helen Shattuck's diary, in her handwriting?"

"We're sure, sir. Eila lived in the same house with her, at Mrs. Wilson's boarding house in Rosemount. She knows Helen's handwriting. I've also seen her handwriting on many papers in my school. We're certain this is Helen's diary, sir."

"But what has this girl's diary to do with either Superintendent Murphy or Bill Scheiner?"

"Helen wrote in her diary that Murphy raped her, sir!" said Tillie in a quiet voice.

Gates raised his eyebrows, but remained silent for a moment. He focused on Tillie and said, "I see. Please continue."

"It's all there, in her diary. After it happened Murphy arranged for her to move out of his house. Then she dated Bill Scheiner. They had sex together and she told him he got her pregnant."

"Did he?" asked the sergeant.

"No sir," replied Tillie. "She writes she was pregnant *before* she had sex with Scheiner."

"Is there any proof of that?"

"Only what she writes in her diary, sir."

"Do we even know she *was* pregnant?" asked the sergeant.

"She says she was and I understand the autopsy revealed it, sir."

"I'll have to review the case," said the sergeant. "If I remember correctly, she committed suicide."

"That's what the report said, sergeant," said Al. "Everybody thought she did. Everybody thought it was Scheiner. Nobody went after Scheiner, because Helen was of age. Then Scheiner took off and left the area."

"You're right, Deputy Freitag. We couldn't go chasing after Scheiner, but now he's back and this diary…" Gates paused in thought for a moment, reflecting. His folded hands were up again in front of his mouth, his chin resting on his thumbs and his two index fingers over his lips. Suddenly he separated his hands and put them on the table. He lifted one corner of his mouth, frowned and said, "Are you suggesting foul play? That Scheiner killed Helen Shattuck?"

"Don't think so, sir," said Al. "In the first place, Scheiner was gone over a month before Shattuck was found dead. He was up in Minneapolis someplace and he doesn't own a car anymore. Ran out of money and had to sell it, I think. In the second place, he's too stupid to pull off something like that. He might have a motive, but I don't think he had the means or the smarts to do it."

"What then, deputy? What *are* you thinking? Helen's uncle, Superintendent Murphy?!" Gates spoke emphatically and then paused before beginning again, this time emphasizing every word. "You'd better be very careful about bringing up something like that. Do you have anything other than this diary?"

"No sir, we do not. Just the diary and Helen saying that Murphy raped her, right in his own living room."

"I see." Sergeant Gates looked back and forth at Al and Tillie. "Deputy Freitag, Miss Tilden, what you have put in my hands is a loaded bomb. Have you spoken about this to anyone else?"

Both shook their heads.

"Do you know if Eila Stricklund has spoken about this to anyone?"

"Eila promised both of us she wouldn't say a word," said Tillie.

"Does Mrs. Wilson know about it?"

"No sir."

"And Michael Murphy?"

"He was there, sir," said Al, "at the school, when I came to talk with Tillie, but I often come to see her after school. He thought I was coming to pick her up again. He knows nothing."

"Good. You did the right thing. I'll report this to Sheriff Wahlberg. We'll handle it from here. Meanwhile, you both have strict orders to say nothing to anyone. The same for Miss Stricklund. None of you says anything to anyone. Do you understand me?"

"Yes, sir," replied Tillie and Al in chorus.

"Very good. Once again, thank you for coming in."

They rose. Al shook Gates' hand. "Thanks, sergeant," he said. "I knew you and the sheriff would know what to do."

As they left, Gates followed them to his office door, closed it, returned to his desk and called Sheriff Wahlberg. "Ray, George here. One of my farmers brought in something you need to see."

As they got into Al's Ford, Tillie asked, "What are you thinking?"

"Not sure," he replied. "I think we did the right thing."

"Do you trust Gates?"

"I think so. Never had much to do with him. Likes farmers. Honest. Seems like a nice enough guy.

"He does, but nice doesn't always count."

"What do you mean?"

"I'm just wondering what he and the sheriff are going to do with the diary."

"Out of our hands now, Til. We can't talk about it. Eila needs to know too."

"Right," said Tillie. "My head's going round and round with all this. Maybe this is a good time to take a drive over the Spiral Bridge."

Chapter 16

Endings and Beginnings

"Children," said Tillie, "it's our last week of school. We have some final tests to take and that's it."

A groan went through the room.

Tillie was addressing her classroom on the morning of Wednesday, May 29, 1935. Bright sunshine warmed the air. Blooms of alfalfa, clover and wild flowers crammed the pastures and fields. Along the driveways and next to the houses of the many area farms lilac bushes joined the display. The smell of the many blossoms filled the air. Larks sang their happy songs as they went about the business of building nests in the meadows. Crows and red-winged blackbirds busied themselves with the same tasks in the surrounding oaks and cottonwoods, now fully budded. The apple orchards also showed signs of their familiar white flowers, promising delicious fruit later in the upcoming summer. Farmers hustled around in the surrounding fields, plowing, disking and making final preparations for the spring planting. The children of Independent School District 132 were so excited about the happy prospect of an entire summer without the daily regimen of school that their young teacher had a difficult time keeping them in their desks.

"Friday will be our final day," Tillie continued. "You know we have a scheduled softball game with St. John's. We'll head there around ten o'clock that morning. We play on their field—and we're going to whip the pants off of them, right?"

A shout broke out from all the students. They clapped and pounded on their desks. In the ensuing chaos one of the sixth grade boys threw a spitball at a sixth grade girl. She in turn reached around with her speller and hit him on the head. Feigning a mortal wound, he fell to the floor and rolled over two times. At this the class increased its shouting, laughing and jeering. Tillie ran into the melee, pulled up the "wounded" suitor by the straps of his overalls and plunked him back into his seat.

Laughing herself, Tillie said, "Ervin, you're not hurt. Quit pretending you are. I saw you throw that spitball. You deserved whatever Frieda gave you."

Then turning to the class, she said, "Now all of you, settle down. We have work to do. I want to meet with the third graders. We need some reviewing before tomorrow's test. The rest of you have some final assignments to complete. We need silence—now!"

When Emil picked her up that night Tillie was smiling, feeling relaxed, confident and self-assured. She had met the challenge of teaching an all-grades classroom and was certain every student had learned enough to advance to the next grade. The year had not been a pushover. Robert's death disturbed her deeply. She often looked at his empty desk and felt a lump rising in her throat. Why did it happen? The question remained unanswered.

Then there was Orville, growing bigger in body throughout the year, but making very little progress in mind. He was such a child, such a sweet child. He, too, grieved for his brother. He missed their games and their conversations. He said very little about it, but she could see sadness in his face since his brother's death. His happy attitude was gone. He seemed tense, almost afraid.

Tillie had asked him frequently if anything was wrong, but he always denied it. As she thought about it, she remembered Hermann Switzer's frightful anger on the day of Robert's death and wondered if he had forgiven Orville. She made a promise to herself to stop over at the Switzers if she could before returning to St. Paul.

Lost in these reveries she didn't even notice that she and Emil had arrived at the Wilson boarding house. Emil stopped his little truck and waited, looking at her with his gentle, fatherly eyes.

"You're quiet today. Not long now before the year is over," he began.

Tillie looked up, surprised. "Oh! We're here. Yes, I mean no, not long now."

"When will you be leaving?"

"As soon as I get everything straightened out. Sometime next week, maybe. I might stay for the week. Al wants me to attend Bill Scheiner's trial. It's supposed to start the first week in June."

"Oh. I didn't know. Why would you attend his trial?"

"Probably because he was once Helen Shattuck's boyfriend. Seeing him—I've never seen him, you know—seeing him will kind of help me put everything into perspective, kind of wrap up everything. Know what I mean?"

"Yah, Tillie. I understand. I only hope for your sake the trial does that."

"I think it will. We'll see. I've never been to a trial before. I think it'll be an educational experience as well."

Emil nodded knowingly and then smiled. Tillie stepped out of the truck, closed the door and spoke through the open window, "See you in the morning, Emil."

Tillie went up to her bedroom, deposited her books and papers on her bed and walked back down the stairs to the front porch. She settled there on the hanging swing, pushed off her shoes, dangled her feet and soaked in the warmth of the late May afternoon. Two hummingbirds whizzed past on the way to Mrs. Wilson's garden flowers. A couple of cerulean colored horseflies droned over to the porch's sill, landed momentarily and then disappeared into the yard. The smell of fresh lilacs growing beside the Wilson house filled her nostrils. She breathed in their sweet scent, closed her eyes, touched the floor of the porch with her toes and gently pushed back. Lifting her toes she let the swing glide gently back and forth, back and forth. Spring had come. Summer was not far behind. A whole world beckoned her to a new life.

As she swung, her mind also went back and forth across the events of the past weeks. Up front, as always, was the thought of becoming Al's wife. She knew her heart. It spoke gently to her about the joy awaiting if she were to sit at his table and sleep in his bed for the rest of her life. She swam in that ocean, diving into the azure depths hidden behind his blue eyes. She imagined herself in his arms, consumed by his embrace, devoured by his presence within and around her. She relished the possibility of being one with him forever. She dreamed of the children she would bear with him and for him. She saw them growing up to become proud and happy men and women, contentedly marrying and nurturing their own offspring. She walked with him hand in hand down that road toward maturity, old age and finally into eternity. She composed poems and sang songs about him. She danced and frolicked in the woods, on the hills and, with the wings of birds, over the clouds. She was in love and she knew it.

But should she give in to the sweet sickness that possessed her? Should she be guided by her heart and ignore the persistent questionings of her mind? Would there not come a day when the blazing fires died to the warm embers that alone endure through the long winter nights? Would their marriage have enough fuel to quicken them again? Did they share more than friendship and youth? Did they have within them the kind of tinder that would be ignited by one another's sparks years, even decades from the present?

She pondered the deadness of the coals in the furnace of her parents' marriage. She was aware of the decade of winter that had settled into their family. She remembered the sorrow in her own father's blue eyes as he endured her mother's daily demeaning remarks. She recalled her mother longing for joy and substituting the fading glory of her petty West St. Paul Professional Women's club for it. She remembered the photos and stories of how her parents met and their laughter in the springtime of their relationship. The spring had turned to summer and summer to fall. With the coming of autumn's winds the leaves had fallen from the trees and the ground had frozen. So now they walked the bleak and barren land and believed there could never be another thaw, another spring, a new beginning. They were too old, too far down the road. They could not break the frozen ground. They could not leave or separate. Both God's law and man's threatened humiliation prevented it. So they walked alone in the frozen waste, sitting across from one another at an icy table, exchanging empty cliches and sleeping alone in bitter bedrooms at opposite ends of the igloo they called home.

Tillie thought of all this and hated it. She hated the very idea of such an existence. She prayed again for her forlorn parents as she had so often before. She prayed for them and she prayed for herself. She prayed that she would not be betrayed by the aromas of her own springtime, the laughter of her dances and the singing of her heart. She prayed for courage and she prayed for hope.

She thought also of Helen Shattuck and of Michael Murphy's mendacious mockery of his niece's virginity, of what he stole from her by his selfish, drunken act. She considered the seeds of despair he had sown within that fertile field. She thought of Helen's pain and final despondency, of Scheiner's rapacious greed for her body and his careless misuse of her helplessness. She remembered Helen's prayers and imagined herself in the depths of the murky cavern into which Helen had been thrown. She remembered and felt a shiver even as she sat in the warm afternoon sun.

She thought also of Orville. She thought of her uneducated attempts to reach the little child hidden deep within the confines of his tiny intellect. She thought of his ability to love, his humility and his need for tender care. She remembered the hopelessness she saw in the eyes of Orville's mother and the fierce hate that blazed in the eyes of his father. Was it hate? Perhaps it was really despair, covered over by a futile attempt to defend a broken and shattered sense of self-respect. Was there a sickness unto death in that household? Would Herman Switzer actually hurt his son, because he believed Orville had killed Robert?

She contemplated the possibility and saw herself sweeping down to rescue Orville and carry him to some haven of safety. She knew he was trapped in a family ensnared by its own demons; she could do nothing. She knew it and for a time tasted the bitter dregs of that mixture. She tasted it and wanted to spit it out and somehow fly away to another world, a world of clear, cool springs of life-giving water. Yet she knew no such world was available, so she simply prayed for Orville's safety and thanked her Lord for giving her this time to be his teacher.

These thoughts skittered within her mind, sometimes filling her with laughter, sometimes emptying her of hope. They went back and forth until she slipped into a deep sleep, right on the porch, her head drooping to her chest as her body moved with the swaying of the swing.

"Tillie, Tillie! Wake up! It's time to eat!" A voice shouted far, far off in the distance. Eila shook her out of her trance.

Tillie crawled laboriously out of the depths of her cavern, and forced her eyes open, hardly aware for the moment of where she was. She squinted in the late afternoon sun, yawned, stretched out both of her arms and said in a husky voice, "Hi, Eila. I guess I dozed off. Let me get my shoes on. I'll be right with you."

Chapter 17

Election

"Tell me again where you got this?" growled Sheriff Wahlberg as he held Helen Shattuck's diary in his huge hand. He chewed on an unlit cigar, flexed his bulging muscles and scowled at Sergeant George Gates sitting across from him.

Gates shifted in his chair, uneasy despite his long friendship with the six foot, four inch Swede. "From Al Freitag and his girl friend. Freitag is one of my farmer-deputies out in the Coates area."

It was the morning following Al's and Tillie's visit to the sergeant-supervisor. Wahlberg had invited Gates into his office for an urgent conference.

Wahlberg ran a hand over his blonde hair and scowled. "I've read the pages you marked about five times. Good God in heaven, George, what should I do with this?" He lifted his two hundred forty pound bulk out of his chair and began to pace the room. Clearly troubled, he waved his arms and spit a piece of chewed cigar into a wastebasket. "There's nothing here the D.A. could possibly use in the Scheiner case. The woman admits she allowed him to have sex with her. Damn it, she told him she was pregnant and he threw her out of his car. That's all we have. There's no evidence whatsoever he did anything more."

Gates followed his boss's wanderings around the room with his eyes.

"What about Mike Murphy?"

"That's it. What about Murphy?" barked the Swedish bull. "Should I take this girl's diary and bring charges of rape against him two years after she says he did it? What have we got? The words of a dead woman. That's it!" Wahlberg slammed the diary down on his desk in disgust. "He'd deny it until hell freezes over. I know the man. You know damn well I do."

Gates shrugged and frowned, feeling intimidated by the big man's ravings. "I know, Ray. This puts you in a bind."

"You're damn right it does. The man's married to my wife's sister, for crying out loud. How am I going to accuse him of rape when all I got is this stupid diary? What's he going to say? What's his wife going to say, for God's sake? How will I ever tell Agnes about it?"

"So what are you going to do? Freitag's girlfriend found it. She showed it to that nurse in Rosemount. Freitag read it. How long will they keep it quiet?"

"That's another thing." Wahlberg's voice became intense. "Murphy lives in Rosemount. The whole Irish Catholic community lives around there. I need their votes if I'm going to win this next election. You know how mad some of them got when we put their kids in jail after that football game last fall. They called it police brutality. I need Murphy to put in a good word for me."

"But you also need the Germans in Rich Valley and around Coates," countered Gates. "There's as many Germans out there as there are Catholics in Rosemount. Who knows what Freitag will say if you simply throw the diary away? Lose the Germans and you lose the election." Gates smashed his right fist into his left palm. "You've never lost an election."

"That's what bugs me. I'm damned if I do and damned if I don't." Wahlberg slumped back down in his chair with a look of frustration. "The D.A. will laugh at me if I try to get him to do something about this. I know him. He'll tell me I got no hard evidence against Murphy or against anybody else."

Wahlberg leaned toward his friend. "Like it or not, Mike Murphy is an important citizen of that community. He's the superintendent of all of Rosemount's schools. Hundreds of people know him and respect him. We can't go shooting from the hip. That's what the D.A. will say. I know it is."

"So what are you going to do? You got to do something with this thing," said Gates as he held out his hands in frustration.

"I don't know. Here's what I'm thinking. Tell me what you think. I'll bring Mike into my office and have him read the pages we're talking about.

Then I'll watch his face."

Wahlberg leaned back with his hands folded across his middle and gazed up at the ceiling as he recited some family history. "You know he's my brother-in-law. He married Agnes's sister. Fed her a line of bullshit and got her to marry him, give up her Swedish Lutheran ties and become a Catholic. My wife's folks nearly died when she did that. They raised their two kids as Catholics, even sent them to the nun's parochial school. They're good kids, don't get me wrong. We love 'em. They're part of our family."

Gates sighed, pursed his lips and shifted again in his chair. "I hear you, Ray. I hate it that you're in this bind."

"So do I, but here's the deal. Murphy's marriage has been rocky almost from the start. He's a proud, stubborn, demanding man. Despite all his education and work with kids, he doesn't have much time for his wife. Never has. Yells at her, complains about her housekeeping and cooking. He's gone most of the time and when he's home all he does is hole up in his basement shop. I know, because she's talked with Agnes about it many times. She even talks about getting a divorce, but the Catholic Church would never allow that and she's too embarrassed even to try. She blames herself; says she ought to do a better job."

"Where have I heard stories like that before? Wives always going back for more beatings and blaming themselves for making it happen," said Sergeant Gates as memories of trying to settle many domestic quarrels flashed through his mind.

"Every lawman has worked with women like that," said Wahlberg. The scowl was back on his face. "Anyway, when I read this diary I start thinking to myself. Maybe he did what Helen said here. I knew her. Sweet girl. Her mother lives up in Duluth now, close to her and Agnes' folks. She married this screwed up guy, weak, alcoholic. Even brought Helen up in the Catholic Church, trying to please him. Then he messed up his family real bad."

"When the Depression hit, he split."

"Right. Helen and her mother were left high and dry. Helen was our niece, too. So Agnes wanted us to take her in, but the Murphy's insisted it was their responsibility. Mike said he could find her a job teaching."

"So what're you going to do?" asked Gates, with a puzzled look on his face.

"Like I said, I'm going to confront him and see what he says."

"What then? What happens when he denies it?"

"I'll tell him I'm keeping the damn diary locked up in my safe. I'll tell him if he doesn't start treating his wife with a little more respect I'll leak the story. I'll tell him I expect his undying support in the fall election. If he does all that I'll keep the diary under lock and key."

"Bribery's a dangerous game, Ray."

"Sure it is, but that's the language Mike Murphy understands. He's a politician too, you know." Wahlberg straightened up in his chair and took a deep breath. "You know what you have to do to win elections and appointments. How do you think Murphy got to be superintendent? It sure as hell wasn't because he's such a wonderful school teacher. He pulled some strings, pushed some buttons. I know what he's like. He'll know what I can do to him, regardless of whether he did what the diary said or not."

"I know, but the same thing is true for you too. Rumors can kill."

"I understand. Mike isn't stupid. He knows which side his bread is buttered on. He'll do what I tell him."

"What about Freitag and that school teacher?"

"That's where you come in, George." Wahlberg pointed his big index finger at the sergeant. "You know farmers. You understand how they think. You handle it. Convince him we don't have any hard evidence on which to proceed."

Gates squinted as he looked at his friend. "Are you saying I should tell him you're calling Murphy in?"

"Come on. You know better than that. This is between you and me. What I say to Murphy nobody need ever know."

"So I tell him the diary is nothing but a diary and we have no way to corroborate what Helen wrote in it."

"Right. Only don't use a word like 'corroborate'. He won't have the foggiest idea what you're talking about."

"Sure." Gates thought for a moment, wiped his lips and then, with a smile, said, "I'll come up with some farmer thing, like him accusing his neighbor of not building a good fence when his cow gets into the cornfield, eats too much and dies from bloating. In that case nobody knows whether it was the cow that broke the fence down or the fence itself was no good. No way to tell. He'll understand."

"Good, very good," chuckled Wahlberg. "Let it go at that. Tell him we're going to keep the diary here on file in case something shows up to prove his neighbor really didn't build a good fence around his cornfield."

Wahlberg broke out into a big smile and bit down hard on his cigar. "We're going to win this damn election, George. You're a good man. After we win I'm making you my lieutenant."

"No way, Ray. I'm happy being a sergeant. I told you that many times. I hate desk jobs. I love being out in the field working with the farmers. Leave it the way it is. We'll work together and you'll win. Maybe you can help me get that other hundred acres next to mine we been talking about."

Chapter 18

Last Day of School

"Well, here we are. Last day of school." Emil smiled as Tillie stepped from his little Chevy truck. "The year went by pretty quick, right?"

Tillie smiled back and looked up as memories of the year flooded her mind. "Sure did, Emil, almost too quickly—almost. But I'm glad it's over. So are the kids. Big game today. We got to beat St. John's. We're all pepped up. Want to come see us win?"

Emil shook his head. "Yah, I wish I could, but I got to take Momma to the doctor in an hour. Her arthritis again. Not easy to get old. I'll see you this afternoon, same time."

Tillie stepped back from the truck. "Okay, but remember we're letting school out around two today. I'll be ready as soon as the bus comes, two thirty or so."

"Yah, okay. I'll see you tomorrow too," said Emil as he put his truck into gear. "Don't forget, we got to clean up the place, pick up your things and lock up the building for another summer."

Tillie stepped back another couple steps as the truck began to move. "That's good. Why don't we plan to do that in the afternoon? Al and I are planning a little celebration tomorrow evening, end of the year thing. His Pa told him Werner and he would milk the cows. They want Al to take me out, have a good time to mark the end of a successful year. So if you and I come by, say around one in the afternoon, work for an hour or so, you can get back home by three. Al will pick me up later on. I'll call him this evening."

"Yah, Yah. Okay. That will work out. See you this afternoon then. Bye, bye." Emil waved as he backed up his little truck, turned around and disappeared down the gravel road, heading toward Rosemount.

Tillie, dressed in her favorite flowered cotton print, walked jauntily into the building. A breeze flowed across her dark tresses and she felt happy, beautiful and alive. She entered the classroom and sorted out the certificates of advancement by grades. This was her final educational task for the year. The rest of the day would be filled with the ball game and the wiener roast.

The only dark cloud on the day was that Superintendent Murphy said he would also show up. Perhaps he would arrive during the picnic and be gone by the time the bus left. At least that way she wouldn't be alone with him.

Several of the children arrived early. Among them was Orville. "Morning, everybody. You're early. Orville, did you walk?"

"Yes, Miss Tilden. My momma said I could. She told me to be careful, but she said I could walk. It's not far, Miss Tilden."

"Yes, I know. It's only about a half mile. Good to see you, Orville."

"Yes, Miss Tilden." Orville had a frown on his face. "This is the last day, isn't it?"

"Yes. This is the last day."

Orville looked down at the floor for a moment and then up at Tillie. His lip quivered as he spoke. "I'm gonna miss you, Miss Tilden."

"And I'm going to miss you too, Orville," she said as she reached out to give him a hug. He wrapped his arms around her.

Tillie noticed Orville's strength as he held her. "You've grown quite a bit during this past year, haven't you?" she said as she gently placed her hands on his shoulders and pushed him from her.

"That's what my Momma says," replied Orville, with pride in his voice.

As they spoke the bus arrived and the rest of the children came tumbling in. Their excited conversation filled the room. They laughed and chattered like a flock of blackbirds that sometimes filled the branches of a big cottonwood directly across the road from the school. The boys bragged about how hard they were going to hit the ball at the game and complained they would have to put up with the girls' batting. The girls in turn insisted that they were as good as any boys when it came to batting and running. So the banter went on as they filtered down the rows of desks and reluctantly took their places.

162

"Today, class," said Tillie, "we're going outside to say the Pledge of Allegiance before the flag pole for the last time. As we say it I want you to remember that we live in the best country in the world. Remember that and then join me in a prayer of thanks for our nation and for a very successful school year. Then we'll come back in and I'll hand out your certificates of advancement. Now follow me. It's the seventh grade's job to run up the flag today."

The twenty-two students of Independent School District 132 marched behind their teacher and quietly assembled before the flag pole in the front of their school building. One seventh grade boy undid the rope and held it taut while the two girls of his grade fastened the two corner grommets to the clasps. Then, as it waved proudly before him, he hoisted it to the top and tied it off again. All of the students looked up at the national standard, held their hands over their hearts and joined their teacher in the pledge.

"I pledge allegiance to the flag of the United States of America and to the Republic for which it stands..."

"Now children," said Tillie, "let us pray." Tillie read from a piece of paper on which she had written her prayer.

"Dear God, we thank thee for this great nation, for our leaders, for President Roosevelt and for all who rule over us. In these difficult times we pray for wisdom and patience and thy blessings.

"Great Father, we thank Thee also for another year here at school. We thank Thee for keeping us safe. We remember Robert and we thank Thee for him. We know he is with you in heaven. We miss him..." At this her voice quivered and she had to pause to regain control of her emotions. "We miss him and, and we wish he was with us today to graduate, but we know Thy will is best.

"Father, give us a good summer too. Keep us in Thy love and one more thing. If it is Thy will, let us win the ball game today!"

The children responded with a resounding, "Amen!" Then they all marched obediently back into the little school where Tillie passed out their certificates.

To Orville she said, "Here is your certificate. It says you tried really hard this year and we're all proud of you. I know you will try hard again next year too."

"Thank you, Miss Tilden," said Orville. "I wish Robert could get a certificate too."

Tillie did her best to hold back the tears that were welling up. She sniffed, wiped her nose with her hankie and continued. "The final certificate today is for our graduating eighth grader, Wilbur Hillert. Wilbur will you please come forward."

Wilbur, dressed proudly in his best Sunday overalls, stepped up and held out his right hand. Tillie shook it, stepped up to him and gave him a big hug. Wilbur's face went bright red when she did so.

"Congratulations, Wilbur. You worked hard. You were a big brother to everyone. Thank you for helping me with the fires and for helping me keep order on the playground. I hear you will be going on the high school over at Rosemount next fall. I know you'll do well."

Everyone clapped and pounded their desks. School was over. The fun was about to begin.

"OKAY, OKAY!" shouted Tillie. "We head up the hill in a minute. To conclude our ceremonies this morning I want you all to stand and sing with me 'America the Beautiful.' We all know the song. We've sung it many times. Let's do it together this one last time."

Tillie sat down at the ancient, off-tune piano and began to plunk out the melody. The children joined in with gusto to sing Katherine Lee Bates well known hymn.

O beautiful for spacious skies,
For amber waves of grain,
For purple mountain majesties
Above the fruited plain ...

With the singing of the final word they all clapped and ran for the cloak room to grab their lunch buckets. Some boys seized ball gloves. Two snatched up bats. In a few moments all were outside, yelling, jumping, laughing and tossing softballs back and forth among them. Tillie joined them, carrying a large paper sack of wieners and buns in one hand. She took her place at the front and led them, Pied Piper style, up the gravel road hill toward St. John's. Orville quietly joined her at the front. She took his hand in hers and they marched joyfully, swinging hands and laughing.

In spite of the laughter and shouting behind her, Tillie could not help thinking about Murphy. What kind of a monster was he? What would he do if he ever caught her alone? A little chill feathered her spine. For a brief moment she no longer heard what was going on around her.

Orville broke in. "We're gonna win today, aren't we Miss Tilden?"

"Yes, yes, Orville. We're going to win!" She smiled and swung his arm and hers high above his head.

In less than ten minutes the troop arrived at the top. The children of St. John's were waiting, assembled in a ragged line behind their teacher, Harold Hartung. As they approached Hartung stepped out to meet Tillie and shake her hand. He looked at her with a warm smile and said, "Good morning, Miss Tilden. I see that you and your students have arrived right on time for our annual game. I must warn you and all the good students from ISD 132 that we are ready for you and are quite determined to win and make it two years in a row."

At this the children from both sides shouted and promised victory. The two teachers walked before them to the ball field, located behind a long row of pine trees at the far end of the church-school's parking lot. A twelve foot high fence of wire mesh stood ten feet behind the batter's box. The infield itself was covered with recently mowed wild grasses. The bases were marked with ragged canvass bags. The outfield was a mowed hayfield.

Teacher Hartung reached into his pocket, withdrew a quarter and said to the crowd gathered around him, "I'll throw my quarter into the air. If it's heads St. John's bats first. If it's tails, then ISD 132. We play seven innings. Whoever is ahead at that time is the winner for this year. I'll be the umpire behind the plate and Miss Tilden will umpire the bases. Let's all play hard, play fair and have a good time. Here goes."

He tossed the coin high above his head. Everyone watched as it bounced to the dusty ground behind home plate, bounced up again and finally settled in a little cloud of gray powder.

"Tails!" proclaimed Hartung. "The valley school bats first."

So the game of slow pitch softball began. Every child was expected to play some of the game and even the smallest batted at least once.

The game waged back and forth for the next hour. The boys from both sides heckled and yelled when the girls came up to bat. The girls jeered back and stuck out their tongues when they struck out. The smaller children were scattered in the outfield since the boys of both schools insisted that they alone could handle the bases. By the end of the sixth inning the score was fifteen to thirteen, in favor of St. John's.

Tillie had a hard time concentrating on her umpiring. She kept imagining Murphy standing behind the home plate fence, smiling at her, waiting, like a huge, red barn cat about to pounce upon an innocent, little sparrow. If he came, would she be able to fly away?

When it was their final turn at bat, Tillie called her students to gather around her in a circle. "Okay, guys," she began. "This is our last time at bat.

165

We need three runs to win. It's now or never. So let's get some hits and drive in those runs."

Eileen Swenson was first up. She swung hard, but struck out. Then it was Orville's turn. Despite the coaching from the boys he held the bat like a broom, with his hands six inches from one another. On the third pitch he managed to touch the ball. It dribbled feebly toward the pitcher as Orville skittered toward first base. The pitcher ran for the ball, but in his haste ran past it, stopped, turned around, reached for it, but briefly fumbled it. He finally got hold of it and threw it wildly in the direction of the first basemen as Orville approached. The ball went over the baseman's head, and bounced out into the hayfield.

The valley school children erupted with shouts, urging Orville to head for second base. Orville, for his part, was confused. It was his first time on base that day. He was surprised he had even made it. When he reached the base he victoriously jumped on the bag and decided to remain there. As he proudly stood on the bag, his classmates continued to shout, "Run, Orville, run to second base." At last it dawned on him what he should do and he headed out.

By this time the first baseman had found the ball and gave it a heave toward second base. His aim was true, but Orville was in the way. The ball bounced off his shoulder and he went flying to the ground, barely two feet from the second bag. He tore his jeans and skinned his knee in the process and began to cry. Tillie, acting as infield umpire, ran up to him and shouted, "Orville, are you okay?"

Orville pushed himself up with tears pouring from his eyes and said, "Yes, Miss Tilden." Then he limped the remaining two feet and sat on the bag to nurse his wound.

The second baseman recovered the ball and pumped it over to the pitcher as the game continued. The next player, Billy Lundgren, a tiny boy in the third grade, popped up to the short stop. Two out. Orville stood on second base bag and reached down from time to time to touch his bleeding knee. A big scab was forming over the wound. His hands were dirty and his face was streaked with tears.

Tillie gazed at him fondly. *He has suffered so much this year,* she thought. She wanted to rush over to sit beside him and hold him in her arms. She wanted to wipe away his tears and tell him he was loved and everything would turn out right. She wanted to tell him he was going to make it safely to home plate and that when he did Robert would be waiting for him. But she knew it wouldn't be so and she felt a deep sadness in her heart.

From the pit of her sadness a sudden feeling of anxiety emerged. *Murphy should be here. He said he was coming. No time for such worries now,* she thought. *Back to the game.*

Wilbur Hillert, ISD 132's biggest boy and only eighth grader, came up to bat. He gripped the bat in his strong hands and waited for the lazy, slow pitch to drift toward him. At exactly the right moment he connected with the ball and sent it whizzing far out into left field and over the heads of the three outfielders. Orville, at the urging again of his classmates, hobbled past third base and on to home plate, hardly three steps ahead of Wilbur. The score was all tied up!

The next batter was Betty Wagner, a fifth grader. She was a good athlete and had learned from her two older brothers how to hit. She hit a hard ball down to the third baseman. He was the best player on St. John's' team. He fielded the ball easily and threw her out at first. The game was tied fifteen to fifteen and St. John's was up to bat.

St. John's was, however, at the bottom of their lineup. Two girls swung out in quick succession. A fifth grade boy plopped a ball over second base. He was held at first with the winning run on base. Now they were at the head of their lineup and an eighth grader, as big and tall as Wilbur, was at bat. Wilbur decided to abandon his position at short stop and headed out to center field.

The St. John's eighth grader let the first ball go by. When the second came, he connected with as much energy as had Wilbur, but Wilbur was waiting for the ball as it flew high out to deep center. He waited patiently for it to drop down, caught it expertly and the side was out. The game remained tied, fifteen to fifteen.

"Game's over!" shouted Harold Hartung.

"No! No! It's a tie. We have to play another inning," came the screams from the players.

"Sorry, children," said Teacher Hartung. We agreed on the rules at the beginning. Seven innings is the game. Today everybody wins and nobody loses. Time for the picnic and hot dogs."

As the children walked slowly to where they had left their lunch buckets, Tillie again remembered Murphy's promise to visit on the last day. Would he be there when they came back down the hill? When the children left, would he stay? What if he suspected something?

Her thoughts were interrupted by Billy Lundgren shouting. "That's my stick," yelled the towheaded third grader. "You find your own stick."

Teacher Hartung had prepared a pile of wood for a bonfire. When he struck a match, the kindling had caught and spread quickly to the larger wood. As the fire died down, the children were grabbing from a pile of sharpened sticks to roast their wieners and place them in buns swabbed generously with ketchup and mustard.

"There are plenty of sticks, Billy," said Tillie, as she placed her hand on his shoulder. "We all need to take turns."

The children drank a sweet nectar made from a mixture of strawberry syrup, sugar and water. Teacher Hartung ladled it into paper cups from big metal pots on a table in the shade of the St. John's school building.

When the meal was over both teachers invited their students to shake hands with one another. They did so with much chatter. Most of them were related in one way or another and had been together at family and community gatherings over the years.

When the ceremonies were over Tillie turned to Teacher Hartung. "On behalf of the students of our school I want to thank you for your hospitality." She winked as she continued, "And please understand. We didn't win, but neither did you and ... wait until next year!"

At this the children of both schools broke out in shouts, predicting victory the next time they met.

Tillie waited for the enthusiastic banter to calm down and said, "Okay, everyone, time to go. The bus will be coming soon." She took her place at the head and led her troop back down the hill.

By the time they reached the school and gathered up their belongings from their desks it was nearly time for the bus to arrive. As her charges stood around her, Tillie made a final speech.

"This will be the last time I see most of you, maybe all of you. So I want to say again how wonderful it has been for me this year. You have come to mean so very much to me and I'm really going to miss you. Keep on studying and learning. God bless you all. Now give me a big hug."

The students all gathered around her, hugging and touching her one by one. Eileen Swenson hung back until the end. As she came up she had an envelope in her hand. "Miss Tilden," she began, "this isn't much, but we wanted you to have this card. We've all signed it. We want you to remember us."

Tillie opened the card. Signatures of all her students were written with pencil and ink on the inside and on the back. She read the card so all could hear.

Days will come and days will go,
Days with sunshine, days with snow.
Wherever they take you,
Wherever you'll be,
Remember these days,
So happy and free,
We passed together,
Both you and me.

Tillie's hands trembled as she held the card and gazed out at her students. Orville was standing beside her again. He looked up her and said, "We all love you, Miss Tilden."

"And I love you too," she said, giving him a hug.

The big orange bus pulled into the driveway. One by one the students piled on. As the bus pulled away they all waved from the windows. Tillie waved back.

Whatever happened to Murphy? she wondered. *He didn't show up like he said he would. Oh God! Did he do that on purpose? Did he figure to find me alone, with all the children gone?*

That cold feeling crept into her heart. She turned and walked slowly up the steps, fighting the impulse to run into the woods on the other side of the road to hide until Emil arrived.

Chapter 19

Final Session

As she was about to sit behind her desk, Tillie heard Superintendent Michael Murphy's car pull into the driveway. She stood in the doorway as he got out of his car and walked up to the schoolhouse.

"Good afternoon, Miss Tilden," he said with a wan smile on his face. "I'm sorry I wasn't here in time to greet your students. I had to make an emergency trip to Hastings."

"I'm sorry too," she said. "They left a few minutes ago. We managed without you and had a good final day."

"Well then, that's fine. Let's go in. We have a little business to finish."

He followed her into the classroom and pulled a chair next to her desk as she settled into hers. Placing his briefcase on his lap, he opened it and pulled out some papers. Placing them on the desk, he put the case on the floor beside him and began, "I have here the final forms that the University asked me to complete. I'd like to go over them with you before I sign them."

Tillie noticed that his hands were trembling slightly. His face had a pallor to it. She considered asking him if he was ill, but dismissed the thought. *Frankly,* she said to herself, *I'd like to get this over and never see the man again. If he's ill, too bad. His problem. Not mine.*

"I have given you excellent marks on all matters. You always had your lesson plans well prepared. As far as I can see your students learned what they were supposed to. Your rapport with the parents was very good. Your dress and demeanor were always of the highest quality. You were very willing to accept guidance and instruction from me, your supervisor. Yes, Miss Tilden, I have nothing but the most excellent things to say about this year. As far as I am concerned you have completed your student teaching experience with a straight 'A' mark. I trust that is satisfactory."

"Yes sir, it is. Will you be signing the report and sending it in? Is there anything I can do?"

"No, no. I send it in, but I have prepared a copy for you. I'll sign both copies now," he said as he pulled out his fountain pen and quickly scrawled his signature on the two copies. "There. That does it. Here is your copy."

"Thank you, Mr. Murphy." Tillie took her copy, folded it neatly and slipped it into the drawer of her desk. Then looking back at Murphy she continued, "May I say something?"

"Oh, yes, by all means."

"I want to thank the school district and the school board for the excellent arrangements they made for my care and transportation during this year. Mrs. Wilson's home is a very fine place. The meals have been delicious. The girls there are wonderful. I've formed some beautiful friendships. I can't say enough about Emil Wunderlich. He's one of the most precious souls I have ever known."

"Very good. I'll pass it along. Perhaps you'd like to drop them a note yourself."

"Oh, I fully intend to do that."

"Yes, yes do that." Murphy seemed more nervous than before as he shuffled his papers, reached down for his briefcase, opened it and deposited them within. Setting the case back on the floor, he cleared his throat two times and with a slight frown on his forehead, asked, "How will you be evaluating me, Miss Tilden? I know the University will be asking you to do that. I was wondering if you would be caring to share your thoughts as well."

Why is he so tense? Tillie asked herself. *He's as wound up as a ball of string. What's all the coughing and frowning about? He seems almost frightened of me. I thought I'd have to be afraid of him. What's going on anyway?*

Besides all that, how honest can I be with him? What will his reaction be if I raise the question of Helen again? He doesn't know about the diary ... or does he? What did he say? Emergency trip to Hastings? Hastings! Why would he go to Hastings? What is the connection? Did the Sheriff tell him?

171

Oh surely not. Why would he? Why would he tell him? But what if he did?

Tillie's mind raced back and forth, much more rapidly now than it had on the porch swing a few days earlier.

I'm all alone here. What time is it? she asked, glancing at her wristwatch surreptitiously. *Two, twenty-five. Emil will be here in about a half hour. Nothing can happen. Maybe I'd better remind him of Emil's coming.*

Wait a second! What kind of game are we playing? He didn't have to tell me he was detained because of an emergency trip to Hastings. He never mentioned Hastings one time this whole past year. Why would he tell me about going there today? Does he want me to know he was there—and he knows about the diary?

What then? If he knows about the diary, he must also know that Al and Eila know. That means that he doesn't dare do anything that will incriminate him.

Why does he imply he knows about the diary? Is he mocking me? Is he trying to tell me I can do nothing—and that I had better not try?

Did Sergeant Gates tell him? No. Gates probably went right to Sheriff Wahlberg. Wahlberg is his boss. Why would Wahlberg tell Murphy? How much did he tell him—if he did? Did he let him read the diary? Why would he do that? What's the relationship between Wahlberg and Murphy?

Oh, dear God, please help me. I wish I knew more. What shall I say? Maybe the best thing is to say nothing about Helen. Must keep it on the topic of school and the children. Yes, that's what I better do.

Murphy kept his tight smile. He noticed Tillie's hesitancy. He picked up the conversation, "I recognize that it is always difficult to critique one's superiors. I don't want to be pressuring you, Miss Tilden. I was wondering if you'd be liking to say anything and, for that matter, if you'd be liking to share any other reflections upon the year."

Tillie cleared her throat. "Yes sir. It is difficult to evaluate one's supervisor. Uh, let me say this: You have been most helpful throughout this year. I benefited greatly from your suggestions about lesson plans and preparation. Your experience in the classroom as well as your experience with these people was very important in helping me to do my job. I could not have done nearly as well without you. I do thank you. I plan to share some such thoughts in my student report to the University."

"Thank you, Miss Tilden," said Murphy. "You are most kind, most kind." He relaxed and sat back in his chair. "Now then, is there anything else you would like to be discussing?"

"Yes sir. It's the Switzer family. Robert's death touched us all. I'm thinking that two years running now the children have had to deal with death."

Oh, dear, thought Tillie, wincing. *Why did I say that? I didn't intend to put it that way. Why did I blurt out about Helen's death? Why didn't I simply mention Robert's?*

Murphy's tight smile became even tighter. "Uh, yes." He stammered. "I, uh, yes, I see what you mean. Difficult for them. Touches the lives of all. This is a close-knit community. Yes, Robert Switzer's death touched the lives of everyone."

Murphy folded and unfolded his hands, took a deep breath and continued. "Uh, but let me say that this isn't the first farm accident we've had around here. No, not the first one at all. Happens all the time." He warmed to his topic.

"Why, I can remember some three years ago a man on the other side of Rosemount got too close to a ditch with his tractor. Rolled right over on top of him. Killed him on the spot. Yes, and they didn't find him until that night. He'd been dead the whole day long."

Tillie sat with her hands folded on her lap, looking very serious as she heard his recitation of local tragedies.

"A high school student was gored to death by a bull. Let's see. That was back in 1930, I believe. I knew the young man. Nice kid."

Where's he going with all this? thought Tillie. *I know farm accidents happen. We all hear about them. What does that have to do with the Switzers? Is he telling me that they'll have to get past it? Too bad? It happens all the time? Forget it and go on?*

"Yes sir. Accidents happen all the time," said Tillie as her pent up words poured out like water from a broken dam. "But that's precisely my point, sir. How do the children understand this? What do they understand? Help me. How does a teacher handle the subject of death in the classroom? Should we talk about it in school? First they lost a teacher and this year a classmate. Frankly, sir, I was not prepared to deal with these matters and I don't think I did a very good job."

Murphy frowned, but kept his forced smile. "Now, now, Miss Tilden, so many questions. I don't think you are suggesting you should lay out a lesson plan for a week on the topic of death, set up grade by grade."

"No sir. I'm not. But how much should we talk about? Is this something best left to the family and to the church? Do we skirt the issues in the classroom and go on as if nothing happened?"

Murphy was clearly uneasy. He tried to turn off the unwanted discussion. "Well, we are getting into a topic that can become quite philosophical, aren't we?"

Suddenly Tillie became very angry. *Here's a man who may have killed his own niece and he's pretending we're talking about abstractions. What kind of lunatic am I dealing with?* she thought.

Her voice rose in pitch and intensity. "No sir, this is not some abstract philosophical discussion about an educational theory. This has to do with a little boy with a limited intelligence who is grieving and who misses his big brother greatly."

Fear, anxiety and hate swelled up in her breast to join her anger. She struggled to control her emotions as she continued. "This has to do with a little boy's father who, I fear, is taking out his anger and confusion on the child. This has to do with a great many unanswered questions floating around in this community about families and children and marriage and sex. Nobody wants to deal with them!"

She was losing control of herself. Her passionate love for her students had pushed her on to a soap box. She almost stood as she proceeded, "It has to do with everybody pretending that things are going well. Oh, we have some money problems and some people are out of work and all that, but beyond that everything's fine! And it isn't!"

Oh, dear God, thought Tillie, *what have I said now? Why can't I control my mouth?* She felt the blood rush to her face. Her heart was beating rapidly. She put her head down and looked at the floor.

Murphy sat with his mouth partly open, as if he wanted to say something, but restrained himself. He blinked five or six times, took a long, deep breath, started to speak, but once again said nothing.

"I'm sorry, Mr. Murphy," said Tillie with a deep sigh. "I'm getting carried away again. I recognize I'll be gone from this community in a few days. I have no right to be so critical. After all I don't really live here. I mean, I do, but I'll not be here much longer. It's just that…" She paused, as if preparing to say more. "No, I've said enough."

Finally Murphy gained control of himself. He spoke softly, measuring each word. "Yes, Miss Tilden, you have said enough. You are young. You are very intelligent, but you do not know some things. Some things you will never know, cannot understand. You will do well to leave them alone."

Murphy's eyes met hers. They looked sad, not angry. They peered out from dark shadows, filled with gloomy memories unknown to her.

"When you are young you want to change the world. You believe that you can. Isn't that why we get into education? As you grow older … well, things happen. The world resists your efforts. You start to get … jaded, cynical and, and … tired."

Now his eyes looked not only sad, but extremely weary.

"I know that you have taken Robert's death very much to heart. You've spoken before about Orville and your concern for children like him. What can I say? Some things you can be doing nothing about. You do the best you can. You try. Quite often you'll be getting no support. Most don't care. So, perhaps we should leave it there."

"Yes," said Tillie, sighing, "perhaps we should."

Murphy reached down and picked up his case. As he rested it on his lap he said, "Once more, Miss Tilden, thank you for being our ISD 132 teacher this year. It's been a good one. It's had its challenges. Nevertheless, thank you. I will remember you and I trust you will think about me—and about what I said."

With that he rose stiffly. She stood with him. He offered his hand. She reached out hers. They shook. He turned and walked quickly out the door, down the steps to his car. In a moment he had started it and was gone.

How strange, thought Tillie. *How very, very strange. What really happened? What is going on?*

As she sat down to straighten out her desk she heard Emil's truck pull up. She glanced around to make sure all the windows were secure, walked to the door of the cloak room, locked it from the outside and joined Emil.

"Good day, Tillie?"

"Yes, Emil, good, but rather strange."

Chapter 20

Nothing We Can Do

When Emil dropped her off Tillie said, "Thanks. See you tomorrow afternoon at about one." She turned and walked up the inside stairway to her room. She was glad for the extra hour. What she really wanted to do was kick off her shoes, flop down on the bed and think about her conversation with Murphy. So that's what she did.

As she lay there she kept wondering if he was telling her that he knew about the diary. How would he know? Why would Wahlberg tell him? In a few minutes her thoughts began to drift. Soon she was lost in a deep sleep.

"Tillie, Tillie, hello Tillie!" She thought she could hear Mrs. Wilson's voice, but where was it? Then she was awake, struggling to lift her head in order to reply. She rolled over on her side, pushed up with her arm and rasped in a soft, husky voice, "Yes, yes. I'm here."

"Telephone call from Al Freitag," came the reply from the first floor.

"I'll be right down."

She rolled her feet over the side of the bed, slipped on her shoes, ran her fingers quickly through her hair, stretched briefly and walked down the stairs to the kitchen. *Why would Al be calling in the middle of the afternoon?*

"What time is it?" she asked.

"Nearly five," said Mrs. Wilson.

"No! It can't be. I've been sleeping for over an hour."

She reached for the phone's earpiece. "Hello. What's going on?"

"Hi. I know we weren't supposed to get together until tomorrow, but I got something important I really need to talk about with you and Eila. Do you suppose I could come over tonight after chores, say around eight or so?"

"Sure, fine with me. Hold a minute." She turned to Mrs. Wilson, "Do you know if Eila will be around tonight?"

"She didn't say anything to me about going anywhere," said Norma Wilson. "Course she wouldn't have to, would she?"

Tillie turned back to the telephone. "As far as I know, that's fine. See you out on the front porch at about eight tonight … Right … Love you too. Bye."

Before dinner Tillie told Eila about Al's coming. Eila agreed to join them on the front porch.

Tillie and Eila were waiting when Al arrived. He walked up to the porch and said, "Hi girls. How about taking a walk with me?"

Tillie stepped down the front porch steps to meet him, gave him a little kiss and took his hand. Eila walked beside her. Al began.

"I was in Hastings this afternoon."

"You were? Why?" asked Tillie.

"Sergeant Gates asked me to come by."

"What did he want?"

"He wanted to talk about the diary."

"Did he say what they're going to do with it?" asked Eila.

"He said they're not going to do nothing."

"Nothing? Why not?" asked Tillie.

"Because you can't tell who broke down the fence."

"You what?" laughed Eila.

"He said that if my cow got into the neighbor's corn I'd have a hard time proving it was the neighbor's fault. Maybe it was the cow's fault."

"Come again?" asked Tillie.

"That was his way of telling me that the diary is only a diary," said Al. "He said they had no real evidence that Murphy did what Helen says he did in her diary. Without evidence and witnesses they can't do a thing."

"What's that got to do with your cows?" asked Eila.

"I get it," said Tillie. "He was trying to talk like one farmer to another. So he was using the analogy of cows and corn. Don't you get it, silly?"

"Kinda," said Eila as she wrinkled her nose and squinted her eyes into a quizzical look. "Seems a dumb way of talking."

Al stopped and looked at the girls. "Anyway, that's the way it is for now. Gates said in no uncertain terms that we have to leave it that way. We're not to talk about it to anybody. He repeated it several times.

"He also said the sheriff is going to keep the diary on file, in case something else shows up. But for now that's as far as it goes."

"Al, a funny thing happened to me this afternoon, now that you mention Hastings," said Tillie as they resumed their walk. "Murphy showed up a little late. Said he'd been detained because of some emergency meeting in Hastings."

"Tillie!" Al almost shouted. "I saw Murphy heading back toward Coates as I was arriving in Hastings!"

"I was wondering," said Tillie, "if he'd been in to see Sheriff Wahlberg."

Al stopped again, put his fingers to his mouth, wrinkled his forehead and said, "I just thought of something. Wahlberg and Murphy are related!"

"What? You got to be kidding," Eila's voice rose.

"Keep it quiet, Eila," said Tillie. "We don't want to get the whole neighborhood in on this." Turning to Al she asked, "What do you mean?"

"They're married to sisters. A third sister was Helen's mother. I forgot all about that until this very minute," said Al.

"How do you know that?" asked Eila.

"It's no secret. Wahlberg has lived around here for a long time. His wife and Mrs. Murphy were originally Lutherans, grew up around Minneapolis. So, anyway, they're all living in the same county. Then along comes Helen and she moves in with the Murphy's."

"Was Helen a Lutheran?" asked Tillie.

"Nope. Raised in the Catholic Church. That's how come she moved in with the Murphy's, I suppose. They're Catholics and the Wahlbergs are Lutherans.

"So, anyway, now we plunk that diary in the lap of Wahlberg and it's all about Murphy raping his niece."

Eila motioned for them to stop and stood in front of Al and Tillie. Her hands were on her hips. She spoke in quick bursts. "And Wahlberg wants to kill the jerk himself, but … Murphy is an important guy in the community … and an election is coming up, right?"

Tillie broke in, raised her hands and shook her clenched fists. "Right. So Wahlberg has Murphy into his office for a little tête-à-tête."

"A what?" asked Al.

"Oh, that's a little French expression. It means they got their heads together to talk this thing out. And if that's what happened, then it explains why Murphy was so nervous this afternoon."

"What do you mean?" asked Eila.

Tillie reviewed her conversation with her supervisor and continued, "I'll bet Wahlberg told Murphy he knows what Helen wrote and he's keeping the diary under lock and key."

"And," said Eila, with a note of excitement in her voice, "he told Murphy he'd better be a good guy and say a lot of good things about the honorable sheriff in this fall's election."

"So where does that leave us?" asked Al, with a puzzled look on his face.

"It leaves us hanging," said Tillie. "The cow got into the corn and died and nobody can do a thing about it."

"You're right," responded Al. "For now we can't do nothing."

"I hate this. I really hate this," said Eila with a grimace on her face.

"I think we all do," said Al. "But like Tillie said, we're stuck. Murphy might have killed her, but we got no proof. All we got is a theory and a dead girl's diary."

Leaning his head back, Al turned toward Tillie and Eila in the rear, "Let's walk back to the house. It's been a long day and I need to get home."

Early the next morning Sheriff Raymond Wahlberg was on the phone to his brother-in-law, Michael Murphy. "Mike, your year is nearly wrapped up," he said, "since our meeting I've thought about a couple other things you and I need to work out. How about breakfast this morning at that little café over in Rosemount, O'Hara's, about seven-thirty?"

"Sure, sure. Whatever you say, Ray. Be glad to meet you."

An hour later Raymond Wahlberg asked for a booth off in the corner of O'Hara's for himself and Murphy. As they ate their plates of eggs, bacon and toast, Wahlberg said, "Quite a couple years you've had, Mike, with Helen dying and all. Now we in the family have her little diary to help us know what really happened."

"Th-th-the diary?" stuttered Murphy. "W-w-what will ya be doing with it?"

"Like I said before, Mike, nothing at all. I'll keep it for now in my safe," said Wahlberg, his eyes hard as steel, "but I was thinking some more about all that. I'm thinking you must be getting tired of all the pressure of being school super."

"Y-y-ya." Murphy continued stuttering. "G-g-gets tough at times, tough, Ray. R-r-real tough." Lines of tension were written across his forehead and around his eyes.

"Sure does. Hard on a guy your age, Mike."

"R-r-right, Ray. G-g-gets me down at times."

"So I'm thinking, brother-in-law, that it's time to step down, find a new profession, move out of Rosemount, try something new. What do you think, Mike?"

"Y-y-you saying I should be quitting the teaching profession, Ray?" asked Murphy. His cheeks were twitching. A forced smile was on his lips.

"Yeah, Mike. I'm thinking that and I'm sure when you think about my suggestion you'll want to say yes. I believe the school board will understand. This is a good time to step down. They'll find somebody new over the summer. Don't you agree, Michael?"

Michael Murphy said nothing for about a minute. He screwed up his face and clenched his fists as he took a sip from his coffee and looked up with a tight grimace on his lips. "R-r-right, Ray. You're right. M-m-maybe it's time for me to be stepping down. But what'll I do?" Fear was etched across his forehead. His eyes were wide. "I-I-I mean, 'tis a teacher I've been me whole career. I don't know much else."

"Oh, don't underestimate yourself, Michael. I got some friends up in Minneapolis in the farm machinery business and they need a good salesman. You're good at talking, Mike. Hard work, but you're an educated man and you've lived around farmers and farm families all your life. I'm sure you'll do okay, even in these difficult times. Farmers can't buy much machinery, but a hard working guy like yourself, well, you can sell something. The machinery people said they'd find you a job, give you a chance to earn a little commission. After that it's up to you."

"Up to me?" asked Murphy. He sat across from Wahlberg with his shoulders hunched. He looked like a Holstein cow had sat on him.

"I got a friend in real estate," continued Wahlberg. "He says he knows somebody who wants to buy your house. Houses are hard to sell these days, but there's a new high school teacher coming to town, as you know, and he might be interested."

"Sell me house?" asked Murphy plaintively.

"Right, Michael," said Wahlberg as he took a sip of his coffee, "I'm thinking you might want to hand in your resignation and move to

Minneapolis by the end of next month. So, what're you thinking, Michael?" "Y-y-you're right, Ray." Murphy continued stuttering. "I-I-I-I'm thinking that's a good idea." He cleared his throat, pushed his eggs aside, rubbed his hands on his napkin and continued. "G-g-guess I've lost me appetite. I-I-I'll be going home now and telling Mary. She's mentioned once or twice that a change would be nice."

"Right, Mike, but the kind of change she's talked about doesn't include you. I'm thinking she ought to have a chance to read the diary, learn about what happened, come to her own conclusions."

Murphy's face was now as red as his hair. He tried to take another sip of coffee, but his hands were shaking so much he spilled it on his trousers. As he reached down to wipe the spill with his napkin, his whole upper torso began to tremble.

"R-r-ray," he said, now nearly out of control. "P-p-please, Ray. L-l-let me tell Mary. For God's sake, Ray, p-p-please."

Raymond Wahlberg calmly sipped his coffee. His steely glare did not change as he continued in a soft voice. "Sure, Mike. You do that. Don't overlook the details or else Agnes and I will have to fill them in."

"A-A-Agnes? She knows, too?"

"Right, Mike." Wahlberg glared down at Murphy. "After all, Agnes was Helen's aunt. I thought she ought to know about it, so I let her read the diary."

"Oh, God, Ray. Now the whole family will know. W-w-what will I do?"

"Well now, Mike, what will you do?" asked Wahlberg with an ironic grin on his lips. He pulled himself to his full height and leaned down toward his brother-in-law like a great grizzly. "Perhaps you should have thought about that when Helen was living with you."

Murphy said no more. He sat across from Wahlberg frozen to his seat, staring blankly.

"You're a smart man, Michael," said Wahlberg as he rose to leave. "You'll figure something out—eventually. Breakfast is on me. When you move out, I'll get some people to help you."

Chapter 21

Storm

Tillie awoke before seven o'clock on Saturday morning. Her sleep had been troubled and filled with dreams. In one dream she found herself alone in her school late at night. Someone was coming up the front stairs. As he entered the classroom she could barely make out his face by the light of the kerosene lamp on her desk. He drew closer and she could hear a slight chuckle. At once she knew the voice. It was Michael Murphy.

"Thought you could pull one over on me, didn't you? You gave the diary to the Sheriff. Now I'm going to be taking care of you, once and for all."

He had a rope in his hand. He approached with a stiff smile on his face, his eyes hard and wild. She was trembling in the corner next to the door of the wood-room. She tried to run through the door into the darkness. He kept coming toward her. Everywhere she looked spiders crawled toward her. She screamed!

Abruptly, she awoke, sitting up, covered with sweat and trembling. It took her a moment to realize she was in her room at the boarding house completely alone and safe. She fell down on her pillow, her mind racing, remembering the events of the day and her conversation with Al and Eila. It seemed like hours before she fell asleep again.

After a light breakfast Tillie returned to her room to begin sorting out her papers and prepare her own report to the university. She kept thinking about

Orville. Was his father punishing him as she suspected? How violent was the man?

She completed her hand written report and wrote a note to the school board, thanking them for the year and the provisions they had made for her care. She thanked them for Mrs. Wilson and her experiences at the boarding house. She smiled to herself while she wrote glowing words about Emil. She wanted to tell them this had been the most momentous year of her life, but decided not to share such personal thoughts.

By the time she had completed her tasks it was nearly noon. She knocked on Eila's door. Hearing no answer, she decided to go down to the first floor. Mrs. Wilson told her that Eila was in the basement washing her clothes. Tillie found her putting the last of her wash through the roller wringers.

"Hi, Till," said Eila. "How'd your night go?"

"Terrible. I had one bad dream after the other all night long."

"Me too," replied Eila. "I kept dreaming about Robert and how he was when we found him. Crazy stuff, all mixed up. Don't want to think about." She shook her head with a sad expression on her face. "What are you up to the rest of the day?"

"Emil's taking me over to school after lunch. We're going to clean a little, close it down and haul my stuff back here. Want to come along, help out an old friend?"

"I would if I could," said Eila, "but I got to catch up on some of my own paperwork over at the clinic. You going out tonight?"

"Right. Al and I are celebrating the end of the year. He's coming by late in the afternoon to pick me up. We'll stop by here, drop off my stuff and then head over to O'Hara's for some food. We got things to talk about."

"I'm sure you do, sweetie." Eila smiled. "I'm sure you do. Guess I'll see you tomorrow afternoon."

At that moment they heard Norma Wilson calling down the stairs. "Lunch is served, girls."

Emil Wunderlich picked up Tillie around one that afternoon to drive her to the school. As she stepped from the car she looked around. "Know what, Emil? This may be the last time you and I ever drive up here. Seems a little sad."

"Yah, maybe," said Emil, "but we got to move on. Every day brings us something new. Looking back is good, but we have to keep looking ahead."

"I know. So much has happened this year. We've had some good talks together. I'm going to miss them."

"Yah, Yah. I'm going to miss them, too … But for now we got some things to do."

With that Emil stepped from his truck and headed for the school building. Tillie smiled and followed him up the stairs as he put in his key and opened the front door. For the next two hours they swept, dusted, moved desks around and organized the books on the shelves of the school's miniature library. Tillie gathered her own books and papers and piled them into four cardboard boxes. Finally she and Emil paused for a break and a cup of coffee from Emil's thermos jug.

"Looks like your part is pretty much finished," Tillie began. "I have some files to sort through and some lesson plans I need to organize yet. No need for you to stay. Al will be along around five. We're going out to eat. He said he'd pick me up, wait for me to change and afterwards we'll go together to O'Hara's. So, as far as I'm concerned, you can go."

"Yah, good. I'll take the boxes back to Mrs. Wilson's place; carry them up to your room."

"Thanks. That's awful sweet of you. One more thing." Tillie reached into one of her boxes. "I have a little present for you in memory of our times together." She pulled out a wrapped present and handed it to Emil. "Open it."

Emil smiled broadly as he removed the paper. "Ach, my oh my."

"Do you like it?" she asked. "I know we've talked about them several times. You even said you wished you had a copy. I wrote a little note on the front page and signed it."

"But this, the complete works of William Shakespeare," said Emil. Tears gathered in the corners of his eyes. "Come here, my sweet little Tillie," he said, reaching out his arms.

Tillie stepped forward and they embraced for a long moment. "Thank you so very much Emil. I'll miss our rides and our talks. You have meant a great deal to me."

Tillie helped him haul the boxes to his truck. "Good bye," he said in a quivering voice. "Thanks again for the book. I'm sure I'll see you before you go back to St. Paul. Thank you."

In a few minutes he was gone and she returned to her tasks. In less than an hour she finished. She glanced up from her desk and a sudden thought came to her. She took out a piece of paper and scribbled a quick note on it. Then she slipped the note between the jamb and the front door, closed and locked it.

Certain Al would see the note when he came to pick her up, she set off down the gravel road to walk the half mile to the Wechsler farm and the Switzer house.

While she walked she thought about Orville. *This is a little silly. Why should I go out of my way to see him? On the other hand, he's such a lovable child and he's had so many terrible things happen to him. I need to see him one more time, try to give him some encouragement. I got the time. Nothing else to do right now. Al can come and pick me up down there as well as here.*

Some clouds were building in the north. The wind picked up as she entered the driveway of the Wechsler farm. The smell of rain filled the air. Al and the other farmers will be happy for a little more rain, she thought.

She walked to the tiny farm house in which the Switzers lived. Several shades of gray in color, it was in dire need of paint. The tattered screen door in the front had a large hole torn in it. One of its hinges was hanging by a single screw. The front porch had a couple floor boards missing on the far left side. A single ancient rocking chair sat on the other. The step leading up to the porch was a concrete block turned sideways. One of the block's corners was chipped. The entire structure looked as sad and lonely as Tillie imagined Orville to be.

She stepped gingerly up the front step and rapped on the frame of the screen door. No answer. She rapped again. Still no answer. She noticed that the front window was open. An equally tattered screen covered it, but probably did little or no good to keep out flies and mosquitoes. She walked to the window and shouted.

"Anybody home?"

No answer.

Perhaps I should try the barn, she thought.

The barn had once been painted red, but sun, snow, wind and rain had gradually turned it to a light pink. In many places the boards had completely lost their painted hue and were various shades of gray like the house. The first floor was built from field stone. Windows were built into the stone about every five feet. Their casings, once white, were now also turning gray. Spiders made their homes in the corners. Large button weeds and various grasses grew all around the building. Buzzing flies filled the air. Wasps flew back and forth from their nests under the eaves. Several chickens clucked and scratched in the grass. The wind continued to blow and the sky grew darker by the minute.

On the end closest to the house a big Dutch door, divided in half horizontally, led into the barn. The top half was open. The ground around the door was caked and muddy. Between it and another large door stood a fence of heavy posts and barbed wire surrounding the cow yard. The tracks and manure of cows that made their way in and out of the barn each morning and evening filled the muddy yard.

The smell of manure, rotting hay and grain seemed overpowering to Tillie.

She stepped carefully through the mud to the door. She could hear some noise inside the building.

"Hello!" she shouted.

No answer. She tried again, "Mr. Switzer! Hello!"

"What do you want?" said a harsh voice behind her.

Tillie turned abruptly, nearly losing her shoe in the mud as she did so. Hermann Switzer stood before her, holding a pitch fork in his hands. His faded overalls bore patches on both knees. Mud and cow manure covered his rubber boots. A dirty straw hat adorned his head. Stubble covered his unshaven face. His muscular arms bulged beneath the rolled up sleeves of his old blue shirt. Cowhide leather gloves covered his calloused hands. He looked at her with dark and menacing eyes.

He sucked on a cud of tobacco stuffed into his left cheek, spat the deep brown liquid into the mud and spoke in a harsh baritone, "You're the teacher, ain't you?"

"Yes, I'm Miss Tilden, your son's teacher. We have met."

"Watcha want?" he asked.

"I wanted to say goodbye to Orville."

"Why?"

"Because I'm leaving in a couple days. Would that be all right with you?"

"He don't need you no more."

"Yes, of course, I'm about to leave. I wanted to … to tell him … to tell him to keep on working."

"The dummy don't need no tellin'." Hermann Switzer glowered down at her. "He don't need no crazy teacher tellin' him nuthin'! Why don't you get the hell out of here!"

Tillie fought to keep her composure. She sensed a wave of panic rising within her. This had all been a mistake, a crazy, stupid mistake. What was she thinking? *Think, girl, think,* she said to herself. *Try to calm him down.*

A few drops of rain fell to the muddy earth. A low rumble rolled across the heavens.

"Certainly, sir. I'm leaving."

"No, I think I don't want you to leave," said Switzer as he reached out with a strong right hand and pushed her toward the barn door. "You come inside. I got something I want to tell you," he said as he swung the bottom half of the door aside with the hand in which he still held the pitchfork.

The gloomy interior became even darker as heavy rain clouds closed in. Another deeper rumble echoed across the skies.

Tillie found herself shoved inside the barn up against the stone wall, whitewash caking off in layers. Smells of manure, cow feed and stale air choked her.

"What are you doing?" she screamed.

"Whatever I want, missy," he hissed. "I got something I want to say to you, same as I said to that damn hussy that tried teachin' Orville before you got here."

"What do you mean?" Tears filled Tillie's eyes. She leaned against the wall, trembling. Switzer loomed over her. Tillie remembered her image of a barn cat about to pounce on a cornered field mouse. She felt small and helpless.

"I mean that you and everybody else should leave us alone. The dummy don't need no teachers. He ain't never gonna learn nuthin'. He's too stupid. What good is he? All he knows how to do is mess everything up. He killed his brother, di'n't he? He's good for nuthin'."

Heavy rain began to fall outside. Moist air and raindrops flew into the barn to form little puddles.

Tillie's breath came in gasps. She fought to calm herself. "Mr. Switzer, I feel as bad as you do about Robert, but it wasn't Orville's fault."

"What the hell do you know about it?" snarled Switzer. "He put the damn tractor into gear di'n't he? He's the one who ground up my Robert!"

"It was an accident. Orville didn't mean to do that," protested Tillie, her voice quivering as she spoke.

"That's what I mean. He didn't know nuthin' about what he's done. He's a stupid dummy!"

The rumbles grew stronger and stronger. Rain beat against the barn's window pains.

"Maybe it would be better if I talked with your wife," said Tillie, searching for some reason to get him to release her.

"Yah, you do that! But she ain't here and she ain't gonna be here for a couple more hours, Missy. She and the Wechslers is gone to Farmington to do some shopping and they ain't coming back until sometime before supper. So it's me and you all by ourselves."

"Is Orville here?"

"Hey, who cares? The dummy's around some place I suppose, but you ain't gonna see him today." Switzer's eyes crackled with hate. He spat spittle mixed with tobacco juices into the gutter beside him as he leaned his pitchfork against the wall. He held Tillie's forearm in his strong grip and pushed her toward a three legged milk stool sitting in the corner.

"Sit down, teacher!" he said in a hoarse half-whisper. "I want to tell you something and I want you to hear me good."

Tillie sat on the stool, rubbing her now bruising left forearm with her right hand. Switzer stood over her, a sneer on his lips, tobacco stains dribbling down his chin.

"You told Robert to take care of his poor little brother, didn't you?" He spoke the words poor little with deep mockery. "You told him to teach his dummy brother how to read. You told him the dummy could learn somethin', din't you?"

"Yes, I asked Robert to help him," replied Tillie. "What's wrong with that?"

"What's wrong with that?" sneered Switzer. "I'll tell you what's wrong with that. The dummy is a dummy! That's what's wrong with that. Dummies can't learn nothin'! That's what's wrong with that! All dummies can do is shovel shit. They ain't good for nothin' else. If you let 'em around any machinery, they'll kill their brothers with it! That's what's wrong with that!"

A flash of lightning lit up the gloomy interior for a second. Ten seconds later the deep sounds of thunder rolled through the dark clouds.

"But Orville can read," said Tillie.

"What can Orville read? Cat and dog? You call that reading? He can't read nuthin'."

"But..."

"Don't but me, Missy. I know about the dummy. More'n you'll ever know. He got his blood from them Italians. I heard it on the radio once. I should a knowed better than to marry one of 'em. They got dummy blood running in their veins. It's damn good luck I got German blood and we had Robert. That wop I got for a wife give me a dummy. Now he's gone and killed my son!"

"I don't understand," protested Tillie.

"Oh, you don't understand?" mocked Switzer. "I thought you was the teacher. You're supposed to know about blood and inheritance and junk like that. What blood are you?"

"I, uh, I am an American!"

"Don't bullshit me!" he shouted. "What blood are you from?"

"I have British, Irish and some American Indian in my background."

"Good. You're lucky you don't have any of that Italian or Gypsy or Jewish blood in you. The guy on the radio explained it all scientific and such. I heard him. They been studying what makes dummies like Orville. So here I end up with one, one that comes from the damn Italians."

The man is crazy, out of his mind, thought Tillie. *His grief over losing his son has driven him mad. Or is it his grief about having a child like Orville? What is this nonsense he's spouting? If only I could remember what I learned! The profs talked about genetics, linking it to Darwin, survival of the fittest, stuff like that. It's all a bunch of theories. Yet crazies on radio shows babble like this, spreading half truths. The Nazi party in Germany talks about it too. Clean up the race, they're saying. What philosopher talked about the master race? Or was it a politician? Lots of Germans are all for what that guy Hitler is saying. How did Switzer hear about this? Al and his family don't talk like this. What can I say to this crazy man?*

Switzer's eyes glazed as he stood there, not looking at Tillie any longer, but looking up, remembering past events, past conversations.

"I told that other teacher—Helen—what's-her-name? I told her what I was gonna do. I told her I was gonna keep the dummy home, make him learn how to shovel shit, 'cause that's all he's good for, but she started shouting at me, saying he was a child of God or some stupid thing. She insisted he had to stay in school.

"Then I told her to shut up. I called her a bitch and a whore. What does a whore know about school anyway? I said. Why don't you and Scheiner get married like you're supposed to? I asked. Then she started crying and screaming. And the bitch hit me. The damn bitch hit me! I wasn't gonna take no hitting from no bitch, so I hit her back. She flew up against a desk and hit her head and she laid there. The bitch laid there, not even breathing."

Another flash of lightning, followed closely by the rumble of thunder. The storm was closing in.

Stark terror rose up in Tillie's chest. *My God! It was Switzer, not Murphy! He killed Helen and now he's going to murder me too!* She looked around for a way to escape, but Switzer stood over her like a wolf with its teeth bared for the kill.

"I tried to figure what to do," he growled. "Then it come to me. So I drug the bitch out to the wood room and I hung her up. I hung her up like a side of beef!"

Switzer suddenly broke out into a long, loud cackle. His voice grew louder and louder as he screamed, "Like a side of beef! Everybody thought she had committed suicide! Damn! Like a side of beef!"

As he spoke he pounded his right hand into his left palm and screamed again, "Like a side of beef!"

Abruptly he fell siient. He returned his gaze to Tillie sitting beneath him on the milk stool. The rain pounded down. It was as dark as midnight. She could only barely see the menacing figure before her. The barn closed in on her from all sides. The heavy stench of cow manure and rotting grain robbed her of the ability to breath.

As abruptly as he had stopped, Switzer began again. "So now you know, Missy school teacher. Now you know. You're the only one who knows and ain't nobody ever gonna know what you know. Ain't nobody even gonna know you been here, 'cause ain't nobody ever gonna find you."

Leaning his pitchfork against the wall, he grabbed her again by her bruised arm, pulled her to her feet and spun her around. He pushed her toward a dark room in the rear of the barn. When he reached it, he yanked open the ancient door and threw her to the floor inside. Forcing her to lie face down, he pulled a piece of rope from a hook on the wall and wrapped and knotted it tightly around her arms. He used another piece to tie her legs.

"Now, Missy school teacher, get ready to meet your Creator!" he shouted. "And when you get to hell, tell that dumb bitch it served her right!"

The ground shook with rumbles of thunder.

Switzer rose to look in the dim light for something, a board, a stone, anything he could use to pound the life out of the hated teacher lying there before him. When she stopped breathing, he would haul her body out to the cow yard. It wouldn't take much of a hole. He could bury her in it, shovel the mud back. Cows would soon come in from the pasture and track over the mud. Nobody would ever know she'd been here. Nobody. If they came looking for her, he'd say he never saw her. Nope, she didn't come here, he'd say. Don't know what happened, he'd say, but she never came here.

In the same moment that he spied a broken two-by-four in the far corner of the dark storage room, a flash of lightning as bright as the sun itself filled the air and a tremendous clap of thunder shook the whole building! It seemed to Switzer and Tillie as if a bomb had suddenly fallen and exploded above them. The light and sound terrified Switzer. He slipped on the slime of the barn floor and fell beside his victim. When he fell he hit his head on the rough stone wall. Dazed by his fall, he lay on the floor, wondering if some angel of death was sent to destroy him as he had been about to annihilate the teacher.

Smoke began to filter down from above. In a few minutes the whole barn was filled with it. The air crackled and snapped. Fire blazed in the dry hay and straw stored overhead.

Struggling back to consciousness, Switzer crawled up on his hands and knees. He breathed in the smoke-filled air and began to cough. *Forget the teacher,* he said to himself. *Let her burn. I got to get out of here.*

On his knees he began to search for the door. There it was, but who was standing there? He could not make out the figure in the smoke, but he heard the voice.

"What did you do to Miss Tilden?" said the voice. "You hurt Miss Tilden. You hurt her bad. You hit her. I saw you hit her. You are bad. You let her go. You are bad!"

"Get out of my way, dummy!" shouted Switzer as he pulled up one leg and prepared to stand.

"No, you are bad," said Orville. He lifted the pitchfork, the same pitchfork Switzer had leaned against the wall of the barn. "You hurt my teacher!" he screamed. "You are bad!"

With those words he drove all four tines of the fork into the abdomen of his father. Switzer's face contorted in unbelief and confusion as his blood and his life poured out from the wounds. He fell to the floor, blood gurgling from his mouth. His hands and feet trembled momentarily before his body stilled.

Orville ran to Tillie, untied the ropes and reached down to help her stand. Both of them coughed violently as the smoke from the burning hay and straw grew heavier. Tillie leaned on her student while he pulled her toward the door of the room. In a moment they were out into the main room of the barn.

"This way, Miss Tilden. We got to get out of here. The barn is on fire!"

Struggling, coughing and crying, the two of them found their way to the Dutch doors and outside into the mud. Rain flooded down. Flashes of lightning lit up the dark sky. Thunder clapped again and again as they stumbled and ran to the porch of the Switzer house. The whole top of the ancient wooden structure, fueled by dry straw and hay, blazed. Billows of smoke and sparks rose to meet the torrents of rain pouring from the skies. Two great armies waged war. The fire was determined to destroy the barn and the rain was determined to prevent it. The rain lost. No matter how hard it fell, the fire kept devouring the dry wood, reducing the entire structure to a pile of broken timbers and ashes.

When Harold and Willa Wechsler drove into the yard with Sally Switzer an hour later, the rain had slowed to a drizzle. The fire still burned. The debris from scorched and broken timbers filled the charred stone walls. Scattered and broken pieces of glass and blackened pieces of wood lay all about the yard.

Tillie and Orville huddled on the floor of the porch, arms wrapped around one another. Both stared blankly out at the rain and smoldering ruin. Neither said anything as the Wechslers and Orville's mother ran toward them from the old farm truck.

Chapter 22

Crazy Man

Sally Switzer knelt beside Tillie and Orville. Orville looked up at her and said, "Papa tried to kill Miss Tilden. I stuck a fork in him. He burned up in the fire."

Sally collapsed, her head falling to her knees. Tillie reached out to take Sally in her arms. All three began to cry. "Oh, no, no, no!" sobbed Sally, her entire body shaking.

The Wechslers stood beside the porch in the drizzle, looking back and forth, first at the porch and then at the barn. Both had tears in their eyes. Harold Wechsler took his wife in his arms and she wrapped hers about him. They stood there. Amid her tears Willa Wechsler kept saying, "Harold, what are we going to do? What are we going to do?"

As they stood in the rain, bewildered by the events unfolding before them, a black Model-A pulled into the driveway behind their own farm truck. Al leaped out and ran toward the porch. He stopped in front of the Wechslers. "How did the fire start?"

Harold turned toward him. His shirt and overalls were soaked by the rain. His face was ashen and streaked with tears. "I think it was lightning."

Al jumped up on the porch and knelt beside Tillie, Orville and Sally. He reached out his arms to Tillie as she rose up to meet him. He held her as she continued to sob.

"What happened, Tillie? What happened?" he asked.

After a few moments, she was able to speak. She sniffed and struggled to find her voice. "Switzer. Tried to kill me. Called Orville a dummy. Pulled me into the barn. Oh, Al, he did it. He's the one. He told me."

"What did he tell you?"

"Said he hit Helen. She hit him. He hit her back!"

"What are you talking about?"

"It's crazy." Her voice was returning. She was feeling a little more composed. "He went down to school to tell her he was going to keep Orville home that fall, because he couldn't learn anything anyway. Then he called her some terrible names and she hit him."

"He's the one? You sure?"

"Yes. He screamed at me and said he was going to kill me too, because I knew about it. Orville saved me. He stuck a pitch fork into him. Oh, Al, it was awful!"

"How'd the fire start?"

"The barn was struck by lightning and the hay started burning. Orville got me out. Switzer's in there—burned up."

Al held her as she continued to weep. He turned to the Wechslers. "We got to get her to the clinic in Rosemount. She's all beat up. Call the clinic. See if anybody is there. Call up Eila Stricklund at Mrs. Wilson's. Ask her to come here as fast as she can."

Harold Wechsler stood as if he were a fence post buried two feet into the ground. He stared at Al, but heard nothing. Willa, however, responded. She pulled her arms from around her husband, walked over to the porch and spoke quietly. "Yes, of course. We'll call. You go ahead and take care of her."

Sally Switzer continued to kneel beside Tillie, staring blankly at the devastation and the rain. Al reached to her. When she felt his touch, she blinked and looked at him. "Sally," he said softly, "help me get Tillie inside."

She nodded her head, got to her feet and spoke in a whisper, "Miss Tilden, let me help you inside. You can lie on my bed. I'll look after you 'til they get here." Turning to Orville she spoke quietly, "Orville, help us with Miss Tilden. We got to put her to bed for a little while."

"Miss Tilden is hurt," he said. "We got to help her."

Al gently lifted Tillie from the porch floor and carried her to Sally's bedroom. Sally pulled off Tillie's muddy shoes and eased her back on the pillow. "Just lie still," she said. "Everything's going to be all right now. Everything's going to be all right."

"I'll be back in a little while," said Al. "Sally will look after you." He gave her a soft kiss and left the house.

Sally left the bedroom for a moment, but returned with a chair, a basin of water, a wash rag and a towel. She sat beside the bed and began to wash Tillie's face and arms. "This will help you feel better," she said.

Tillie smiled weakly. "How are you?"

"I'm fine," Sally returned the smile. "Orville and I got some things to do now, but we're going to be fine."

"What really happened?" asked Tillie.

"You should rest," said Sally.

"No, I need to know. Please."

Sally frowned, put the basin on the floor and began. "Hermann and I never had a good marriage. I should of never married him. I knowed from the beginning he was, well, weird. He always made fun of me being Italian, called us wops, like we was some kind of wicked, stupid people or something.

"I tried to tell him some great people were Italians, people like Christopher Columbus and such, but he always laughed at me.

"Then, when Orville was born and we knowed he was different, well, he got stranger than ever. He started crying and cussing real bad."

Tillie tried to pull herself up, winced at the pain and slumped back. "Did he hit you?"

"You just lie quiet," said Sally. "Sometimes he hit me, but then he'd apologize and we'd make up."

"Why was he so crazy about Orville?"

"He was ashamed of Orville, I think."

"Ashamed?"

"Yah. Sometimes he said we was cursed."

"I don't understand."

"Well, you know Hermann never learned to read, but he listened to the radio lots. He heard this guy talking about how we get to look like we do and even how it is that some are smart and some, like Orville, is not so smart. The radio guy said lots of dumb people come from Italians and stuff. That got Hermann really going."

"Got him going?" repeated Tillie softly. She was beginning to shiver.

Sally pulled a blanket over Tillie and settled back on her chair. "I mean he decided that Orville had my blood and Robert had his German blood. He talked about it all the time."

"How could he decide that?" asked Tillie, with a puzzled look on her face.

"I don't know. I think he made it up and then convinced hisself that it was the truth. He decided Orville didn't need no more school, 'cause he said he was nothing but a dummy and was never going to learn nothing."

Orville had pulled a stool into the room and was sitting on it to listen. He was peeling an orange as he asked, "Am I a dummy, mommy?"

Sally glanced over her shoulder. "No, honey. You ain't no dummy. You don't learn as good as Robert did, but you ain't no dummy."

"I can read, can't I?" asked Orville.

"Yes, honey. You can read."

"Hermann said he went to the school to talk with Helen," said Tillie. She was feeling warmer with the blanket over her.

"That October," continued Sally, "Hermann said he had made up his mind and was going to tell Miss Shattuck that Orville wasn't coming back. So after the boys got home that day he went over. He wasn't there very long. When he came back he didn't want to talk about what she said. All he said was that she was looking real bad and he didn't want to talk about it. He told me that I wasn't ever to tell anybody, ever, that he was over there."

"Did you?"

"No. I was scared of him. Like I said, he hit me sometimes and I was scared of him."

"Orville didn't stop going to school then, did he?"

"No. Hermann said he'd changed his mind and we wasn't going to talk no more about it."

"Sally, when you heard about Helen's hanging herself did you wonder anything?"

Sally wrapped her arms around herself, remembering her thoughts. "I did, but what could I say? Now today it all comes together. He killed her. Maybe it was an accident, but no matter, he killed her and he covered it up."

"Why do you suppose he told me?"

"I think it was 'cause Robert died. He got really crazy after Robert died. Sometimes he'd talk to hisself, sitting out on the front porch rocker for hours. He'd say things like, 'God is mad at me. I know he is. He's mad at me. I shouldn't a ever done it. He's mad at me. That's why he let the dummy kill Robert. I know it.'"

"Did you ever ask him what he meant?"

"Oh no. It wasn't possible. He'd a hit me if I'd ever asked him 'bout that. He was all mixed up inside. I figured it was best for me to say nothing.

"Anyway, I think he couldn't hold it in no more. When you came here today, it all came back and he went crazy."

"He was going to kill me," said Tillie. She shivered again.

"Here now," said Sally, "We talked enough. You try to close your eyes and rest. Orville and I'll be in the kitchen."

When Al left the Switzer house, he found Willa and Harold still standing in the rain, staring at the smoldering ruins. "Willa," he said. "How about I make the phone call instead and you and Harold see what you can do to get the cows milked."

From the Wechsler house Al phoned Eila at Mrs. Wilson's. He told her Tillie was hurt and asked her to come out to take Tillie back to Rosemount while he helped the Wechslers with their cows. She promised to grab some bandages and head out at once.

Al's second phone call was to his own house. Ma Freitag answered. "Ma," he said, almost shouting, "I got to talk with Werner."

"But Werner and Pa are out in the barn milking," she said.

"Yah, I know, but I got to talk with him. Hang up. Go out to the barn and tell him he's got to call the Wechslers. It's very important. There's been a fire!"

At this moment, a third voice broke in. "Al, this is Arlene. I'm on operator duty today. Did I hear you right? Is the Wechslers' barn on fire?"

"Yah, Arlene, that's right," said Al. "I'm glad you broke in. Lightning struck. The barn burned down."

"Al, I'll call around the area. See if we can get some people over to help."

"Thanks, Arlene. Do that. Ma! You still there?"

"Yah, I'm still here," she replied.

"Go tell Werner. Tell him to call me. I'll stay by the phone for a little while."

The phone clicked as Ma hung up. Al paced back and forth in the kitchen of the Wechsler farm house. In five minutes, the phone rang again. It was Werner.

"Brother, thanks for calling back so quick. There's been a fire. I know you got to help Pa with our cows, but I need you to come over here as soon as you're done. I got to talk with you."

"Okay, brother. I'll be along as soon as I can. Can you handle things until I get there?"

"Sure, but you come when you can." Al said no more. He hung up the receiver. He knew he could say nothing about Switzer's death over the phone. Who knew how many people on the party line were listening? As it was, Arlene would be spreading the news far and wide. There had to be an investigation into all of this. He'd need the sheriff himself in on this one.

By the time Al stepped out the back door of the Wechsler house the rain had stopped. In a couple places far above, clouds were breaking and a streak of sunshine was trying to come through. He walked quickly to the cow yard where he found Harold and Willa Wechsler in ankle deep mud. Harold was opening the gate separating the yard from the fenced lane out to the pasture. Twelve patient Holsteins stood bunched together, ready to follow their evening routine. As Harold pulled back the gate they plodded slowly into the muddy yard and stood gazing with big dark eyes at the remains of the barn.

Turning to Harold, Willa said, "Harold, we got to get the cows milked."

Harold came out of his fog, "Yes, we do, but how?"

"We'll tie them to a fence post one at a time and we'll milk them, rain, mud and all. We got to, Harold. We got to. We can't leave them. They'll get sick and die. We got to."

"Willa," said Al, "I'll help with the cows."

"All our pails is burned up," said Harold as he walked stiffly toward the smoky mess that once was his barn.

"No they ain't," said Willa as she took his hand and walked beside him. "We still got some in the milk house. They ain't all burned up. We got some milk cans too."

"Willa, you get a couple big buckets," said Al. "I'll go get a sack of oats from the granary and some bushel baskets. We can give the cows something to eat while we tie them up and milk them. Okay with you, Harold?"

"Sure, sure," Harold said, still somewhat in a daze. "Sounds fine."

In a little more than an hour the dozen cows were milked, fed and watered and turned back to the pasture.

By the time the milking was completed, a crowd had gathered in the yard in front of the burned out barn. Several women brought food. Two of them went into Willa Wechsler's kitchen to make a large pot of coffee. In a few minutes they were outside pouring it into large mugs for anyone interested. Both of the Wechslers declined food, saying they weren't hungry.

Al took two mugs of hot coffee and walked back to the little Switzer house. He pulled off his mud-caked shoes and stepped inside. "How's Tillie doing?" he asked, handing Sally a mug.

"I gave her a drink a water, washed her face and arms. We talked for a while," she replied. "Now she's asleep."

"How are you doing?"

"Fine. Orville is fine, too."

Their conversation was interrupted by a knock on the front door screen. "Hi," said Eila. "Got here as quick as I could. We had a couple emergencies at the clinic. Can I come in?"

"Come on in," said Al. He rose to greet her and gave her a little hug. "Tillie is asleep right now, but when she wakes up I need you to take her home. Before we go into the bedroom, I want to tell you what happened." He motioned for her to sit.

Al reviewed what he had heard from Tillie and Sally filled in with what she and Tillie had discussed earlier. Al shook his head several times and frowned at Sally's story. Eila listened, but said nothing. Finally, she said quietly, "Maybe I better get Tillie back to town."

Eila, Sally and Al went to the bedroom. As they entered Tillie opened her eyes. "Hi Till," said Eila.

"Hi, Eila," said Tillie in a quiet, drowsy voice. "When did you get here?"

"Just a second ago, hon. How about I take you back to the house?"

Tillie nodded and tried to sit up. When she did so she screamed out in pain. "It's my arm," she said. "It hurts real bad."

Eila asked Sally to bring a basin of water. "Tillie, lie back. Let me look at you," she said. In the next minutes she bandaged the wounds on Tillie's head and knees. Then, carefully wrapping her left arm, she put it in a sling. Turning to Al, she said, "Let's get her to my car."

"I got you," said Al, as he bent down and lifted Tillie up in his arms. Sally, Orville and Eila followed Al as he carried Tillie to Eila's car. Al set Tillie gently in the front seat. In a moment, Eila was in the driver's seat. Before she left the yard, Al said, "Eila, don't talk about this to anyone. If Mrs. Wilson asks, tell her that Tillie got hurt trying to help put out the fire. Don't say a thing about Switzer. It's very important. Hear me?"

"I understand. We'll get Tillie cleaned up and I'll use your story." With that, she drove out the driveway a moment before Werner Freitag arrived to park his truck beside Al's Model-A.

Chapter 23

Sheriff Wahlberg

"When you called," said Werner to his brother, "it sounded like there was more going on than a fire."

"Sure is," said Al. "Come into Sally's house. We got to talk."

They both turned to follow Sally as she walked slowly to her house. Orville walked beside them. Seated again in the little kitchen, Al asked Sally to re-tell her story about Hermann Switzer and Helen Shattuck. When she was finished, Werner thought for a moment and said, "We got to call the sheriff. This is really bad stuff."

Werner called Hastings from the Wechsler house. When Sergeant Gates came to the phone, Werner explained, "Sergeant, Harold Wechsler's barn is burned to the ground out here in Rich Valley. We can manage that, but we got some other things going on. I can't talk about it on the phone. I need you to come over as quick as you can. The Wechsler's farm is down the hill from St. John's Lutheran Church, past the school house a little ways. And, Sergeant, bring the sheriff!"

Gates, long experienced in the problems of telephone party-lines, said only, "Certainly, Freitag. We'll be along as soon as possible. In the meantime keep everyone away from the barn. Don't want anyone hurt. Hear me?"

"Yes sir, we'll do it. See you soon." Werner hung up the ear piece.

Once outside the two deputies moved the crowd back from the smoldering fire. They found some steel posts in Wechsler's machine shed, pounded them around the outer perimeter of the ruin and tied some twine from post to post. Then they tied a rag on the twine between each post and said, "Everybody has to stay back behind this line. We'll look into the barn later on, but right now we don't want anybody getting hurt. It's probably best that you go back home. Harold's cows are milked. Nothing more we can do tonight."

Slowly, the crowd began to disperse. Several promised Harold and Willa they'd be back in the morning to help with the cows and the milking. As the last of the crowd were leaving, two squad cars from the Dakota County Sheriff's department pulled up. Sergeant George Gates drove the lead car with Sheriff Raymond Wahlberg beside him in the front seat. Al and Werner walked over to greet them.

"Looks like you men have things well in hand," said Wahlberg as he stepped from the car. Turning to two uniformed deputies in the other car, he said, "See that everyone leaves and make sure no one gets near the fire scene. I'm going to need you men to stay here for the night."

Turning back to the farmers, he continued, "George indicated something serious went on here. Fill me in."

Al recounted what Tillie had told him about Switzer and Orville. He reported that Eila had taken her back to Rosemount. Werner completed their report with Sally's tale about Helen Shattuck's death.

"Where is Mrs. Switzer now?" asked Wahlberg.

"She's in her house. Her son Orville is with her. She said she'll be there when we need her."

"Anyone else know about this?"

"No sir," replied Werner. "The Wechslers, of course, but they're not saying anything."

"And Eila Stricklund?"

"She knows, but we instructed her to keep it to herself. And I believe she will."

"Good. Now let's walk around the barn and see what we got here."

The troop marched over to the barn where Harold and Willa were standing. "I'm sorry about your barn, Mr. Wechsler," said Sheriff Wahlberg.

"Thank you, Sheriff," replied Harold. "It was lightning. Happened so fast."

"Do you have insurance?" asked Wahlberg.

"Couldn't afford it. Not making enough money. Hardly making enough to keep ourselves going as it is."

"I understand. Hard times."

"I don't quite know what we're going to do now," said Harold with a quiver in his voice. "Don't have money to rebuild."

"Harold," said Werner, "don't worry about that for now. You got lots of friends and family around here. We'll help you out."

"Thanks, Werner," said Willa. "I know you will."

"Is everything secure?" asked Wahlberg.

"I think so," said Harold.

"Good. Then let's go to your house. We need to talk. You know what I mean."

Wahlberg, Gates, Werner and Al followed the Wechslers to their house. When the men were all seated in the front room Willa hurried to the kitchen to prepare some of the coffee and cake her neighbors had left behind. As she served, Sheriff Wahlberg began.

"Harold, I'll get right to the point. The body of your hired man is in that rubble. Freitag reports that he tried to kill teacher Tilden after confessing to her that he murdered former teacher Shattuck back in the fall of '33. At the time we recorded it as a suicide. This, of course, changes everything. Tell us what you know about this."

"Sheriff, I don't know much. I knew Hermann was strange, but he's been my hired man a long time and he did his work good. He and Sally lived in that old house ever since their boys were born. What can I say? I never suspicioned nothing about him being involved with the teacher's death."

Willa poured coffee into Sergeant Gates' cup. "We knew Hermann had some crazy ideas about Orville. He really didn't want the boy to go to school."

"Sure, we knew that," continued Harold, "but he let Orville go anyway. We tried to get him to send the boys up to St. John's, but he wouldn't have nothing to do with that. He wouldn't go to church. He went once in a while, but most of the time he said he didn't believe all that stuff and preferred to stay home. Sally, she come quite often though, even joined the church after they was married."

"Sally's a good woman, real patient," interjected Willa.

"Hermann was proud to be a German. He talked with me about it some. Said Germans are the smartest people in the world and God chose us Germans to run it. He even complained once in a while about why he was dumb enough to marry Sally, her being an Italian and all. Stuff like that."

"He was really broke up when Robert got killed," said Willa. "Course, so was Sally, but Hermann, well, he started getting real strange after that. Sometimes he'd yell at Orville something fierce."

"I felt so sorry for the poor little kid," said Harold with a twinge of sadness in his voice. "He'd run off somewhere and hide for hours. I know he hit the child quite often."

"Once or twice Sally started to say something to me when we was working out in the garden," said Willa, "but then she'd stop herself. I kind a suspected something was going on, but there wasn't nothing more we could do."

"So, from what I hear," continued Wahlberg, "you both believe Switzer was capable of the things reported."

Harold looked down into his coffee cup. Willa paused in the doorway of the kitchen as she said, "Yes sir, we both knew Hermann was capable of violence. It doesn't surprise us at all."

"Then you'll be willing to share your observations at a hearing in a week or two?"

"What's that?" asked Harold.

"Well, you see, when something like this occurs we have to go before a judge and spell out everything that's happened. It's clear Switzer tried to kill Miss Tilden and little Orville saved her life. It also appears we'll have to change the record about Helen Shattuck's death. So, in order for all this to get straightened out we're going to need your help. That's what I'm asking of you."

"Does that mean we got to go to Hastings for this—what'd you call it—hearing?" asked Willa.

"Yes, Willa, it does. I apologize for asking this in the midst of all this tragedy, but it's very important. Do you understand what I'm saying?"

"We understand," said Harold, "and we'll be there. Just tell us what to do."

"Thank you. Now I want to do something for you." Turning to Sergeant Gates, Wahlberg continued. "Sergeant, tomorrow go to the bank at Rosemount and tell them we're setting up an account to receive donations for the Wechslers. Then get articles in both of the local county newspapers about the fire and about how to send donations. When you get back to your office, send letters to the several area churches, inviting them to tell their parishioners about the fire and the need Harold and Willa have."

"Yes sir, I'll take care of it first thing tomorrow," replied Gates.

Turning to Werner, Wahlberg said, "Werner, you suggested you could arrange for some help around here, did you not?"

"Yes sir, I did," said Werner. "As soon as we get the lumber together, all of us in the area will get together and have us a barn raising. I'll get the word around. Count on it."

"Good," said Wahlberg. "One more thing, Sergeant. Call Art Olsen over at the lumber yard in Farmington. He owes me a favor. He knows what I mean. Tell him I expect him to supply the barn lumber at his cost."

Gates made a few notes on a pad and stuffed it back in his shirt pocket. "Got it. We'll do it."

"Got to go. Harold, Willa, thank you again. Two deputies will remain here through the night to guard the barn 'til it cools down. We'll take away the remains of Switzer's body tomorrow. Willa, thank you for the coffee and cake."

Taking Harold's hand, he said, "Harold, you have many friends. We're in this together. Remember that."

Harold's eyes filled with tears as he replied, "Thank you Sheriff. Thank you and God bless you."

Wahlberg marched his entourage out to the yard, over to the front door of the Switzer house and knocked gently. Sally Switzer appeared behind the tattered screen door. "May we come in for a moment, Mrs. Switzer?" She nodded and they entered.

Taking her hands in his, Wahlberg said, "Mrs. Switzer, may I call you by your first name?" She nodded and he continued, "Sally, I am most sad about what happened. This has been a very difficult time for you and for your family. My deepest condolences for your losses. The people in my office will do everything we possibly can to put this whole thing to rest. In the meantime, what do you need?"

Sally's face was tear streaked, her hair in shambles. She looked down as Wahlberg spoke. At his question she raised her eyes slowly and said, "Thank you Sheriff, but there ain't nothin' much to do right now. I think I'll spend a couple days with my sister over at Coates. Maybe me and Orville will move back to South St. Paul to live with my other sister."

"Good. The Freitags and your church people will be here to help you too. Sally, in a week or so there's going to be a hearing before a judge about all this. May I send a car out to Coates to pick up you and Orville so you can tell your story?"

Wahlberg was still holding her hands as she replied, "Is that really necessary, Sheriff?"

"Yes, Sally, it is."

"Then I guess we'll do it. I'll be glad to get past it all. There's been so..." Sally began to weep. "So much hurt. So much hurt."

"I understand," said Wahlberg. "It will soon be over. Thank you, Sally, for giving us this moment."

Wahlberg slowly released her hands, turned back toward the front door and walked out. As he left, Werner moved next to Sally, put his arm across her shoulders and said, "Sally, I'll take you and Orville to Erma's on my way home and explain to her and Reinhold about what happened. She'll want you to stay with them for a while."

Sally nodded her head and said, "Thank you, Werner. I'll get a few clothes together for me and Orville. It won't take but a minute. Tell Willa and Harold where we're going, will you?"

"Sure," said Werner. "I'll be waiting outside."

Gates was already in the squad car with the motor running. Wahlberg stood next to it as he addressed Werner and Al. "Good job, deputies. Check back with the Wechslers tomorrow afternoon." Sitting down on the front seat and closing his car door, he said, "George, let's go. We got work to do."

Werner led Sally and Orville to his truck. Just before he got in, Al walked up to him. "You know, brother, there's a whole lot more to this deputy business than I realized."

Chapter 24

What Will Be Will Be

Al parked his Model-A in front of the Wilson house. Mrs. Wilson was waiting for him. "How's Tillie?" he asked.

"She's upstairs resting. Eila brought her in all bandaged up. Said they stopped over at the clinic. What happened?"

"She went down to visit one last time with Orville Switzer. While she was in the barn it was struck with lightning and caught on fire. The Wechsler's hired man got burned up in the fire. She's lucky to be alive," said Al, purposely omitting certain relevant facts. "Do you suppose I can see her?"

"Yes, I think so. Eila's with her. I'll take you up. Let me check with the other girls first."

Al settled on the divan in the front parlor as Mrs. Wilson disappeared up the stairs. In a few minutes she returned. "Come this way. Eila's with her. Tillie has been waiting for you." She led the tall farmer up to Tillie's room, knocked softly on the door, opened it, and led Al in. She excused herself, but left the door open, according to house rules.

Al listened at the door to be sure she had reached the bottom of the stairs. Tillie was in her bed with Eila sitting beside her. Tillie smiled as Al bent over to kiss her softly.

"Hi, big man. I guess we won't be going to O'Hara's tonight," she said wearily.

"Nope, I guess not."

"Eila called my folks. They're on their way out. They're going to take me home. I'll be back in a few days to get the rest of my stuff."

"Good. Are you going to be okay? I mean, nothing's broken, is it?"

"Nope. Just some big bruises on my arms and wrists, a whole bunch of scrapes and scratches and a big knot on my forehead."

"I'm glad. You've been through enough for a lifetime."

"No argument there, sweetie," she replied, her voice a bit stronger.

"We talked with the Wechslers," Al spoke softly. "Sheriff Wahlberg says there'll be a hearing in a week or so. He wants you there. Think you will be able to make it?"

"Yup. I'll make it. Probably won't look my prettiest, but I'll be there. What's happening to Orville and his mother?"

Al went through the details of their meeting with the Wechslers and told her about Werner driving Sally and Orville to the Wieselmann home. "I'm going to let you get some rest now," he said. "I'll wait downstairs until your folks arrive."

He kissed her again softly on the cheek and left the room. Tillie closed her eyes and in a moment was asleep.

About eight that night Dr. and Mrs. Tilden arrived at the Wilson home. Al met their car. "Tillie is resting and doing as good as can be expected," he said. He quickly detailed the day's events and pointed out that only Eila knew about Switzer's death. "We got to keep quiet about this stuff until the hearing," he continued. They agreed and followed him to Tillie's room.

Within a half hour they had her down the stairs and propped on some pillows in the back seat of their car. Before they left Dr. Tilden turned to Al and Eila. "Thank you for taking care of our daughter. We'll keep in touch by phone. I'm sure Tillie will want to see you in a couple days. Thanks again for everything."

After the Tilden automobile disappeared down the street, Eila turned to Al, "You know what, big guy? I was thinking that Tillie has had quite a year."

"I think you're right," said Al, "quite a year indeed."

Dr. Stephen Tilden turned his Desota onto the highway and headed north toward St. Paul. For long minutes no one in the car said anything. Finally, Iva Tilden could restrain herself no longer. A tirade of remonstration poured from her.

"I knew it. I knew this whole thing was wrong. I tried to tell you, Tillie. I tried to tell you and your Poppa that it was a mistake to come out here. I could feel it in my bones.

"And now look at you, nearly killed! We could have been following a hearse today instead of driving you home. I'm sick at the thought.

"I'm so glad that you decided to come home. That's where you need to be. You need to rest up in your own bed. You need to be with your family instead of those stupid farmers. You need to finish school and get a good position in the city."

Quite suddenly Stephen Tilden slammed on the brakes of his car and pulled it screeching over to the side of the road. His face was red and his hands were clenched around the steering wheel. He looked forward as he spoke.

"Shut up, Iva! Just shut up! Have you no feelings? Have you lost all common sense? In the name of heaven, can't you see what's happened to your daughter? Do you not understand the trauma and the pain she has been through? If you love her you will shut your mouth and quit your crazy lecturing!"

Iva Tilden began to speak, her eyes wide with shock, "Why I never. What are you saying? How dare you lecture me."

"I said shut up, Iva, and I meant it. If you don't shut your mouth this instant you can get out of the car and find your own way home. Hear me?"

"Are you threatening me?"

"Out, Iva, right now!"

"Stop it! Stop it, both of you!" moaned Tillie. "You're worse than a couple of kids. I can't stand any more of it. Please, please be quiet. Poppa, please, drive me home."

No one said another word as Dr. Tilden put the car in gear again and returned to the highway. In less than an hour he pulled the car up the drive to their garage, parked it and got out. With their daughter between them Stephen and Iva Tilden walked slowly up to their house. Tillie's teenage sister, Mattie, held the door open as they climbed the two steps leading to the back porch. Together they helped Tillie up the inside stairs to her room and tucked her into bed. Her mother handed her three aspirin with a glass of water. "Take this dear. You need to sleep," she said.

"Tillie's been in a fire, nearly lost her life," explained Dr. Tilden to Mattie "but she'll be fine."

"How? What happened?" asked Mattie, her voice quivering.

Poppa motioned for Mattie to come to his room. Iva turned away and disappeared into her own. When Mattie was seated Poppa detailed the events of the fire and explained that Hermann Switzer had died, carefully omitting any reference to Switzer's attempt to murder Tillie.

"We thank God your sister is alive," he said.

Mattie began weeping as she thought about how close her sister had come to death. "Oh, Poppa, so do I."

"Nothing more we can do for now. She's bruised, but she'll recover. Time for us all to get some sleep."

Mattie tiptoed down the hall to check on her sister. Assured she was asleep, she slipped into her own room and closed the door.

Tillie woke twice during the night, once screaming. Both of her parents ran to give her more aspirin and to calm her down. They sat, one on either side of her bed, until she fell asleep again. Without saying a word, they returned to their respective bedrooms.

The second time Tillie awoke she was certain she had heard Orville calling her name. She sat up straight in her dark room, trying to see if he was near. Another dream. She shuddered, fell back on her pillows and stared into the gloom. *What will happen to Orville?* she thought. In a few minutes she fell asleep again with a prayer in her heart for his safety.

Tillie was dozing fitfully the next morning when Mattie carefully opened her bedroom door. Quick witted like her sister, but still very much a teenager, she smiled and entered. Tillie opened her eyes and said, "Hi kid."

Mattie sat on the edge of the bed. "Morning sis. It's about nine. You hungry?"

"I think so." Tillie yawned and stretched out her arms from beneath the blankets. "My stomach is starting to tell me I forgot to feed it last night."

"Great! I'll bring something to you."

"Don't think that'll be necessary, my dear little sister. I'm not so broken I can't get out of bed."

She sat up and began to move her legs toward the edge of the bed. Suddenly alarms went off in her head as pain shot from her back and arms. "Owee! I guess I'm not going to be moving quite as much as I thought." She slumped on her pillow and stared at the ceiling. Squinting her eyes and pursing her mouth, she let out a little puff. "Everything hurts. My head hurts.

My back hurts. My arm hurts. Maybe I'll take you up on that offer."

In a few minutes Mattie returned with a tray of toast, scrambled eggs and orange juice. She helped Tillie prop herself against her pillows and placed the tray on her lap.

"You were pretty beat up last night when Momma and Poppa brought you home. What happened anyway? All I got from Poppa were some sketchy details. He was gone to work before I got up today."

Tillie drank some orange juice. Between bites she outlined events on the Wechsler farm. When she was finished, Mattie asked, "What's going to happen to little Orville now?"

"I think they'll say he was protecting me."

"Yeah, but it must be awful to know you killed your father."

"Right. First he caused his brother's death and now he has killed his father. I don't know what that's going to do to him or how he'll deal with it. His mind is slow, but he feels deeply."

"Is there anything you can do?"

"I doubt it, but I'm going to try. Al told me Orville and his mother were moving to Coates with her sister for a while but she was thinking about moving back to South St. Paul. She has another sister there. As soon as I know where they live, I'll stop by, keep in touch."

"Sounds like a good idea." Mattie took her sister's hand. "Gollee. To think I almost lost my favorite sister!"

"Your only sister! Scares me to think about it, too. I dreamed about it last night. It was like it was happening all over again."

Mattie gave her sister a hug. As she did so she tipped over the juice. "Now look what you've done," said Tillie with a wry smile. They both began to laugh.

"I'm so glad we can still laugh together," said Mattie. "I don't ever want to lose you."

"I don't want to lose you either, little sister. Now take this bedspread downstairs and clean up your mess while I finish my eggs."

Chapter 25

GED

"I'm going to the grocery store. We need eggs, bread and fruit," Mary Murphy shouted down the basement stairs.

"I'll be here when you return," replied Michael Murphy. "And Mary, I always loved you, even though I haven't always showed it."

"Sure, Michael. Sure."

A double barreled shotgun rested on Murphy's worktable in the basement of his house. He slowly pushed two shells into the chambers and clicked the weapon shut. He looked at the two sheets of a letter he had written, laying beside the gun, took his pen in hand and signed his name. Folding the sheets, he placed them into an envelope, licked the cover and sealed it shut. On the front he wrote, To Mary Murphy.

Reaching under his worktable he recovered a familiar flask of whiskey from a bucket of rags. "One last time, me little bottle, one last time," he mumbled as he took a mouthful, swallowed and breathed deeply. Setting the bottle on the table, he said softly, "Good bye, Mary ... Ah, sweet Jesus, please forgive me, but I can't be finding another way. I can't."

Placing the barrels of the shotgun in his mouth, he reached down to the triggers with his thumbs, paused for a moment and then pushed.

The front page story in the St. Paul Pioneer Press the next day read:

SUICIDE AND MURDER CONNECTED
Michael Murphy, long time Superintendent of Schools for District 132 of Rosemount, was found by his wife in the basement of their home last evening, dead from an apparent shotgun wound. Some observers suggest a connection between Murphy's suicide and last week's death of Rich Valley farmhand Hermann Switzer. A hearing will be held today in the Dakota County courtroom of Judge Jacob Breitlinger.

Spectators and reporters from the Twin Cities and surrounding areas packed Judge Breitlinger's courtroom that Friday morning. The gray-haired Judge, sixty some years of age, wore thick, horn-rimmed glasses. He entered, took his place and everyone sat down.

Tillie, sitting next to Al, whispered, "I can't believe it. Murphy dead. I don't know what to say."

"He couldn't face what he did to Helen any more," whispered Al.

"I guess," she said as she screwed up her face. "It's all so awful." Looking to the bench, she asked, "What's this judge like?"

"He has a reputation for being tough, but fair. He's been on the bench here in Hastings since before I was born. People say he listens and usually makes good decisions."

The District Attorney called Tillie, the Wechslers, Sally Switzer, Al and Werner to testify. They filled in the details of the fire, Switzer's attempted murder and Orville's rescue.

Sheriff Wahlberg was the final witness. When the District Attorney asked if felt there was any connection between Hermann Switzer's death and Michael Murphy's suicide, Wahlberg replied, "Only indirectly. Michael and I were both uncles of Helen. Our whole family has mourned her death for over a year. We were puzzled by her apparent suicide. It seemed so unlike her.

"Now we know what happened. Horrible as it is to think about, at least we have an explanation. We can finally give her a proper Christian burial."

"You and Michael Murphy were brothers-in-law," continued the D.A. "I ask you again. Do you see any connection between Murphy's suicide and Switzer's death?"

Wahlberg adjusted his huge bulk, squinted and stared at the District

Attorney. "I'm not sure what you're asking, sir. Perhaps you could rephrase the question."

"Do you believe that any action of Michael Murphy contributed to what Herman Switzer did to Helen Shattuck?"

"No, I do not."

"Thank you," said the D.A. "You may sit down."

Judge Breitlinger declared a recess and returned thirty minutes later. He ruled that Orville's killing of his father was justified defense of Tillie Tilden. He also instructed that the cause of Helen Shattuck's death be amended in the record to second degree murder and declared the two cases closed.

Bill Scheiner appeared on Wednesday of the next week before Judge Breitlinger. On the advice of his court appointed attorney, Scheiner pleaded guilty to robbery and the attempted murder of Deputy Al Freitag. The District Attorney considered Helen Shattuck's diary irrelevant to the case and left it in the possession of Sheriff Wahlberg. After hearing the report from the two farmer deputies, Judge Breitlinger sentenced Scheiner to fifteen years in the State Prison at Stillwater.

Al, Werner, Tillie and Eila went to lunch at Richard's-on-the-River, a popular local restaurant in Hastings, beneath the Spiral Bridge, overlooking the Mississippi river.

"That was short and sweet," said Tillie.

"We caught him red handed," replied Werner.

"What do you mean 'we', big brother?" Al laughed.

"Okay, you're the big, brave hero," admitted Werner.

"Hey, guys," Eila chimed in, "I think you're both heroes. By the way, whatever happened to the other guy?"

"His trial comes up this afternoon," said Werner. "I think the judge'll be a little easier on him. He doesn't have a record like Scheiner. Did you know Scheiner had been jailed five times for being drunk and disorderly?"

"Quite a guy. To think that for a time I was attracted to him. He was fun, but he never had any self-control."

"Look where it got him. Fifteen years behind bars," said Werner.

"I wonder where we'll be in fifteen years," mused Al.

"Forget fifteen years. What about next year?" asked Tillie.

"Yes, Tillie, what happens after college?" asked Eila.

Tillie glanced up at the Spiral Bridge. "You know," she said, "this year has been like that bridge, going round and round, but now I'm on top and I know where I'm headed. I will go on for my master's degree to learn about kids like Orville. We have to help kids like him. I plan to make that happen."

"That's great, Till," said Eila with a wink, "I believe you will, but I was thinking about something else."

"Like what?"

"Don't 'like-what' me. What's happening with you two?"

Both Al and Tillie blushed. Tillie turned to Al. "We haven't settled that yet, have we?"

"Ah, Tillie," said Al, with a big smile on his face. "You know how I feel,"

"Yes, I do, but what about that other stuff?"

Both Werner and Eila asked in chorus, "What other stuff?"

"Werner, you know about the patent," said Al. "We've talked about Minnesota Mining's offer. The farm won't support all of us if either you or I get married. So I'm accepting their offer."

"Hey, hold on here," said Eila. "Here's one little gal who's completely in the dark."

Al explained to Eila about his offer to go to Dunwoody Institute and work for the 3-M Corporation. Then he continued, "I've checked with the high school in Rosemount. They'll give me a test at the end of August and if I pass it, they'd give me a high school equiva..." Turning to Tillie, he asked, "What's that called again?"

"A GED, a high school equivalency diploma. It's the same as if you had actually finished high school."

"Right, but I'm going to need a teacher to help me get ready. I was wondering if you knew of one."

"Sure do," smiled Tillie. "I think she's available all summer long."

Printed in the United States
20265LVS00007B/1-69

9 781413 709537